What the critics are saying

"Burke's skills at creating outrageous, loveable, larger-than-life characters shine in this darkly romantic erotic read."
- *Ann Leville, Sensual Romance*

"Once again, Ms. Burke has delivered a story you won't want to put down until you finish it."
- *Nicole La Folle, Timeless Tales*

Ellora's Cave Publishing, Inc.
PO Box 787
Hudson, OH 44236-0787

ISBN # 1-84360-622-4

The Slayer edited by Martha Punches.
Cover art by Bryan Keller.

Warning: The following material contains strong sexual content meant for mature readers. *THE SLAYER* has been rated NC17/Borderline Hard NC17, erotic, by a minimum of three independent reviewers. We strongly suggest storing this book in a place where young readers not meant to view it are unlikely to happen upon it. That said, enjoy…

THE SLAYER

Written by

STEPHANIE BURKE

This book is dedicated to the Wild Wonderful Women of Flamekeeper! Thank you so much for hanging in there with me, for listening to me whine, for helping me make decisions about where my plot lines and my worlds would take me! You guys are always there, offering encouragement, advise, insults as needed, and your unwavering support!

Thank you to Chari and Bri for being the perfect smart*sses! Smarter*sses make smarter victims! I am just glad that everyone has such a great sense of humor.

Thank you to the writers of Ellora's Cave! Kate, Rod, Shelby, Treva, Jaid…it was fun torturing you! We have to do it again!

A very special thank you to CMA, Chesapeake Martial Arts, http://www.cmakarate.com. Especially (in no real order): Master Kim Heaney, Mr. Harry Schcrieber, Mr. Tony Shcrieber, Ms. Elizabeth Seuferlin, Mr. Jack Seekford, and Ms. Melissa Heaney. Without your help, caring, and ability to break down the hardest forms and make them something that an observer like me can understand, rationalize and detail, The Slayer would have fallen on its proverbial butt! Kye and Tali have a lot to thank you for!

And as always, thank you to Dennis for providing enough frustration, encouragement, and comedy in proper doses, to help me get through this! Love ya, you pierced, tattooed Irish Viking!

Chapter One

God, he hated enemas! There was no worse feeling in the world, but he had to do what he had to do! With a grimace of disgust, he quickly got the job done then wearily headed for the showers.

He wanted to wash away the feeling of dirt and disgust before he soaked in the vanilla scented waters he had earlier prepared.

The sweet comforting smell of the perfumed steam was incentive enough for him to hurry with the proficient scrubbing he gave his body in the shower in order to soothe his soul in the steaming hot waters.

As the last of his unsettling feelings rolled down the drain, he wearily dragged his body out of the brass and glass alcove and crossed the room on silent feet. Walking quietly had become second nature to him.

With a barely audible sigh, he settled into the still stinging hot water, shuddering slightly as it first burned then eased his muscles, warming them up, helping to prepare him for what was ahead.

He soon relaxed against the lip of the tub, closed his eyes and let his thoughts drift.

Would tonight be the night? Would his soul find the peace that it so craved? Would tonight be the night that ended it all?

The discreet beeping at his wrist told him his time was up. Not that it mattered anyway, he thought as he rose from the now tepid water. He had wasted enough time pampering his flesh. Now it was time to do his duty.

His wet hair hung to his knees and clung to his body like dark silken ropes.

He liked it that way. It made him stand out. If they were watching for him, waiting for him, it would make him easier to find. And with his exotic looks and devil-may-care attitude, he stood out.

Wrapping a large bath sheet around his dripping hair, he smiled as the scent of vanilla and cinnamon followed him, wafting in the air around him. It was a comforting smell, but also the smell of remembrance. He would remember always. He would make them remember, for what little time they had left on this mortal plane.

The scars that scored his back moved with his skin, only their discoloration making them stand out. He worked hard so that no scar tissue would hinder his movements, worked for years to make the skin as soft and supple as the rest of him. He needed no impediments to his movements to slow him down.

His skin itself was a bit of a miracle. It was what happened when you mixed a full blood Crow warrior with an African/Chinese woman. As a result, he had a golden bronze complexion that could easily slide into the shadows as well as worship the sunlight like many others. He loved the skin that he was in; he relished the feel of it stretching out over his muscular body, framing the thick wiry muscles that made up his form.

He didn't exactly have a swimmer's build, he was a little too thick for that, but he wasn't overly muscle-bound either, perfect for practicing martial arts and for slipping into shadows at a moment's notice.

His eyes were a strange combination of green and gold; at any time any one of the colors could take control, often making one eye seem green and the other gold. It had a way of unnerving people, and that suited him just fine. He wanted to unnerve people, to make them back off without a word. It made his job easier.

"Thank God androgyny is in," he muttered to himself, as he stood in front of an expansive wardrobe that consisted mostly of leather.

With his delicate features, he could easily make himself look ultra-feminine with a few strokes of a makeup brush or a certain way he styled his hair. But the masculine jaw line and the way he moved marked him unmistakably as male, unless he wanted to make another impression.

Now, as he tugged the towel away from his hair, tossed back the chin-length bangs that framed the front of his face, and whipped the long mass back over his shoulder, he decided that tonight called for something special, something that would keep them guessing.

Quickly he fashioned a long braid with the still slightly damp knee-length hair. He left the chin-length fringe to frame his face, making it easy to shake over his eyes and hide his face from scrutiny. He smiled as he tied a small chain of bells at the end of his braid. It didn't matter that they tinkled lightly as they brushed against his bottom; he could make them silent when he chose. But that sound would likely drive his intended target mad as he tried to discover where the light, joyful sound came from.

He had to admit to himself; sometimes he was a bit like a cat, toying with its prey before moving in for the kill.

In the length of the braid he placed seven long metal points, thin enough to be hidden totally in his hair, but strong enough to bring death at a distance. More people should have such accessories, he decided. Then again, why give his secrets away?

Tucking his hair behind his almost too-delicate ears, he returned his attention to the closet.

What to wear, what to wear, what to wear? Why, leather of course! That's what was mainly there!

Now the color, black, white, dark blue, red…

The white.

He smiled as he pulled the snow-white butter-soft pants from their hanger.

He would have to be careful about the blood, he decided. He really liked those pants and no matter how you scrubbed, blood always left reddish-brown stains on white leather.

Slowly, he eased the almost living material up his legs, loving the feel as the leather instantly formed an attachment to his skin. These pants were so tight that underwear was all but impossible.

He didn't mind. He hated underwear anyway.

The pants closed with a thin leather thong that laced across his tight abdomen, emphasizing the muscle definition there as well as exposing the thin line of soft dark hair that started just beneath his navel.

He smiled as he bent and stretched a bit, making the pants conform to his every movement, before he reached in and pulled out a pair of white calf-high boots.

The boots were cross-tied with silver buckles, leaving spaces for the several knives and secret pouches that easily and safely fit beneath the straps. These boots were also made of leather and had very low heels, heels that could be twisted the right way to expose secret compartments that would provide protection for a man in his position.

Now all he had to find was a shirt.

Glancing in the mirror to his right, he decided he definitely looked more Oriental today. That made his selection easier.

Roaming deeper into his closet, he pulled out a knee-length tunic with side slits that ran to his armpits. The only things holding it together were two long white leather thongs at the sides that matched so well with the black and red dragon and tiger pattern on its back. The Oriental-style cut of the tunic included a banded collar and shoulder fasteners of white roped silk. The red silk garment was light and easy to move in.

After securing the inside and shoulder fasteners, he stepped back to examine himself in the mirror.

He looked…he looked like an erotic Asian fantasy. But that was not enough.

Walking over to a special make-up table in his closet, he sat down long enough to apply eyeliner to emphasize the slant to his eyes and enough powder and rouge to make people wonder about his gender.

The result was breathtaking, to say the least. He looked beautiful, he looked sadistic, he looked like a wet dream wrapped in leather and placed on display for some foreign emperor's whim.

Most importantly, he looked distinctive, memorable, and nothing like his true self.

It was time.

Taking an ankle-rubbing black leather cloak from its place by the closet, he shrouded himself in mystery and headed for the front door.

Before he exited, he patted the hidden pockets, making sure all was in readiness.

With one last look around, he closed the door.

He was sure that he would be home soon, washing away the night's excess, checking his clothing for wear, replenishing lost supplies, and then hopefully, he could get an uninterrupted day's worth of sleep.

Hopefully tonight would be the night when he found and destroyed the man who had made him what he was, destroyed his whole life and cursed him with this half life filled with a compulsive-obsessive need to seek out his revenge, to destroy and kill any who got in his path.

Hopefully, tonight all of his demons would finally be put to rest and the innocent avenged.

But deep in the cold shrunken place that he called a heart, he knew that it was not to be.

Turning, he walked away from his comfort place, his lair, his prison, and walked softly into the night, the tinkling of the bells in his hair the only signal of his passing.

Chapter Two

His boots made a clipping sound as he walked across the wet concrete. The sounds of the nightlife surrounding him were muted, as muted as the emotions he felt when he watched humanity parade by in a never-ending party.

People laughed, people cried, people dressed in their disguises, and they lived as if their problems and joys were the only important things in the universe.

He knew better.

Slowly, his head down, he made his way to his destination, walking past the scantily dressed females and their weary and posturing males. If you want to impress someone, but not knowing who it would be, it's the clothes that are important.

And he looked the part of being important.

"Right this way, sir…" a low voice trailed off as if uncertain of his gender. The bouncer dressed in black motioned him forward, past the red velvet rope that held the masses back. "We need more of your type inside."

"My type?" he asked, the colors in his eyes violently fighting for supremacy, swirling pools of green and gold.

"Party people," the bouncer said to him. "There is a movie company filming here tonight and we need to make it look good."

"Film company?" he asked as he stepped past the tall, burly man.

"What are you? Some kind of parrot?" he laughed. "The boss wants us to pack the place with interesting individuals, and you are one of the more interesting things I've seen in a long time."

He shrugged and stepped into the dark foyer of the club, noticing the black velvet curtain that separated the necessary security from the view of the never-ending party going on inside.

"This way," another brusque voice growled as the first bouncer went back to his door duties.

This bouncer was not as big as the first, but the jaded look in his eyes showed only disdain for the people who partied there.

"Arms spread, legs spread I need to use the magic wand!"

He gestured with the small metal detector he held in his hand.

"A necessary precaution," he said as he moved into position so the guard could check him.

There was a beep, and suddenly four equally large disagreeable men emerged from the shadows.

No matter, he had scented them before he moved into position.

The bouncer with the wand narrowed his eyes and he ran the detector again over his back, finally smiling as he realized it was the bells in his hair making the wand beep.

He motioned his back-up to return to the shadows and glared at the man dressed so distinctively, even for the weirdoes that hung out in this Goth club.

"Bells?" he asked, sneering a bit.

"What sweeter sound can fill the ears and ignite the senses?" he answered, shaking his hair, his voice low and calm, mellow even.

"Yeah," the bouncer answered. "Well, a freak is a freak is a freak. And you are the freakiest thing that's passed through here yet! What are you, Disco Ninja Vampire with a makeup fetish and an urge to boogie the night away?"

"Something like that," he smiled. He slowly moved past the bouncer. The man was still mumbling about the trash filling the place each night as he turned to frisk some women coming in the door.

"Where are you, my dear?" he murmured to himself as he stepped into the club and was hit by the 'club scene' non-stop energy.

The mass of people, almost all dressed in black, seemed to bounce in unison, a sea of gyrating bodies, all moving to the same beat.

The music was so loud and bass-filled that it vibrated through the floors, moving him to the specified rhythm that the DJ was spinning.

Brilliant blue flashes of light shot through the air and the crowds, appearing almost hypnotic, as they burst upon the ever-moving sea of black crowding the dance floor.

He inhaled deeply, identifying the intermingled smells of sweat, cologne, perfume, and over-heated bodies—some in rut, others fearful. But they smelled of life, of humanity, and not of the death that he half expected. But that would make his night too easy, and he never trusted anything too easy.

"Excuse me," a man stuttered as he danced in his direction. "But my friends and I have a bet. Are you a man or a woman?"

He looked curiously at the drunken individual, and smiled a slow chilling smile.

"I am whatever I need to be for the moment," he answered, as he turned away from the drunk. He would not consider him a man! A true man would not have to find courage in drink to ask a simple question.

"Hey!" the man cried, reaching out to grip his arm. "You didn't answer my question, freak!"

In a movement almost too fast for sight, he gripped the drunk's wrist, whipped his arm over his head, spinning the suddenly babbling man backwards, and pinning his arm behind him.

"What I am is none of your concern," he hissed in the drunk's ear. "You are ready to go and make nice with your friends, are you not?" he asked.

The drunk, stunned by the swift move and the pain in his arm stopped babbling long enough to nod his head.

"Stay out of my way," he whispered, as he backed up a step before releasing the defeated man.

When the drunk turned, ready to take a swing at the man — it had to be a man — and redeem himself in front of his laughing buddies, there was no one there. Only the slight tinkling of bells and the delicate scent of vanilla.

Silently, he made his way through the crowds, eyes open to detect any unnatural movements, nostrils lifted in expectation of the smell he counted on finding.

Moving silently to a carpeted staircase, he managed to make his way to the highest ground possible. He found a seat at a small round table when its previous occupants moved off towards the stairs and the dancing.

Untying his cloak, he ignored the small gasps of admiration and surprise around him.

His back was almost in a corner, protected on both sides, but it also made him stand out in his bright white and red gear.

That was okay. He wanted to be noticed. He was here to serve a warning.

His quarry had to show sooner or later, so he settled back for a long wait, but kept all senses at attention.

"You are not like the others," a voice said, as a woman stepped up to his table. "I have been watching you."

She shouted to be heard over the loud music and conversation in this place, but his ears picked up on her words just fine.

"Why?" he asked, his voice still low, almost a whisper. Was she an agent of the man he was seeking?

"Because you make no effort to fit in. Mind if I sit?"

"If it suits you," he said, making no move to stand or offer her assistance.

Stephanie Burke

He moved his cloak closer to him, closer to silent death that existed inside its pockets.

"You are not what I expected to find here tonight."

"And what did you expect to find?" he asked as he sank deeper into the shadows.

"That you would come in with a load of body guards and protection. Like the cowardly worm that you are."

"Indeed?" he questioned, as his eyes slowly ran the length of the woman.

She was small, only came to his shoulders, which made her roughly five-feet-two in her high heels. Her hair was a deep dark color, could be brown, could be red, but it was too dark to tell, even with his eyesight. Her face was covered in white paint, although he could tell that her skin tone was almost as dark as his. Her eyes were another mystery, but they appeared to be deep brown or black—soulless eyes, as if her life had been slowly drained away.

He knew the feeling. He saw those very eyes every time he looked into the mirror.

Her lips were painted a garishly bright yet deep red, the color of fresh blood from an artery. Her eyebrows were painted on high slashes that gave her the look of a demented geisha.

She was dressed in a skintight black leather outfit that hugged her body so tightly, he could have seen what she had for dinner…if he chose to look.

Instead he inhaled, smelling the scents of a recently digested meal, the fruit juice she had drunk, and the smell of cold determination. She smelled like death, making home deliveries.

"Indeed," she confirmed. "That is why it is going to be so much fun to kill you, Mr. Balthazar. Enjoy hell."

"My name," he said slowly as he tensed his body in anticipation of an attack. "Is Kye."

"Your name is dead meat!" she replied as she threw a small flash bulb on the table.

Instantly it exploded in a blinding flash of light, and a strange but not unpleasant smell filled the area.

"Odorless garlic?" Kye asked as he raised an eyebrow. He had not moved from his seat, but now all pretense of relaxation was gone from his body.

The music began to swirl and pound madly, the beat matching the rapid pace of his blood through his chest. The wild bass beat reached something deep inside of him; something untamed that showed in his eyes. Eyes now fixed on the woman, eyes promising retribution.

"How can you…?" she began, eyes wide open as realization dawned. But before she could speak, another short woman ran in her direction.

"Wrong man!" she hissed as she moved closer, but then Kye smelled what he was looking for. The smell of old blood and quiet, walking death.

In an instant, he leaped over the table, shoved 'Elvira's' shorter sister behind him, and swung his braid in a full circle, its arc coming dangerously close to the new woman's face, the bells tinkling merrily, a harbinger of death.

"No!" the woman behind him screamed, sidestepping him in a move he had not seen but had expected. He always overestimated his opponents, and this small woman was no exception to the rule.

She ducked the final spin of his braid, dropping into a full split to get beneath his guard, and thrusting both fists upwards towards his chest, fast as lightning.

He countered her move by dropping into a split of his own and gripping her up-thrust arms, holding her immobile for a second.

The people around them screamed and gasped, but all got out of the way of the tableau.

Some wise person decided this was all part of the film that was being shot and eagerly called out encouragement. Only trained stunt people would be able to move like that, so they settled back to enjoy the show.

"Where are the cameras?" someone called out, transmitting his mistake to the rest of the crowd, calming the screams and the frightened panic.

"They must be hidden," someone else shouted, as more people moved in to witness cinema being born.

"Who are you?" Kye hissed, holding the woman immobile for a moment, ignoring the crowd, although he kept his senses attuned to the second woman, the one this hellcat had tried to protect.

"What are you?" she returned, as she suddenly dropped her whole body back, yanking him off balance as she quickly positioned her feet flat on the ground to give her more leverage.

He countered that move too, by using his superior strength and muscle control to quickly slide out of the split to a standing position, yanking her to her feet and unbalancing her so that she fell against his chest.

"A woman who made a mistake, I think," she hissed against his chest, where her face was plastered, but not trapped.

Showing off her flexibility to the delight of the crowd, she swiftly twisted her wrists, reversing his hold on her and thrusting him backwards.

He moved back a step to maintain balance, but also to give her time to make the next move.

"You guys," the other woman, the unnatural one hissed. "We are in big trouble! The onster-may is ere-hay!" She grabbed the hellcat's attention as well as Kye's.

"What?" they both asked, as they dropped their guard to stare at the woman who danced nervously from foot to foot.

"He is oming-cay this a-way!" Her voice rose in pitch to show her fear.

Then Kye smelled him.

Fresh blood mingled with old blood, the stench of fear, the smell of vanilla. His quarry had arrived.

But he hadn't come alone.

There had to be five men, all of the same breed, with him.

"We are in eep-day it-shay!" the woman hissed as the first of the henchmen, to the delight of the crowd, came on the scene, guns drawn.

"Lights, camera, action!" some wise ass called out, laughing at his own wit.

But Kye knew what he faced. In this scene, there would be no one to call cut once the action began. He was fighting for his life, and looking down at the woman that stood so close to him, realized she knew the score too.

Chapter Three

With a curse, Kye thrust the female behind him, found his center of gravity, and met the charge head-on.

As the first man rushed forward, Kye was already moving into action.

Springing into the air, his left leg curled under him, his right fully extended, he whirled into a roundhouse kick that threw the man violently backwards and to the side.

Even before he hit the floor, Kye had landed neatly on his feet, knees bent, hands fisted before his crouched body, eyes meeting those of his next challenge.

The DJ, by some quirk of fate, decided to add extra laser lights, as the electric blue flashes filled the area, surrounding the combatants. The loud, rollicking beat of Prodigy's Slap My Bitch Up, filled the air, the beat matching the blood racing through Kye's body.

"Appropriate," he murmured under his breath. The four remaining guards paused. "Who's my bitch now?"

"Kill him," a voice said from behind the men, his face hidden in the shadows, but his scent, that disgusting smell of old blood and death, was unmistakable. "Then bring me his head. I wish to meet this phantom who has been plaguing me—well, his corpse at any rate."

"He's not the one?" the painted lady said from behind him, just as the next two men launched their attack.

Bending at the waist, Kye leapt into the air, executing a perfect helicopter kick, turning his body in a complete circle, the heels of his white leather boots connecting with the men's chins, knocking one off balance. The other shook off the blow, regaining his balance as Kye landed on his feet and drew his body upright, his long ponytail swinging around his neck, the bells tinkling to the delight of the crowd.

Smiling, the henchman raised his fists in front of him, blocking, as he nodded to his opponent.

Returning his grin, Kye, with one hand, swung the end of his braid around, freeing his neck as he began a series of movements with his feet, movements that resembled a boxer's footwork.

Nodding, the man followed suit, moving his feet rapidly while keeping his eyes trained on the man...woman...thing in white.

Kye smiled. "Let's dance," he murmured as the music began to swell and he waited for the first attack.

With a loud scream, the man rushed forward, executing a perfect drop kick.

Kye stood still, watching until the last possible moment, then he side-stepped, spinning around behind the man before his feet touched ground, and landing a good solid kick to his back, sending him crashing to the floor.

Before he could recover, someone grabbed him from behind, trapping his arms at his side and using their larger size and girth to bend him forward.

"Got you now, you mother..."

His remaining words were cut off as Kye swung his head backwards, striking his captor in the nose, breaking it with a loud crunch, before he jerked his arms up and forward, breaking the now panicking man's hold.

Turning quickly, Kye delivered a blow to the underside of his chin, snapping his head back as he thrust with his other hand, striking him in the center of his body, sending him crashing to the ground.

That left one man standing.

Turning to face this final obstacle, he suddenly became aware of two things. The music changed to Daft Punk's One More Time, and the final man held a weapon in his hand.

Taking no chances with hand-to-hand combat, the final man did what he figured was the smart way to kill a man.

"This gun beats Kung Fu anyway," he taunted as he stepped closer.

"A Smith and Wesson," Kye purred, his eyes glowing with admiration as he whipped his braid around his neck. "A classic!"

"They never go out of style," the man agreed, "unlike your superhero outfit. What are you, The Ghost of Ninja Past or something?"

"Or something," Kye said with a smile, before, lightning fast, he whipped one of the spines from his braid and sent it sailing towards his target.

The man, seeing the move, stepped to the side to avoid being hit, taking his eyes off of Kye.

That was all Kye was waiting for.

Silently, and with preternatural speed, he leapt forward, knocking the gun aside and lifting the now frightened man three inches off of his feet.

"What are you?" the man hissed, his eyes wide as he saw his own death in those dark glowing orbs.

"I am a classic case," Kye replied, as he lifted the man higher, using his fingers to cut off his oxygen supply. "I never go out of style. You should like that."

While the man gasped and kicked, Kye carried him over to a nearby railing, noting the shocked anticipation from the crowd as they watched, eagerly seeking out movie death and bloodshed.

"You will deliver a message for me," he said as he easily lifted the man to lean over the banister.

Looking, the now terrified man gulped and tried to breathe as his eyes took in the panoramic view of the floor one story below. The people moved and gyrated as the DJ segued neatly into Let the Bodies Hit the Floor.

"Oh, they're playing my song," Kye purred as he eased his grip on the now morbidly still man.

"Please," the man gasped, as he was allowed a little air.

"Tell him I am coming for him. Tell him Death is now risen and is hungry. Tell him to prepare to meet his master in hell."

As the man shook in terror, the crowd began to murmur in confusion and fear. This was way too real to be a movie! Yet what else could it be?

"Tell him!"

"I-I will!" henchman number five gasped, then screamed as Kye released him.

The man flailed his arms and legs wide, expecting to feel the emptiness of cold space before the feel of hard bones and floor cushioned his fall.

Instead, he felt two hands suddenly grip his ankles, holding him solidly and surely.

"Remember," Kye said.

"Remember!" the man screamed, tears beginning to well in his eyes. "Remember that the painted freak is coming to kill him!"

"Good, though I'm not sure about the painted freak," Kye said, considering the merits of letting the man go.

Then he shrugged and pulled him upright, letting him flop to the ground amid the stunned crowd.

Turning his back to the man, who was no longer a threat, he stepped over the four fallen bodies in an effort to find the two women — the vampire and the painted lady.

"Now, for you!" he declared as he approached his table, ignoring the clapping cheering crowd.

The woman was gone! Both of them were gone! On the table was his black cloak, the powdery garlic residue shaken off. But the woman who sought to assassinate him was nowhere to be seen.

"Great moves!" one man said, running up to him and clapping him on the shoulder. "You have that Bruce Lee, Jackie Chan thing going!"

Snorting, Kye retrieved his cloak, patting the pockets and finding no immediately empty spaces that told of a theft. Still ignoring the man's babbling, he swung the cloak around his shoulders, concealing his body and face in the enveloping darkness within, his bells tinkling merrily as he turned to the man.

"Go away," he said softly, watching as the man's words tapered off and died.

"When is the movie coming out?" the man asked again, as he backed away from the mysterious actor who had performed his own stunts.

"Movie?" Kye asked, then smiled. "Next year. It will be called Death Had Two Faces."

The man blinked, then nodded. "I like it," he said, then turned to face the man again, but he was gone.

"Hollywood types," he muttered to himself then stepped over the extras still lying on the floor, and headed towards the bar.

Outside, the lone cloaked man moved quickly though the crowd, emerging at the exit and disappearing into the night, leaving behind the faint scent of vanilla and cinnamon.

Two glittering pairs of eyes watched his passing and noted his progress.

The Slayer

Chapter Four

Kye brooded.

He walked the darkened streets like a caged animal, daring anyone or anything to attack, giving him an outlet for his pent-up frustrations.

So close, and yet so far away!

He'd almost had Balthazar! He had his trail, knew that he would be putting in an appearance, yet he'd slipped through his hands.

All because of some two-bit, painted hussy and her blood-sucking friend!

Almost had him in his grasp, almost held him in his hands, massaging his neck until death, almost was able to put an end to his miserable existence.

Almost, but for the girl in black with the painted face.

As he stalked along the streets amid the illusion of water reflecting the buildings and the night sky in its asphalt mirror, he wondered again if ridding the world of Balthazar would make any difference.

There was so much scum on the Earth, so much pestilence and human filth. Would ridding humanity of the fiend's existence make this hellhole a better place to live?

He doubted it, but it would make his remaining time tolerable.

There were so many people, human and other, just waiting to pick up the reins and wreak havoc on the city. So many plain, evil, mean, bad people, both mortal and partially mortal — in his opinion nothing was immortal. It just took longer to kill them.

As he walked, the tinkling of his bells filled the silent air around him, a warning, an enticement, and a threat to all that heard. A few people on the party strip, still seeking entertainment of the unusual and wild kind, ventured through the streets, but bypassed the grim figure dressed in black. That was too much unusualness for their taste.

"Walk away," he mumbled as he passed them, ignoring their curious stares and amazed gazes. It was almost his feeding time, and he didn't want to make a meal out of anyone who would be missed.

As he walked, his keen hunter's eyes surveyed the landscape, searching for the perfect victim, the perfect meal.

There!

He found it!

Sleek and fast, smelling of fresh meat and some unnameable spice.

He would enjoy this to the fullest! His hunt had been worth it!

Even so, anticipation of this new food source did little to appease his anger at letting Balthazar slip through his fingers or the part the painted woman and the bloodsucker played in his escape. The thought of a full stomach satisfied some inner craving that was getting harder and harder to pass up with each moment.

As he drew closer, his eyes began to tear and his mouth to water. He could almost picture himself sinking his teeth in and devouring, feeding like the lone alpha male in a pack of wolves. His eyesight sharpened as his senses went on alert!

It was time!

Closing in on his prey, he pulled close the black cloak around him, masking his face and body, protecting his clothes from the carnage that was sure to follow.

He began to sneak up on the intended, salivating at the thought of what he would do!

"One, with the works," he growled, to the delight of the woman behind the hot dog stand.

"Baby! What are you doing out here this time of night?" the laughing woman said as she clapped her hands in delight.

"Angel, baby! How could I stay away from you?"

Laughing, the short dark woman clapped her hands again in joy, before reaching out and touching the side of his face.

"How come you walking around like a two dollar whore, baby? You turning tricks?" She giggled at the slow grin that spread across his face.

"Your tip paid off," he told her with glee. "He was there, but there were extenuating circumstances."

"Circumstances?" she asked as the rising joy in her face melted into a look of disbelief. "But it was all set up! It was perfect, baby! What happened?"

"A female with Terminator delusions and some decent training happened, Angel." He narrowed his eyes in memory. If only he had not been distracted…

"Her people are not as well trained as you," Angel said quietly, as she eyed her mysterious friend. "Who was she?"

"Someone bent on killing. And I haven't decided which side she is on."

"That…that is…not good," Angel said as she tucked an errant strand of hair behind her ear and let the rest of the chin-length, thick mass fall over the right side of her face.

"Hey! Don't do that!" Kye demanded as he reached out and gently brushed the hair away from her face, exposing what she so dearly tried to hide.

"Kye!" she cried out in protest, her brown eyes widening in shock and a bit of fear. "No!"

"Hush, Angel," he said as he gently caressed the scarred cheek with his left hand and cupped her chin with his right. "You are beautiful and should not be in hiding."

Large tears welled up in her eyes as she stared at the man who had taken her heart so many years ago; who had saved her life and had given her a reason to fight for the best of all reasons, revenge.

"I am an old fool who was a bigger fool when she was younger," she whispered, as she, just for a moment, nestled her face into his hand, then dropped her head.

"You were young and innocent, Angel, a victim! His victim. And I swear to you on my brother's grave, on the burial mound of my father and the ashes of my mother, that you will be avenged."

"What was taken away, Kye, what was such a vital part of me, is gone! Nothing can change that," she argued as tears began to fall down her face, following the path of the crescent shaped scar that ran from the side of her eye to the corner of her mouth, emphasizing the deliberateness if its nature. Its two bisecting lines in the center of the arch marred her almost perfect features, marking her for the world to see as his...thing.

"No, Angel. No force on earth can return what was stolen, but I can bring you some satisfaction."

"But it may be too late! Time is running out, Kye! I am wondering if it is worth it to go on!"

"Are you worth so little, baby?" he asked as he gently urged her head up to meet his gaze. "Are you worth so little? Is your struggle, your fight so easily discarded?"

Angel looked up at Kye, a tear trembling, threatening to fall from an eyelash, and slowly shook her head. "No."

Her eyes, her deep brown eyes, were fathomless pools of misery; a pain so deep filled them that it almost physically hurt to stare into them. But there was also a returning strength, a steely determination in them that almost overwhelmed the anguish.

"What..." she cleared her throat and tried again. "What did the woman look like?"

"Painted, baby! All painted up like a two-bit prostitute."

"Kind of like you?" Angel chuckled, as she sniffed and stepped back from the man that had come to mean so much to her, as she stopped drawing his strength.

"No one is as good looking as I!" he retorted, pleased to see her mind back on track.

Angel was a beautiful woman, despite, no, in spite of the scar. He would have taken her to his bed in a moment, if he still had those desires and if she would have submitted to his taking. Women like Angel were rare, women of indomitable spirit and determination. She would fight for their mutual cause to the bitter end, and then, while the light of life was extinguishing from her body, she would take a few enemies with her along to the final destination.

"If you say so, baby!" she laughed, as she reached down into her cart and began to prepare his sausage just the way he liked it, with everything and extra hots. "Now tell me about this female Terminator who has you thinking. Maybe I can get the 411 on her and her companion."

"Angel-cakes, I always think," he said. He watched with hungry eyes as she prepared his dog the way he loved.

"True enough, but tell me about her anyway."

"Well, she had the most garish make up job I have ever seen. She looked like a reject from a geisha academy, but her catsuit was eye-catching."

Chapter Five

"How could I have made such a foolish mistake?"

"You are human."

"I know, but how could I have been so wrong?"

"You are human."

"I know, but I could have killed an innocent man! How could I have done something so stupid?"

"You are human!"

Tali glared at Mari.

"You are not helping."

"Maybe I could take you more seriously if you removed that god-awful paint from your face, first."

The short woman glared at her even shorter companion before sighing and sitting at the vanity table.

"Thank you," Mari sighed as she reached for the jar of cold cream and the cotton balls. "Honestly, you would think you'd never made a mistake before."

"But attacking a totally innocent stranger, Mari! I lost my shot at Balthazar and maybe my only chance to get this close to him."

"Well, you got some exercise out of the deal," the short, curly-haired woman said, as if trying to find the bright side as she scrubbed the paint from her friend's face.

"Ouch! Watch it!" Tali glared in the mirror at the unrepentant face above her. "Why did you use this crap if it's so hard to get off?"

"Because you wanted to fit in. And I don't think the man is totally innocent."

"He was a stranger and didn't play into my plans!"

"Stranger, but not innocent. He wasn't even human!"

"Really?" Tali snorted. "It was just my luck to pick up on Bruce Lee's confused younger brother," she sighed, as she pressed the play button on her radio that was centered in the chaos of the vanity table.

"He wasn't human," Mari stated again, with authority.

The beginning strains of Enigma's Return to Innocence filled the air in the small basement apartment.

Situated in one of the worst sections of town, it was the perfect place for two women such as they. No one would ask questions if they disappeared, so long as the rent was paid on time, and their comings and goings were not noticed, let alone mentioned. People here were too poor, strung out, or beat down to care. Perfect for two women who were almost too poor, beat down, and frustrated to give a damn.

"How do you know?" Tali asked. She watched in the mirror as the paint disappeared under the attentive actions of her friend. Her plain, normal, everyday face was exposed. The music soothed her nerves as she tried to let go of the tension that had filled her body from the beginning of this night's clusterfuck!

So she almost injured an innocent man. Not!

Okay, so she attacked an innocent man and figured she had almost met her match in him. At least in wardrobe and make-up. His ability as a fighter was still to be questioned.

Damn! Why couldn't she get him off of her mind?

"I know," Mari said, as she finished removing the last of the war paint and stared at the smooth cocoa brown skin of her companion's face. "I know because I am not human."

Tali froze.

At moments like this, she almost forgot that Mari was indeed not human! She forgot Mari needed a steady supply of blood to remain fresh and lifelike, but she was not human.

"So you run up yelling in pig Latin?" she asked as she again shook with the painful hatred she felt for any of Balthazar's ilk.

But Mari was different! Mari was her friend, she reminded herself. Mari had saved her.

"Well, I could have engaged in fisticuffs, but I thought it would be more prudent to warn you the big guy was on his way in."

"True," Tali agreed, then sighed, the soothing music and the haunting voice of Enigma forgotten in the face of this news. "So tell me, old wise one, who is he?"

"Watch it with that old shit," Mari snorted, then got a thoughtful look on her still features. "It looks like I have to put in calls to Chari and Barbi. They may know something about him."

"Isn't that putting them in danger?" Tali asked, as she examined her friend's face, noticing the small look of unease on her cafe au lait complexion.

"They are in danger already, Tali. I wasn't able to get them out, but it is good to have a voice on the inside. I'll find out what they know about a painted freak."

"With almond shaped eyes," Tali added quickly.

"With almond shaped eyes."

"Deep green and gold eyes."

"Green and gold," Mari said, as she carefully watched her friend.

"And his hair was super long, as if he never cut it."

"Long hair," Mari said slowly. "Check."

"Long dark hair and he smelled like vanilla."

"Okay! What is going on with you?" Mari exploded as she watched Tali close her eyes and inhale deeply as if she were getting a whiff of the mystery man in question.

"Whatever do you mean?" Tali said, suddenly snapping back to full attention and hitting the stop button on her tape player.

"Don't play coy with me, Missy! I changed your diapers and swatted your ass when you needed it done! What is going through that peanut brain of yours?"

"I don't know…"

Hissing, Mari let the inch long fangs explode from her gums as she swung her charge around to face her.

"No bullshit, Tali! What is going on?"

Ignoring the vamping fit Mari was throwing, Tali calmly stared at her friend and companion of many years, as a slow shark's grin spread across her face.

"Oh shit!" Mari breathed, as her fangs sank back into her mouth.

"He makes me feel."

"Oh no, Tali! We don't know anything about him!"

"Tell that to my body, Mari!" She laughed, as she rose to her feet and dropped a small kiss on the woman's cheek. "But I doubt it would listen."

"You want to get laid!"

"I want to get laid and he has such a perfect body, Mari! You didn't get to touch it! It was hard and soft! And he smelled so good!"

"How dare you sink into feminine sensuality when we have work to do," Mari tried to argue, but there was really no heat in it.

"I can't help myself!" Tali sighed. "I'm in lust!"

Sighing deeply, Mari shook her head as she went to place a few phone calls.

"That bad?" she asked as she watched her charge flutter off towards the shower.

"Hurts so good, Mari! I have to admit, I copped a feel! He was fully packed!"

"I don't want to hear this!" Mari laughed as she shook her head.

Her baby had grown up. Now she wanted to test her wings.

If she thought that it was odd to call a woman almost thirty years old a baby, Mari had to take into consideration that she herself was over four hundred. Tali a was baby to her!

"And his eyes, Mari! His eyes, they kind of swirled."

Mari quickly made her calls and asked the right people the right questions.

She wanted Tali to have a fling if she wished, but she wanted to know all about this mystery man and what his purpose was.

If he was to interfere with their plans, erotic plaything for Tali or not, he would die.

They had sacrificed too much, lost so much, to let him go before they got their revenge.

Balthazar's ultimate destruction was the only thing good enough to pay off the debt. They would collect, no matter what!

Chapter Six

"Murder by numbers, one...two...three. It's as easy to learn as your A, B, C, D, E's."

Kye sang softly as he peeled the leather from his body. He'd lucked out with this one! No blood stains.

With the music playing softly in the background, Kye thought back on the night, reviewing all that he had learned.

Angel's network had been notified and the answers he sought would soon be his.

Angel, he thought.

Beautiful, sweet Angel. Another victim of Balthazar. Would he never be rid of that evil? Would he forever find nothing but the broken bits and pieces left in his wake?

Angel, beautiful Angel, was different.

With her inner and outer scars, Angel was the most appealing thing he had seen in years—besides the mysterious woman in black.

It had been years since he first met and almost killed Angel, because of the scents she carried. Something in her eyes had moved him to be cautious.

He soon discovered the beautiful, exotic dancer was another pawn who had suffered at Balthazar's hands.

She was about to kill herself when he stepped in.

Death by the waters of the Inner Harbor was not a pleasant thought. Neither was becoming food for the crabs and fish that inhabited the less than pristine waters.

He sighed as he remembered that night.

It was summer and the night air was filled with excitement. Couples ran along the streets, enjoying their youth and their so-called rebellion. Tourists packed the more popular hangouts, along with pick pockets, thugs, panhandlers, and one man dressed in black seeking vengeance.

It was her scent that caught his attention.

A smallish woman dressed in the typical black of the Goth scene rushed past him, arms bent protectively across her chest as she rapidly walked past the popular historic Fells Point Bars and headed to the little used area on the docks.

She looked to be in pain or searching for her next meal, so Kye gave in to his instinct to follow. It was not unusual for Balthazar to drain his followers and laugh as he watched the poor bastards struggle not to break his rules by eating the next person that crossed their path. Oh no! Balthazar made it a rule to only attack the dregs of society and targets of his own personal choosing.

For fun, he would drain his nearest and dearest guards, filtering the blood of the commoners, he called it. The poor bastard that got drained had to hold in the hunger and the desire to bite until the appropriate target was found. Often the bastard would follow and laugh as his people fought against their natural instincts to keep his rules. He said it made them stronger.

Kye thought it showed just how much of a braying ass the man was.

On this night, he could not detect the cloying scent of vanilla in the air.

Another victim of his Majesty's Enjoyment, he thought. Suffering without the audience this time. So he followed to put the poor bastard out of her misery and take out another layer of Balthazar's security while he was at it. The lost warrior would be easily replaced, but it just gave Kye satisfaction to harass the bastard. Elite warriors were not easily replaced.

"Going to rape me?" the woman asked, as he followed, making no attempt to hide his presence.

"What?" Of all the things he expected, the low dead voice was not what he thought to hear.

"Going to rape me? Cause if you are, you are too late. I am all raped out. If you want money, I don't have that either. You can do us both a favor by killing me now and getting it over with so I won't have to do it myself, or you can just walk away and leave me to get the job done."

"Why on earth would I want to rape you, let alone kill you?" Despite the fact you are an evil thing being prostituted by the world's biggest asshole, he said silently to himself.

"Because that is all I have left and it ain't worth much anymore."

She stood, facing the dark murky waters of this forgotten part of the bay. Her short black leather skirt rode low on her thin hips and her hair covered a goodly portion of her face. The light seemed to pass right over her, neither illuminating her face or form. It was like she didn't exist for the light — like she was no longer worthy of it.

Kye sniffed the air around her and could not detect the traces of old blood, but he could smell hunger, neglect and semen. Maybe she was not of his ilk, he thought. Maybe she was a personal target of the man, suffering at his hands only to be later taken care of when the mood struck him. Balthazar thought he was that powerful. Then again, maybe she was just another willing fuck toy.

"So, you want to do it or you want me to help?" he asked as he closely watched for her reaction.

"Please make it quick. I have suffered enough."

She tilted her head to the side and let the hair cascade away from her neck, exposing it to whatever weapon of choice he had in his possession.

"From what you have been playing with, I'd say a quick death would be too easy."

Kye had no compassion for those who let themselves be used.

"Then get the fuck away from me and let me do it myself! I have had enough! No more! No more begging, no more waiting, no more broken promises and pain! I have had it!"

She turned to face him and he almost took a step back as he saw the anguish in her eyes.

"Kill me or get the hell out of here!" she ordered.

Her eyes were dead flat things that he had seen only in his mirror.

"Do it or go!"

"And if I want to watch, to make sure you do it right?"

She sucked in a breath, then turned without a word to face the waters again.

"Then watch closely and see how it's done."

From seemingly nowhere, she pulled out a small handgun. It glinted dark gray in the non-light of the forgotten alley, the stars and the moon effortlessly highlighting its purpose and intent. The barrel easily slipped between her lips. With both hands she got a good grip on the barrel as she began to squeeze. Then something flashed silver in the dark of the night, something precious and enviable and wholly unexpected in their tragic beauty.

Tears.

It was her tears that forced Kye to move, to attempt to break the sound barrier and reach her.

Just seconds before she completed the pull that would have made stopping the bullet impossible, his finger sank behind the trigger, making it impossible to start the unstoppable cycle.

"Why?" he asked as he snatched the gun away and got his first close-up look at the woman.

Evil shed no tears! It had no regrets. She may be touched by darkness, but she was not fully tainted.

"Because he took my baby!" she sniffled, as she fought to pull the gun away from him. "Because he took my life! Because he took everything away from me! He is a monster and he wants my soul! Better I end it all! I have nothing left to live for!"

She broke down in sobs, leaning against the stranger who promised death, and unknown to her, was death's largest ally.

"Who?" He had to know. Was she some plaything for the hydra or was she a direct pawn? Was she one play toy for the taking, or had she escaped, luckier than she knew, without her spirit but with her soul?

"Why? Are you going to drag me back to him? Are you going to share what's left of my body? Better to murder me now! If you have anything left resembling a heart, kill me now!"

"Who?"

"Why? Why do you want to know?"

"Who?"

He gripped her shoulders in a punishing grasp and gave her a shake that ended her growing hysteria and brought her eyes up to his.

"Balthazar!" she screamed. "He cut me! He took my baby from my womb! He did this to me!"

She brushed her hair from the side of her face and showed the crescent shaped scar, still fresh and pink.

"He took my baby!" she sobbed as she beat at his chest, giving vent to the rage she was unable to free when in his presence. "I want my baby! I want my baby! I want my life!" she sobbed as she collapsed against his chest. "Kill me! Go on! Kill me!"

Not an accomplice and not a soldier, he thought as held her with one hand against his chest. The other slowly lifted the gun to her temple.

"It is so easy to end it all," he purred. "So easy to end the pain and the suffering. So easy to pull this trigger and let your brains run onto the ground."

She sniffed a bit and looked up into his eyes, eyes that were deadly serious and intent. Suddenly, she was a bit afraid of death, for surely she was lying in its arms. The sweet kiss of release it offered no longer looked so sweet.

"It is so very easy to end a life," he breathed as he stared in her eyes, letting her know that this moment would define whether she lived or died. "So easy and such a waste."

He ran his hands along the scar, making her remember the things of her past.

"Such a waste to end such beauty and strength. Such a waste to end such delicious hate."

"I...I..."

"But it doesn't have to end," he added, as he pressed the gun harder, making the muzzle of the barrel mark its imprint on her temple and in her mind. "We can turn that hate into revenge."

"Revenge?"

"Revenge," he assured. "A slow, painful revenge that can be sweeter than any release you have ever dreamed of. Tell me now. The bullet and I will have no trouble helping you slough off this mortal coil. Or you can come with me."

"Is this about sex? Because if it is..."

"This is about life, and ending his."

"Balthazar?"

"He made me what I am. And I want to thank him for his...gifts."

She trembled in his arms, shuddered at the thought of paying back the bastard for even one-tenth of the misery he had dealt her.

"I may be pregnant."

"By him?"

"Yes," she breathed. "He said if I let him...have me, he would give me back my baby."

"So you whored for him."

"And his friends," she said, anger beginning to fill the void left by the loss of her child.

"How long?"

"Fifteen years."

"You are not pregnant."

"But each month, he…"

"You are not pregnant. Evil like that isn't allowed to procreate. They reproduce copies of themselves, make carbon copies if you will. But he cannot get you pregnant."

"Then he never was going to give my baby back. He lied to me."

"For fifteen years of lies and pain. Do you want repayment?"

"Revenge!" Her eyes glowed hotly in her face, their flat look replaced by the multi-dimensional anger she felt, the hatred that now poured though her veins stronger than before.

"After fifteen years, you know things."

"I know people."

"Join me. I can bring him down for you."

"I want to be there! I want to see him bleed!"

"Join me."

"Who are you?"

"I am Death."

* * * * *

And three years later, he had never met a more determined woman. She was a creature beautiful in her hatred, proud in her anger. She stirred his loins in a way few had been able to in the past.

That was, until he ran into the faceless butch bitch in black.

42

Angel would never share his bed, although she knew she had an open invitation. Maybe this woman would be...more accommodating.

"Maybe there is a use for you after all, my mysterious little painted lady," he mused. "At least a use before I have to kill you."

"When you get a taste of this experience,
And you're flushed with your very first success
You must try a twosome or a threesome
You'll find your conscience bothers you much less.
'Cause murder is like anything you take to!
It's a habit-forming need for more and more.

You can bump off every member of your family,
Or anyone else you find a bore.
Murder by numbers
One two three
It's as easy to learn as your ABC's."

Chapter Seven

Chari shivered as she sat, waiting.

Nothing could be worse that the waiting. She knew he did it on purpose. Making her wait, making her think about what was going to happen, making her anticipate each and every mark on her body.

Chari hated waiting.

"I should just leave," she said as she adjusted her collar for the fifth time. "But he would just come after me."

Her collar was a special one, made for his special woman.

Each of his women had a talent he loved to showcase.

Barbi could climax at will, something that made him feel like a great lover when actually he was just the object she used to get herself off and pretend she wasn't living in hell.

Marti was a dancer. She was more limber than a snake and it was as natural to her as breathing. Even her walk was sexy.

Chari could swallow an eggplant! She was born with no gag reflex and hated the day she had jokingly swallowed a banana for her boyfriend in a bar. That twit had sold her, as if he had the right, for a hundred dollars and season tickets to the Orioles games. The damn team even had the nerve to come in last in the league!

Because of her special gifts, she was the woman Balthazar had to have…for the moment.

She remembered her boyfriend had excused himself to go to the rest room and the stunningly handsome young man who had walked up as he left.

"You are so very beautiful, I had to come over and appreciate the blessing the Lord bestowed upon you."

"Um, thank you," she answered, flustered by his attentions.

He was a good-looking man, the rat bastard monster!

His curly hair was a deep brown and so glossy it shined. His eyes were an interesting combination of red and brown, the color of aged sherry. He was a few inches taller than she, which put him around six feet even. His whole form just dripped of grace and class.

She was flattered. Who wouldn't be?

"No, thank you for brightening up an otherwise dull and lifeless night."

He turned and walked away with the music of Men Without Hat's Safety Dance blaring behind him. No other comments were made and the boyfriend was soon back and ready to leave.

Shaking off the strange encounter, Chari left, feeling beautiful and desired and oddly elated at the strange man's compliment.

They were both singing the chorus, "It's safe to dance," and having a blast as they left the hot, packed club.

But all of that changed as a stretch limo pulled in front of them, cutting them off.

The door slid open and that handsome face peeked out from the eclipsing blackness of the car.

"Can I offer you a lift?" he inquired as he stared at her boyfriend.

"See ya, Chari! It's been fun," the bastard said, before he turned and walked away.

"David?" she called as he turned away, leaving her standing by the expensive car.

Before she could do more than that, a hand reached out and yanked her into the car.

"Let me go!" she shrieked. Suddenly afraid and fighting for her life, she was easily held.

"Silence!" he had roared, as he held her struggling body across his lap.

"Get the fuck off of me!" she had screamed, squirming and fighting. She felt the car move and that added another element of fear, and energized her enough to continue fighting the man that held her.

"Such language from such a pretty mouth," he growled and suddenly she was flipped onto her back to stare at the monster above her.

"That is the only reason you are here, you know? That pretty little talented mouth."

Even as she fought him, he stared deep into her eyes and she felt a sudden lethargy take over her body.

Slowly, her will to fight was drained away as she lost herself in those red-brown orbs. She had no will; she was falling, her soul slowly leaving her body.

"That is so good, pretty one. I have never had such a charming honey-skinned angel in my fold before. Especially one with such a talent. You will fit in with the rest."

That was all she could clearly recall, that and when he put the damned collar around her neck—for greater control, he said. That was almost twenty years ago.

In that time, his many lessons stung her pride and made her wish for death.

"Use teeth and I will pull them out. Then we won't have a problem, my little plucked Chari. Hands and knees, bitch! When I walk into a room, you greet your Master properly." And her personal favorite, "Lick it, suck it, but never bite it. Your Master is too pretty for scars. Keep crying and I'll give you something to cry over."

The same lessons, year after year as time seemed to drag on.

As a lesson to his most disobedient woman, Chari, he had skinned one of his lesser women alive, and made the rest watch.

His cold ruthlessness put a fear into her that nothing could erase. Still, time lapsed.

More women were added, a few more punished or out-and-out murdered, and Chari still looked the same.

He had done something to her that night, taken something away, and in return, he had given her this never-ending youth. She could not even hope to escape his clutches in death.

But this last phone call, the one from Mari, changed a lot of things.

Mari was one of the lucky ones. She had escaped and he thought she was dead. So had everyone else until Chari started receiving untraceable calls on her private line.

Each one of his angels had a private line, a gift he gave them, so they could call each other from room to room. But Mari had figured out a way to patch in an outside line.

Since Balthazar's women had to remain at home base while he traveled around being the big shot man of the city, it was easy to get in contact with a few of the girls who hated the man and wished to see him dead.

Chari was just one of many, but she was closer to the man because of her unique talent. He always wanted her around to service his friends or himself. She was very highly prized.

Mari's call had given her a new purpose; put some of the old fight back into her.

If anyone could gather up info about a new enemy, an enemy he feared, Chari would be the one.

So she sat and waited, her naked body tense with anticipation, heat flowing through her veins. She would service the monster; she would get so close to him he would not want to move two feet without her present. She would get the information Mari needed.

Then she would piss on his grave.

* * * * *

Kye rolled over in his bed, glared at the sunlight flowing through his windows and decided it was time to rise.

Naked, he padded across his floor, ignoring the cold on his bare feet, and stepped onto his workout mats.

Old habits die hard, he thought as he first dropped to his knees and offered thanks for seeing another day. He then prayed for strength, strength not to kill himself until his task was complete. Strength to massage the neck of that unholy creation named Balthazar, until he ceased to breathe.

Prayers completed, he rose and walked past the pictures of his family, prominently placed on a bare white wall, and promised vengeance.

Turning, he began his morning workout, stretching and limbering his muscles until he was as flexible as a reed. Then he began his kata, his special and unique series of movements, punches and kicks. It was a mishmash of several fighting skills from Aikido to Karate with jujitsu and street fighting added.

His bastard fighting skills had saved his life on more than one occasion and constantly grew as he faced new challenges out on the streets.

Now, he planned for surprise splits and females who were more butch than he. The addition of these new moves only made him more aware of the strange woman.

He wanted, no, needed to know more about her and her plans. She could be an ally or a very cleverly disguised foe. Time and Angel would tell.

Bowing, he stepped off of the mat and made his way to his bathroom.

Kye could not abide a dirty body. Before he did anything, he bathed.

As the smells of vanilla and cinnamon filled the air, he basked in the hot water of his shower.

There was no time for a bath today. He had to try and discover Balthazar's next move.

The man knew he was on his trail and was beginning to act nervous.

That had to be the reason for the bodyguards that had attacked last night. He had Balthazar worried; not scared but worried. Fear would come.

Kye had a list of the man's business interests in this city and knew he had plans to move into the overseas market before too long. Now was the time to strike, before he moved back to his place of origin, before he could call on old allies to aid and abet him. The game used to be about power, now those of his ilk were after money. It was easier to terrify the masses when you could hire out the bad guys. If he ever gathered enough money to buy into the big leagues overseas, then the monster could effectively disappear.

Balthazar had been around for many years, spreading his own special brand of terror against those who opposed him. The man's quest for magical and arcane knowledge was his greatest asset and weakness.

It had cost Kye his family, but it had also created one of the man's most feared enemies. Kye would deliver death to the man, and then he would end the existence he had been forced to live.

After toweling off in the bathroom, Kye slipped on his favorite slippers and proceeded to his kitchen and his newspaper, his large flaccid cock swaying with every step.

Looking in the fridge, he backed away as the cold air threatened shrinkage, but pulled out his two needed breakfast goodies, a box of cold Apple Jacks and a bag of blood.

Grabbing a bowl, he mixed the happy green and orange cereal rings with the cold thick liquid and began to consume them with great delight.

Who said sweet breakfast cereals were just for kids?

As he munched, he absently flipped on his radio and opened his paper.

There had to be something there, some clue to Balthazar's next move.

As the Eurhythmics' Annie Lennox crooned about sweet dreams in her monotone, Kye's eyes lit up.

"Gothic Rage" the banner said. "The newest hot spot for alternative music and lifestyles." Translated, that meant, 'come out and dress as wild as you want. S&M in the back rooms and sex swapping in the basement. BYOD, bring your own drugs and partners— sanity an option.' It was too good to pass up! Balthazar had to have a hand in this! It was one of the ways he recruited for his growing army.

"I wonder if Morticia will show up," he mused as he reached out and flipped off the radio.

Shoveling another mouthful of breakfast into his mouth, he contemplated what to wear to impress her. Maybe his black I wanna get laid pants or his blood red jumpsuit, both in leather. She was bound to be there, even if she was an enemy out for his blood.

Speaking of blood, he stared down into his soggy cereal and cursed. They never stayed crunchy in blood.

Wrinkling his nose in displeasure, he quickly finished the cereal, vowing—lactose intolerant or not—to find a better way to have his favorite cereal. He could have a glass of blood and still have a complete vitamin and protein rich breakfast.

Chapter Eight

Kye inhaled deeply, the stench of human misery and self-deprecation, and smiled. It was a scent that went rather well with the desperation that also filled the air in the club.

Gothic Rage was a hole in the wall. It was a two-story disaster that the owner had had to bribe the zoning board to get an operator's license. They had gotten by the liquor license laws by making it BYOB. Not that he would trust anything from behind the bar anyway.

The stereo pumped a hard-edged grinding version of Metallica's Enter Sandman by the Mighty Mighty Bosstones. It, at least, was worth listening to.

Keeping that thought in mind, Kye slid between the gyrating sweaty masses that packed the floor, the posers looking for excitement, the newbies looking scared and uncertain, the veterans looking bored and jaded. Just another typical evening in the pit.

"Hey," a woman purred as she bumped into him and turned to face the stranger in red. "Where did you come from?"

"The seventh level of hell," Kye lightly replied as he pulled her hand from his chest where it was steadily inching its way down. "Want to join me?"

She eyed him with an experienced look in her eyes.

His tight red leather vest did nothing to hide the ripcord muscles that covered his body, but it neatly exposed a large amount of bronze skin. His matching red pants left nothing to the imagination, the tight drawstring starting below his navel and carrying the eyes to the prominent bulge below. On his feet were a red pair of leather moccasins, calf length, and original as the green/gold eyes that stared at her coolly.

His hair was a free-falling cascade of night, an endless black waterfall highlighted with several thin braids that tinkled as the movements of the crowd brushed against him. The scents of vanilla and cinnamon surrounded him like a cloak, but it didn't bring to mind baking cookies with her mama. It smelled strangely of death.

But it was the sinister look in his eyes, the cruel twist of his lips and the total control he exuded over himself, that made her back off.

"Honey, I don't even want to know where you have been, let alone join you there. I like my sanity."

"Then why are you here?"

"Everyone needs a thrill now and then. You were my thrill of the night. Do me a favor, let me know when you start killing people, so I won't get trampled in the crush."

That said, she turned and made her way to a spot against the wall, all prepared to wait and see what unfolded.

"Smart woman," Kye breathed as he made his way across the dance floor to the stairs that led above. He caught no sign of Balthazar, but the evening was still young.

* * * * *

Tali slowly made her way into the club, hoping her hunch would play out. It was a message in the paper that had drawn her to the last club, where she'd met him! Maybe he would be here and she could get some answers.

Her near-nude body, dressed in shredded black tights that gave enticing peeks at bare flesh, a black leather schoolgirl skirt that barely covered her privacy and a poets blouse in the whitest of whites, slashed to about an inch below her breasts, drew a lot of attention. Her face, painted to look like a fashion doll on crack, didn't help matters either, but she was used to being observed.

"If he's not here, Balthazar may be and the evening won't be a total waste."

"Who are you trying to convince?" Mari muttered beside her as she ruthlessly pushed people out of her way.

She had not yet heard from Chari, and needed information on this man her charge had decided to bed. There was something about him, something that unnerved her.

"I am trying to convince no one, Mari. But if I can kill two birds with one stone..."

"Don't make me ill."

"Hey! Just because you don't like sex, there is no reason for you to come down on my head!"

"Do you not remember our purpose?" Mari hissed as she grabbed Tali's arm.

"How can I forget, with you hounding me every second of the night?"

"Well...hell!"

Mari realized that she had been riding Tali harder than usual, but things were coming to a head and soon! Reports were saying Balthazar was getting desperate to complete his plans. If that were to happen, he would be a force to be reckoned with and humanity, as a whole, would be jeopardized. So yes, she was riding Tali harder than normal. Time was running out!

"We will find him, Mari!" Tali blithely went on as she pulled her arm from the woman's hand and continued her trek into the club. "There is something about that stranger that calls to me!"

"Yeah," she snorted. "About eight inches erect!"

Before she could find the perfect retort, the music dropped and the hypnotizing drums began a heartbeat of rhythm that signaled the next song.

"You let me violate you

You let me desecrate you

You let me penetrate you

You let me complicate you

Help me…"

Kye saw her from across the room.

The quasi-innocent schoolgirl outfit did nothing to hide her from him. The smell of a recently fed vampire was also near, so he figured it was the female who she traveled with.

Now why was she here? Was she here as a decoy, a rogue hunter, an accomplice?

"I broke apart my insides

Help me."

His body began to quiver from within, as if something long hidden was trying to break free.

"I've got no soul to sell

Help me."

For a moment, for just a moment, the world narrowed to her. He could see every move she made, feel her every breath, smell the scent of her soap and the heated leather that half covered her flesh. Every movement seemed graceful and slow. Then, as if she felt his gaze, she turned to face him.

"The only thing that works for me

Help me get away from myself."

The moment her gaze met his, an invisible electric flash seared his brain. Unknowingly, his feet began to move towards her, drawing him nearer to her, closer to the heat of her flesh, the smell of life that clung to her, the cold determination in her eyes.

"I want to fuck you like an animal

I want to feel you from the inside

I want to fuck you like an animal

My whole existence is flawed

You get me closer to God."

"Who are you?"

He could barely make out the words her lips formed as he pushed through the crowd.

"You can have my isolation

You can have the hate it brings

You can have my absence of faith

You can have my everything."

The driving beat of the music flowed with the pilfered blood that mingled in his veins.

He wanted her.

If she was with Balthazar, he would fuck her, then kill her.

If she was a decoy, he would fuck her then drain her.

If she was an ally, he would fuck her, and let her live.

He felt his gums tingle as he moved closer to the one marked by him. He felt the growing pressure as the twin needles of his existence fought to break through the barrier of flesh. Then as he took another step, he tasted the sweet tang of his own blood as they exploded free, the half-inch incisors that were usually retracted, until he felt keen desire or excitement.

"Help me

Tear down my reason

Help me

It's your sex I can smell

Help me

You make me perfect

Help me become somebody else."

"Who the fuck are you?" Tali near screamed as the dark creature of her imaginings moved toward her at a terrific rate.

"Get back!" Mari hissed as she tugged at Tali's arm. "He may be out to do you in!"

"Mari!"

"Go!"

Turning, Tali made her way through the crowd determined to reach the second floor where she could watch this graceful monster, where she could get a sense of whether she should be running to or from him.

"Through every forest, above the trees

Within my stomach, scraped off my knees

I drink the honey inside your hive

You are the reason I stay alive."

"Tali," he hissed as he watched his quarry attempt to flee. "Sweetest Tali. You are mine."

Chapter Nine

Chari smiled at the tall, dark-haired man who sat in the black leather chair.

His hair was a deep brown that seemed to suck all the light from the room for its inner glow. His eyes were the same shade, startling in their intensity. His full lips parted slowly as he ran his tongue across them, making the surface glisten, adding to the glittering nimbus that surrounded him. He was sex incarnate, desire unfulfilled, the bastard of a monster who controlled her life.

"What do you want, my pretty little bitch?" His voice, smooth and deep as chocolate rolled in aristocratic tones, filled the room and sent her nerves screaming in fright.

She closed her eyes and remembered that same voice gently demanding she breathe through her nose as her face ground in his wiry pubic hair. Shuddering, she cast aside that memory and forced herself to move across the room.

The tight collar around her neck seemed to squeeze tighter as she moved closer to him, watching him become bigger in her sight as she walked across the room.

"I...I...think..."

"No, darling," he purred as he gracefully rose to his feet. "You are not here to think."

His gaze took in her naked form, the frightened doe eyes that stared back at him, the golden collar around her throat, her mark of ownership, and he waited.

"I want..." her gaze dropped to the floor even as her inner voice screamed at her cowardice. Her body trembled and she took several deep breaths before forcing her eyes back to his.

"You have no wants, but for what I allow. Your will is my will."

Her gaze dropped back to the carpet, the bright red carpet and her toenails painted a bright red to match.

"Master," whimpered as she felt her eyes burn and blinked rapidly to hold back her tears.

"I am waiting."

"I wish…to…go with you."

There, she had said it! Sweat broke out on her body as she realized what going with him entailed. She would be his main entertainment, his to lend out, his to torment at his discretion.

But it was worth it! If she could bring him low, if she could help destroy him…

"Why is that? I suppose you suddenly have a great desire to be around me?"

"I…"

"All of my angels are so fragile, so delicate, so easy to break. Yet you approach me, as you never have. Is all not well with my little golden throat? Have you not been given enough attention?"

Chari shivered at his words, but managed to hold her ground. Her traveling with him was imperative! If they were ever to bring him down, it had to be from within. Ignored and treated like an object, she was not very trusted, but being invisible had its advantages.

"I…I don't want to be left…alone."

Tears welled up in her eyes and poured down her cheeks as she stood there, shivering, caught in the burning light of his gaze. She felt as if the room had darkened to pitch black, faded away, taking everything with it except for the unholy light from his eyes and her trembling form it spotlighted.

Never had she felt so all alone.

"You want me to believe you find my company pleasurable? That you want to spend more time with me? Chari, do you take me for a fool?"

"No, Master!" she gasped as she forced her eyes to meet his. "I don't want to be alone."

Her trembling became visible shaking as he stared at her, through her, dissecting her words and twisting them around in his mind, searching for the truth.

Raising one hand, he snapped his fingers and Chari fell to her knees. Like Pavlov's dog, she had been conditioned to respond to his every gesture, and this one was the first she had learned. When the Master snaps his fingers, you fall to your knees and give due respect.

Bowing over, she pressed her head to the ground, making her body a small a target as possible, and waited for his next command.

He tapped his thigh twice.

Like a trained animal, Chari crawled to his side. She rose up on her knees enough to kiss his hand before falling prostrate back to the floor.

"Far be it from me to deny your wishes, my pretty bitch. You may accompany me, but you know the price."

She shuddered as the sound of the zipper echoed through the room. She knew what she had to do, but the end result would be more than worth it.

* * * * *

Tali scrambled up the stairs to the top landing, looking over the crowd of black- dressed people, searching for the thing that was after her.

She felt a strange, erotic thrill as she realized he was looking at her. But then she had to decide if it was her desire or horror that caused her to stare.

The man, the creature she was running from, froze, went deathly still, and locked all of his senses on to her. He moved, oblivious to those surrounding him as he stalked her. Suddenly, she felt like an animal that just realized it had become prey.

She froze there, staring into his eyes, watching the green and gold swirl around in ever changing cycles as he moved closer to her. Those eyes mesmerized, they held her in their sights, and she felt her will drifting away. The thing that scared her was that she liked it.

If Mari had not urged her to run, he would have been on her in an instant! But she wondered, even as she ran, if she would have enjoyed it. He looked as if he wanted to possess her body and soul, as if he was going to absorb her being into his, creating a new and even more dangerous creature.

Mari had shaken her out of her daze and now Tali fled, but from what?

The music changed again, to Mud Vein's, Dig. The rapid gunfire sound of the drums seemed to match the beat in her heart as she pushed past people to make her way to the balcony railing.

Staring over the edge, all she could see was a sea of bodies jumping to the beat of the music, see the flashing of the strobe light as it made everything seem to move in slow motion. She smelled the scents of anger, frustration, desire and confusion that wafted up from the wildly gyrating people.

She could not see him.

But she could feel him.

His eyes were watching her, burning into her from some great unknown spot. She knew it!

Pressure seemed to build in her chest, making her want to scream just to give some release, but she could not afford the loss of control.

She swung around, searching for Mari. Maybe this wasn't such a good idea. But when she saw the ad in the paper, she knew she had to go and see if this was one of his clubs, one of his spots, part of his plans. She also knew deep in her heart the strange man would be there! She counted on it. Now she wondered if that old axiom about being careful about what you wished for, 'cause you just might get it', was true.

She had to get out!

Turning, she ran for the exit, all training dropped as a very human flight-or-fight reaction set in. Mari was nowhere around and she needed time and space to think, to breathe.

She flew down the stairs, pushing people aside as if they didn't matter, knocking a few down, leaving a trail of shouted profanity behind that question of her parentage.

Almost blindly, she saw the back door and darted for it, fleeing as if she could feel his hot breath on the back of her neck and his hard hands reaching for her.

Without a thought, she slammed into the door, forcing it open, and ran smack into two of the largest men she had ever seen.

"Well, what do we have here?" one asked as he adjusted the crotch of his black leather pants. "Another chicken to add to the coop."

"He'll like this one," the second man in black denim jeans and a leather vest laughed. "You can smell the adrenaline in her blood. Wanna sample her before we lock her in with the others?"

"Oh fuck!" Tali gasped as she moved into a fighting stance.

She took one moment to glance around the room she was in, and shuddered at the severe space. The color scheme seemed to be basic black, but the problem was the walls lined with dangling silver cuffs. That and the shredded bits of cloth that had to have been, at one time, clothes for the other victims of the not-so-dynamic-duo.

Her wholly feminine reaction to the man in red disappeared as she discovered what she was looking for. This operation, this whole club, was nothing more than a human blood farm, and it was round up time.

"You always sample them," laughed leather man. "I'm surprised the boss hasn't come down on us yet."

"As long as we don't mess with the high test stuff, he leaves us alone," denim answered, before he turned to face Tali again. "And this chippie is easy pickings."

He laughed at her defensive stance, laughed as the smell of fear poured off of her, sickeningly sweet to his nostrils. He laughed, his mocking tones threatening to steal her defenses as she prepared to attack.

"Think the chicken's gonna run... Oomph!"

Since leather was distracted, Tali decided to attack first, ask questions later. As he spoke, she let her leg fly; delivering a roundhouse kick to his midsection that knocked the wind out of his lungs and doubled him over in pain.

Spinning around, she dropped to her knees just as leather man kicked out at her.

He never expected her to get below his kick to deliver a smashing open handed punch to his crotch.

He folded like a deck of cards.

"Bitch!" he hissed as he doubled over and lost the contents of his stomach on the concrete ground.

Turning again, she spun back to leather man, only to feel his arms surrounding her.

"Nice try, cunt! Your ass is mine!"

With a scream, she threw her head back, smashing her skull into his nose with a crunch, and winced as she felt his blood begin to drip onto her hair.

"Bitch!" he bellowed as he tightened his hold on her, not releasing her as she expected.

Taking a deep breath, she let her body go limp and her sudden dead weight pulled him off balance. With a muffled curse, he began to fall, which gave Tali enough time to twist to the side to avoid being crushed by his weight.

She almost made it, but his hold refused to give. His body smashed hers into the floor, forcing the breath from her body and causing her sight to go dark for a moment.

"Shit!" she muttered as she rapidly blinked her eyes and decided upon her next plan of attack.

"Hold her!" denim snarled as he painfully pulled himself to his feet. "I got her!"

She felt an additional hand grip her leg and pull.

In an instant, she found herself yanked from leather man's bulk to lie flat on her back, looking at death in denim.

"Um, wanna fuck around?" she asked, forcing humor into her voice as she tried to buy time to figure out a way out of this mess.

"Bitch, do you think this is a fucking game?" he hissed and bared his teeth.

There at the top of his gums were two very large white fangs, fangs that dripped saliva, showing his impatience to drink her dry.

"Hell!" she gasped as she turned and tried to scramble to her feet.

"No more games!" he bellowed as he reached for her.

His preternatural strength made it easy for him to grab her by the back of her neck, to drag her kicking and screaming to him, to wrap his arm around her and hold her in place.

"I am going to enjoy this!" he hissed, his hot fetid breath wrapping around her, choking her, smelling of the stench of death.

"But I will enjoy this more."

Before Denim Man could blink, there was a whistle of sound, then a light crunch. Tali was again splattered by blood as the silver blade of a throwing needle exploded from his back. He released her to turn and face his new challenge.

"Hello! Good bye."

Tali turned, and fought to hold back a scream. It was him!

Kye stood in the doorway; his red leather shining like old blood as it skimmed his hard body. His eyes glowed eerily, shined with the heat of insanity, swirled in an ever-changing kaleidoscope of green and gold. His hair fluttered around his body, wrapped around his arms as he held his hands out to the sides, waiting. The smell of vanilla, cinnamon and man filled the room, washing away the stench of death that the two men carried with them.

Tali inhaled deeply, again feeling frissons of excitement down her spine at his very glance.

"What...?" Denim snarled, but was cut off by the man in red.

"That cunt is mine," he snarled, daring the man to respond.

And he did. He was stupid.

"Cunt?" Tali wailed, turning furious eyes to him.

"Fuck you!" Denim answered at the same time.

Kye smiled, exposing his fangs even as his eyes seemed to go cold and dead.

"If you insist."

Chapter Ten

Tali was tossed aside like an empty sack as Denim reached back and pulled the thin spine from his neck. It exited with a slick wet sound and pinged as he dropped it to the floor. He turned angry red eyes to his attacker and hissed, exposing his stained fangs and pointed tongue.

"Yeah, mama!" Kye hissed, as he flexed his fingers, popping each knuckle with a loud snapping sound. "Bring it on!"

That was all the urging Denim needed. With a roar, he sprang forward, arms extended, fingers flexing as if he already held Kye's broken body in his grasp.

Kye waited until the last second, ducked under the arms and came up inside his grasp, both hands grabbing each elbow as he halted Denim's rush.

Denim stopped, blinked twice at how easily the shorter man in red got within his body space and how easily he stopped him.

"Big mistake," Kye sighed as he tightened his grip until the larger man's skin began to part beneath the pressure of his fingers.

"Ahhhh!" Denim roared. He threw back his head as he felt fingers sliding through flesh and muscle. Blood, dark blood, old blood, stolen blood, bubbled around Kye's fingers and still he applied pressure.

Denim fell to his knees, unable to bear the pain as fingers began to caress his bones, and then began applying pressure to them.

With a loud snap, both arms dangled, the bone snapped clean in two, the muscles shredded.

"My arms! You broke my fuckin' arms!" Denim screamed, his voice drowning out the muffled beat of the music, covering the sound of Tali's heartbeats as she stared wide eyed at the man in red.

"That didn't take long," Kye muttered as he stared down at the sorry sight that lay at his feet.

Tali whimpered. It was only a small sound, but it drew his eyes to her.

"Now, I will have what I came for." His voice was low and melodious as he absently kicked the sobbing man out of his path and raised one of his crimson stained hands to his nose.

"What...are you?" Tali managed as she scrambled backwards and bumped into Leather Man but still managed to keep her balance.

"Old blood," Kye muttered as he wrinkled his nose at the smell of the blood on his fingers. "And of a poor quality. You need to leave crack-heads alone. This shit will kill you!" he said to Denim as he curled up in the fetal position, his cries dwindling to whimpers.

Tali made to rise, but then his eyes pinned her where she lay on the ground.

"You are not his toy," he stated as his lips spread into a full smile, exposing his fangs.

"Holy shit!" Tali breathed as she scrambled to her feet. She took one step back and this time, tripped over the still body of Leather Man and again found herself on her bottom, but this time, looking up at him.

"You are not one of his, if his toadies were trying to harvest you. So this is your lucky day."

"Lucky day?"

"Yeah, very lucky. After I fuck you, I will let you go."

"Oh, um...gee thanks, but I think I'll pass."

"No choice."

"You would rape me?"

"Darling, you can't rape the willing. You were so hot for me I could smell it over the stench of Balthazar's men. You want me."

Tali blinked as she sat looking up at him. Was she that obvious?

"Um, just because…"

"No games, Tali. Isn't that what that undead bitch called you? Tali?"

"Mari is a friend!"

"You can't trust the undead."

"And I should trust you?"

"Trust was never a question Tali," Kye said as he stepped closer to her. "It is neither wanted nor required. As for being undead, I'm not. I am something else."

Tali scrambled backwards, dragging her legs over Leather Man as she struggled to get away. She managed to make it to her feet as Leather Man suddenly regained motor-skills and lurched for Kye.

"Got you, mother fucker!" he hissed as he tackled Kye around the legs and knocked him flat on his ass.

"My leather!" Kye roared as he flopped backwards and his head met the concrete floor with a satisfying crunch. Kye moved no more.

"Got that sucker!" Leather crowed as he pulled himself to his knees. "You as good as dead, freak!" he yelled at the prostrate Kye. "I got you good!"

He turned dead eyes to Tali, who stood there, again stunned at the rapid change of events. If he wasn't of Balthazar's get, then who was he?

"Your next!" he roared at Tali. "You don't kick a man in the nuts and think you can get away with it!"

Tali drew her attention to the matter at hand as she took a step back.

"You kind of deserved it, big guy."

"You are not going with the others."

"Where are the others?"

"Don't matter! They are there and you are here! You gonna pay!"

"Me? What did I do?"

Keep them talking, Tali, she coached herself as she moved to give herself better room. As she moved, her eyes darted around the room, picking up each escape route and declining them as poor choices.

Tali knew she was a small woman and that he had vampiric strength she did not. The best way to win was to outsmart him, or to run away until she had the advantage. But there was no place to run, just a large wooden door that led to some unknown destination. Maybe another room, maybe an alley, but the unknown in front of her was enough to deal with right now.

"You caused all of this! My partner will be down for a few hours and then I have to dispose of this freak!" He gave Kye's prone body a swift kick that lifted him a few inches from the floor and rolled his body to his side. "Because you made so much work for me, I am going to enjoy draining you!"

He grinned; his fangs exposed in the dim light as saliva slowly dripped and hung on the very tips.

"Didn't anyone ever tell you not to play with your food?" Tali asked as she realized she had no choice but to fight. "It might not like the games you play, and get mad."

"Gonna play your little kung-fu games?" Leather Man sneered as he moved closer, ready to overpower her.

"No, I am!"

They both turned as Kye rolled to his back, raised his legs and kicked them down swiftly as his momentum pulled him to his feet.

At this point Tali didn't know if she was glad to see him, or glad to see they would fight, giving her a chance to escape. But either way, he was giving her an out.

Grinning, Leather Man turned toward Kye, who was now tossing his hair over his shoulders.

Then in a lightning move too quick to be seen, Kye was on Leather Man, his fingers wrapping around his neck, digging in deep.

Leather gurgled as Kye, despite his shorter stature, lifted the man completely into the air, before he started digging his fingers in deep.

Again blood spurted and coated his hands as he tightened his hold.

He turned to face Tali, a bored smile in his lazy eyes as if the two hundred pound man who struggled and choked on his own blood while being held two feet off the ground was of no consequence. He even positioned the man so that his flailing feet would do no more damage to his pants.

Tali, standing there, did the only thing her mind demanded she do.

"Shit!" she screamed as she turned and made for the door. Fuck the unknown! What she was facing in the room was enough to make her turn tail and run!

Her body hit the door and it sprang open, almost dumping her into an alley as she raced to get away from the creature that had just taken out two vampires as easily as someone taking out the trash.

She had enough presence of mind to force the door shut before she began to race down the alley.

The sound of a loud crash made her look back as she continued to race away.

But all she saw was wood splintering, raining down like ice in an ice storm, before something was knocking her to the ground.

Screaming, Tali turned and saw something out of her worst nightmare.

Kye sat on her chest, the bloodlust riding high in his body as he pressed her flatter onto the wet ground.

Tali opened her mouth to scream, but he quickly covered her completely with his body. Some weird part of her mind marveled that they were a perfect fit, before common sense ruled again and she let out a roar of panic.

"Shh!" Kye hissed, as he brought up one blood-soaked hand to place a finger at her lips.

Trouble was, he realized, he had forgotten he was still holding what was left of Leather Man's throat in his hand.

Tali screamed again.

Staring at the piece of flesh in his hand, he tossed it aside and again placed his stained fingers across her lips, leaving the iron stench of blood in her nose as well as red-brown stains on her face.

"Stop screaming. He will grow another one," he said as he stared steadily into Tali's eyes.

"What are you?" she breathed as she stopped screaming long enough to calm herself and plot her escape. Her body trembled beneath his and strangely enough, her arousal came back.

I am such a slut, she thought as she tried to calm the pounding of her heart. She was a warrior, trained to handle these situations! Now she had to start thinking like one.

"What I am is of no consequence. But you may call me Kye. You will scream it as I pound your ass into bliss."

Well, that sounded…good actually, but she was fighting for her life here.

"You think rather highly of yourself, for a bloodsucker," she hissed. "From where I lay, you are just like the rest. A little sunlight, a little garlic, a blade through the neck, and you are all dead just the same."

"You are welcome to try," he whispered as he noticed the bloodstains on her face and bent low to lick them away.

The rough warm brush of his tongue sent shivers down her spine and reminded her body of how she had wanted this man, this creature, this thing.

"I may just do that," she whispered as he wiggled his hips enough to part her legs. He settled neatly between her thighs, the force of his body no match for her torn stockings or her leather skirt.

She opened her eyes in amazement as she felt his rock-hard arousal brush against her suddenly damp underwear. If what she was feeling was real and all him, he could certainly pound her into submission.

"Yes, it's all me," he purred as he began to lick at her lips.

She gasped as his free hand released her arm, and began to trail down the torn material of her shirt, his nails scraping delicately along her quivering skin.

She strained her eyes to follow, but threw back her head as his hands cupped her breasts through the thin, soiled material.

His hands were so hard, so masculine, so hot they seared her flesh through the thin barrier of her blouse. Her nipples peaked instantly and he chuckled as her hardened flesh pressed into his palms, begging for his caresses.

Grinding his hips in an exaggerated fucking motion, Kye grinned in her face, then gripped her nipple between his thumb and forefinger.

But instead of pinching her tender flesh, he began to rub and roll her, heating her nipple with the precision of a surgeon and sending bolts of pleasure from her nipples straight to her groin, making the damp crotch of her panties absolutely soaking wet.

"That's...um...impressive." she managed, trying to distract herself from the flashing heat that filled her body and tried to cloud her mind.

"Um-hmm," he purred as he lowered his mouth, letting his fangs scrape at her lips before moving into position to get the kiss.

But just seconds before their lips connected, Kye let out a gurgle and his whole body jerked. Blood, bubbling and bright red flowed from his mouth.

"Another time, then," he muttered as he rolled to the side, a large sharp spear of wood from the splintered door, protruding from his back.

"Let's go!" Mari screamed as she reached down and pulled a dazed Tali to her feet. "Let's move it! This will not hold him long!"

"Damn," Tali whispered. Confused, she made her feet move towards Mari as she guided her out of the alley. She turned back to stare at the hard body that now lay on the ground, breathing deeply as if recovering his strength to do something else, as Mari started running.

"I saw what he did to the others, Tali! He almost had you!"

"So close," Tali whispered as her traitorous body screamed for him, for the release he had promised.

"I don't think he works for them," Mari continued as they raced for her car. "But he is still unknown."

"His name is Kye," Tali said as they reached the car and Mari all but threw her in. "Kye and he is not one of them."

"Then what is he?" Mari turned the key in the ignition and that old Doors classic, When You're Strange, began to fill the silence as she waited for an answer.

She pulled out into traffic, breathing a sigh of relief when no one raced from the direction of the alley, screaming for their blood.

"Well?" She spared a moment to glance at Tali before turning her attention back to the traffic.

"He is something else."

"When you're strange, faces come out in the rain

When you're strange, no one remembers your name."

"He is Kye."

"When you're strange

When you're strange
When you're...
...strange."

Chapter Eleven

Chari lay on her bed, tears streaming down her face as she hugged her pillow.

God, she hated him! She hated his smell! She hated his voice! She hated the damn taste that she could not get out of her mouth! He tasted like death!

"I hate him!" she roared finally, as the tension building up in her body demanded a release. "I could kill him, that bastard! I hate him! I hate him! I hate my life!"

Then with a roar that filled the room with the sound of futile frustration and anger, she hurled the pillow across the room, barely missing the woman who now stood in the doorway.

"Oh shut up, Chari!" Marti sniffed. "You don't have enough reason to hate him. He didn't kill your family."

"Fuck off, Marti!" Chari screamed. "You don't know shit!"

"I know that weeping and wailing will get your ass skinned quicker than the last girl."

"She was an idiot!"

"Now she is a dead idiot!" Marti closed the door and walked inside. She watched as Chari tried to recover from her latest session with the boss. "You don't want to follow in her footsteps, baby. You've survived too much."

"I am going with him."

"Where is he going?" Marti's eyes lit up.

"Anxious to be rid of him?" Chari asked as she stared at her long-time friend.

"Something like that."

"Well, we are going to the city soon. There's trouble there."

"Trouble?"

Chari looked up at Marti, wondering why she was asking all of these questions.

"Yes, trouble. Why do you want to know?" Could Marti be spying for him?

With those thoughts, she sat up in the bed and eased away from Marti.

"Just curious," Marti answered, not wanting to scare off her source. "Barbi and I need a bit of relief. He's been working us overtime. Something is obviously wrong."

"I just know we are going to the city," Chari said, still guarding her words. "Probably tomorrow night."

"So soon," Marti sighed, staring off into space as her thoughts swirled through her mind. She had plans to make.

"Something has him worried. He has called up the big guns."

"Big guns?" Now it was time for Chari to do a little digging.

"Yeah, some chick from New York, Raqi or something. Her and this bitch named Bri. I know a lot about Bri, but this Raqi is unknown. But I hear she is tough."

"Where are you hearing this?"

Now it was Marti's turn to ease away from Chari. This sudden trip with the boss could mean she was working for the man, that Balthazar had finally broken her and turned her into one of his pets. She had to be careful about weeding info from this one while keeping her own counsel.

"Put your ear to the ground, girl. It's all over the citadel."

Chari just stared at her.

"Well, you hang tough, woman! If something is brewing, we need to know about it to protect our own asses! You know?"

"I hear ya," Chari answered as Marti rose and left the room, the gold chain around her naked waist swinging as she walked.

"What are you up to, Marti?" she whispered to the empty room.

"I have to call Angel," Marti muttered to herself as she raced away from the woman she now suspected. "She will be mighty interested in this."

* * * * *

Kye grunted as blood loss made his fangs retract into his gums. Reaching back with one arm, he managed to get a grip on the piece of wood that protruded from his body.

"Damned bitch ruined my leather," he muttered even as he cursed his own stupidity.

He let sex cloud his training. That had never happened before, and it never would again. He should have smelled the undead woman's presence even before she got close enough to stake him. But then he was covered in the stench of the undead left by the two assholes he'd put out of commission for a while.

"I wonder if their throats grow back," he mused as he gave a grunt and ripped the wood from his body.

"Damn!" he bellowed as he closed his eyes in pain. He felt the warm gush of his blood and knew that too much had been spilled this night. He needed to replace what was lost and he needed to do it soon.

But for now, he lay on his stomach in the cold alley with the stink of dirty water soaking into his wounds. He closed his eyes and thought of the delicate feminine smell of her, the taste he had almost had, and how delicate those muscles felt under his body.

"Shit!" he cursed quietly through the pain that had suddenly resurfaced in his mind and body. "I am laying here getting a hard on for the little slut and probably getting an infection from lying in this alley!"

Snarling, he pulled himself to his feet even as he felt the wounds begin to knit together.

If any splinters were left, they would work their way to the surface and be expelled through his skin. He healed quickly and cleanly, though he would be feeling the bruise for a few days.

"I can't believe she staked me through the heart!" he muttered as he stumbled from the alley. "Bitch reads too much Bram Stoker!"

Even as he stumbled, he knew he could return and find out where the 'cattle' were being shipped. Not that he gave a damn, but it would move him closer to Balthazar.

One step closer, he thought. Closer to the time when this shit-for-life existence could end.

But he was still going to fuck the girl. He may have to kill the vamp with her, but he was still going to fuck her good.

A slow grin spread across his face as he made his way into the shadows and moved slowly towards home.

The object of his lust now had a name.

"Tali," he chuckled as he made his way around the club. He could barely make out the song playing, then laughed as he realized it was The Crystal Method's Calling All Freaks.

"That's the name of the game, indeed," he laughed. "Calling all freaks. Tali, here I come."

Chapter Twelve

Balthazar smiled and spread his legs further apart, as he watched the woman with the smoldering dark eyes.

"What have you got for me?" he asked as he smirked at her.

"Well, the trouble is in Baltimore. I suggest we get there and handle it before it becomes a big problem."

"When I want your suggestions, Raqi, I will beat them out of you."

"Master," she calmly replied while dropping her head in a show of respect.

"Take Bri and Sheri. I must keep my clients happy. The shipments must continue as planned."

"And for the one who disrupts your plans?"

"You know what to do, Raqi. But I want him brought back alive. I will deal with him myself."

"As you command."

The sound of her heels clicking across the marble floor was all the noise that could be heard as Balthazar settled back comfortably in his chair.

He closed his eyes for a moment, let his head fall back against his chair, then was all business once more.

Picking up the phone, he quickly typed in a series of numbers and waited the three seconds for connection.

"Hendrix," a sharp male voice answered.

"How many?"

"Balt…Sir. We managed to get fifteen out before Sloan and Maxwell had their unfortunate accident."

"I want the mill started up again tomorrow. I need to double my order. And make sure you get some of the more exotic ones. Variety is the spice of life, Hendrix."

"Understood. About Sloan and Maxwell?"

"Tell them to report to recycling. I have no use for men who can't follow simple orders."

"Understood."

"And Hendrix? I am coming for a visit. Don't fuck up again."

"Sir! It was my people…"

"Your people are a reflection of you, Hendrix. Screw up this badly again and I will personally see to your recycling."

"Yes, sir."

He hung up the phone with a click and sat back again to bask in his power.

He ran his hands through his waist-length hair and frowned as he felt a tangle. But then, with all that was going on, he had paid little attention to his appearance.

"Oh, the trials of being a leader," he sighed as he again reached for the phone.

After another series of numbers were punched in, he waited almost a full minute before the line was answered.

"I'll be there soon," he said into the silent headpiece. "Nothing you can do will stop me."

"We have stopped you before," the proper British voice showed no worry. "We shall stop you again."

"Complicity will be your end," Balthazar answered in an emotionless voice. "And I plan on using it against you. You have been warned."

"And you are being ignored. You do not exist to us. Therefore, you are nothing to us."

Snarling silently, Balthazar slammed the phone down and glared at it with all the venom he felt in his soul.

Damn them, he thought. Damn them for not taking me seriously! I will exact my revenge and I will have my way!

"Why aren't you swallowing?" he growled as he turned that gaze to the woman between his legs.

Picking up the pace, Chari began the rhythmic contraction that he had drilled into her.

Swallowing a twelve-inch cock was not easy, but she had done this too many years for survival to let her concentration break now. If he knew she was memorizing every word he said, she would be worse than dead.

Closing her eyes, she began to hum as her nose buried itself in his sparse pubic bush, inhaling the scent of vanilla...and desperation.

Her right hand dipped low to cup his testicles gently, rolling them around, feeling his lifeless seed building and making them rise against the base of his cock.

Her left hand sank below them, gently massaging the inch of penis behind his balls and pressing against his prostate externally.

She winced as she felt his fingers tighten in her hair, then around that hated collar around her neck.

"Oh, yes," he breathed. She felt his heart pump the stolen blood through the veins that corded his thick male flesh. "Just like that."

She increased her swallowing motions, humming harder, feeling the vibrations strike his penis and making him groan lower.

She began to bob her head up and down, slowly at first, then increasing her movements until he was panting and sweat began to bead on her brow.

Come, you bastard, she thought as she worked harder and harder. Come on and end this!

But just as she felt him swell larger with his need to explode, he reached down wrapped his hands in her hair and pulled her upwards.

"Not so fast, my little bitch," he gasped, his eyes glowing faintly red and his fangs slowly dropping from his gums. "I plan on dumping this load somewhere a bit softer than down your throat."

Chari shrieked as Balthazar slammed her on the desk and thrust his hips between her legs.

Eyes wide in panic, Chari reached out to grip his shoulders, but with a low laugh, Balthazar gripped her fists and slammed her hands down on the desktop.

"No!" she gasped, fighting, struggling to free herself from his clutches, but all her efforts proved futile.

Chuckling, he released one hand to grip her chin, to force her eyes to meet his.

"You want this," he purred.

"No!" Chari tried to turn away, to break the physical hold he had on her, but too late. The mental grip he now held was far more powerful.

"You want this," he replied again, his voice holding amusement.

"I...want...I want..."

Then her eyes glazed as they stared into the fathomless depths of his, she felt herself tumbling, circling, felt her will draining away.

"I do so love it when you fight," Balthazar laughed as he released her now leaden arms to roughly explore her body.

She whimpered as his hands caressed her suddenly stiff nipples, her quivering stomach, her soaking wet opening.

Still laughing at his toy, Balthazar positioned his thick cock at her entrance and roughly slammed home, lifting her body from the desk with the force of his thrust.

"I should do this more often, my angel," he laughed as her mouth gaped open and pure ecstasy spread across her face. "Fucking you is almost like getting a virgin."

But Chari paid no attention to his words only wanting to get closer to the source of the pleasure.

Laughing, Balthazar began to rhythmically pump, ripping wails and screams from her throat even as he bent forward and stared deeply into her eyes.

"Come," he ordered, and in an explosion that wracked her body and shattered her mind, Chari came.

But even as her body reached dizzying heights, Balthazar snatched his enchantment away.

Suddenly Chari was aware of what she was doing and who was bringing her to release.

"No!" she wailed the second lucidity returned to her, as her inner muscles clenched around the thrusting flesh of her Master.

Before another thought could pass, Balthazar leaned forward and buried his teeth in her neck.

"Oh!" Chari screamed as pain and waning pleasure again peaked within her

Sighing in contentment, Balthazar drank her in, took her life's blood and shuddered as the electric high of the blood-rush swamped him.

Growling deeply, he tore into her flesh, again and again, reveling in the sheer pleasure of the bite. Shuddering and slamming deeply into her, Balthazar lost all control, his seed exploding from his body as he tore his teeth from her neck and let out a loud roar.

Crying, Chari held on to him, weak from her release and blood loss, as he shuddered once more in her arms then pulled away.

"Very nice," he whispered as he pulled away from her and settled back into his chair.

Opening a drawer, he pulled out a towel and blotted his body before tucking everything neatly away, his eyes amused and on Chari's face.

Chari sat on the desk, shock running through her body. How could she release for such an evil twisted creature?

Tremors of pain and pleasure stirred through her body, her blood dripped down her shoulder, her body still quivering with aftershocks of her orgasm.

"If you are done," he said finally, ignoring the look on her face and the blood dripping down her arm. "Go and pack. I think I will take you with me after all. You are good for…relieving my tensions."

With one finger, he traced the flow of blood down one arm, catching it before it touched his desktop.

"And go and clean yourself up. Try to be a lady, for goodness sakes. My constituents will think my tastes run to hookers and cheap whores."

On weakened legs, Chari stumbled from the desk gracelessly, stomach rolling by what he forced her to do.

His laugher followed her down the hall. His seed dripped from her body. Her blood ran down her chest.

She was almost at her breaking point.

But then she remembered what she had learned.

Her laugher, nearly hysterical, preceded her down the hall, signaling her return and making the newer girls dread their existence.

But Chari laughed. She was going with the monster. She had information to tell Mari. Hell, she may even open the doors and lead the angry mob to his door. Balthazar would fall!

Her laugher, tinged with madness, raised the hairs on her own arms, but suddenly it felt good.

Down, down, down, she thought. The beast was going down! And she was going to be the instrument of his destruction.

Chapter Thirteen

"Damn that woman!"

Kye groaned as he rolled over, the tatters of his leather spread around him like the dead bodies in an aftermath of war.

He was sore all over, damn that female and her pet vamp!

Squinting at the clock, he noticed that over twelve hours had passed, which made it roughly one in the afternoon.

He had things to do.

His first order of business was to try and scrub the remaining muck from his body. Unlike in the movies, when a major wound healed, there was more than just a little dried blood to deal with.

There were bits and pieces of his flesh glued to bits of fat and bone fragment that the wooden door shard had left behind after he ripped it out.

As he rolled out of bed and stared at his ruined sheets, he once again cursed the fates that made him lust after the woman and let his guard drop.

Good thing he remembered to pull back the comforter, he thought. Good silk was hard to replace.

Kye stumbled across the floor and made his way to the bathroom, ignoring for now the mess left behind. There would be plenty of time to clean up after he washed and fed his body.

How could he still be hungry? he wondered to himself as his stomach gave an affirming grumble. He had drained no less than twelve blood bags last night, half of his emergency supply, and he still felt…peckish.

"Too bad vampire blood has no nutritional value or taste," he grumbled out loud. "Else I would hunt down that small nuisance of a vamp and drain her to the point of death, and leave her there while I had fun with the…with Tali."

He smiled at the memory of her shocked face, how her heart fluttered underneath the weight of his body, how the delicious taste of her fear drove his sexual urges to a point they had never reached, at least not in a very long time.

Tali, with her tight hot body, her dangerous moves, and her sneaky friends.

"My new fuck toy has a name," he chuckled as he started the shower and stepped under the warm cascading water.

"But I must not forget my goal," he said out loud, to drive the point home to his lascivious heart. "The time for fun is when the work is done." It seemed that the little one and her sidekick were out to destroy Balthazar as well. They may know something he could use to bring the man down. He still had not heard from Angel. He would have to call as soon as his morning chores were done.

Okay, he knew of one collection point, and he figured if he returned to the club in broad daylight, he would stand a better chance of finding the missing kids and returning them to their homes.

Not out of any sense of right or wrong, but because it would slow down Balthazar's production and royally piss him off. It might even force him to make a trip so he could face the bastard again.

Even as he thought about the man with his suave good looks and sophisticated charm, the side of his neck began to burn. He knew they were just memories, but memories had the power to harm.

Like his brothers' last tortured words before he flung himself into the murderous rays of the sun.

"I am sorry, little brother," he cried, a moment of lucidity replacing the red tide of madness that had taken over his mind and body. "Forgive me. Forgive me and make him pay."

Then there were the screams, the God-awful screams that tore him from his sleep, turned his blood cold, and left him a shaking hull of himself. The smells—even now he could remember—the sweet rotten smell of burnt human flesh had filled his nostrils and mouth as he shouted his brother's name until his own blood filled his mouth. And the sight. How could you ever forget the sight of the person you loved above all others writhing on the ground, exploding into small smoldering fires as bits of burnt flesh fell around? Then the agony of watching the body attempt to repair itself each time a cloud crossed the face of the sun or when the sun disappeared for the night, leaving a pain- filled mass of ash and burned meat to mend itself, to become recognizable as human again, just before the sun burst through the dawn and started the slow combustion of the body, now recognizable as your loved one, all over again.

For three days and nights, Kye watched his brother's torment, watched his suffering, powerless to help, tied down with ropes to a steel chair that would not break.

Kye had rubbed his wrists to the bone to try and get to his brother, to try to end his suffering if anything, but all in vain.

At last, it was the vultures that put an end to his brother's misery.

On the fourth day, they feasted.

Kye remembered each detail, remembered each peck and tear as the carnivorous birds ate at what was left of his brother until it ceased to heal.

He watched, tongue swollen and eyes bruised, body too dehydrated to even cry, as his brother finally found peace.

He was still staring at the remains a day later when the passing band of escaped slaves, fleeing the brutal whips and slashing hounds of their former master, found and freed him.

They cared for his dehydrated body, his lacerated wrists, the huge chunk of flesh missing from his neck.

The spot still burned with his memories, even though it was healed and no one would ever know such a mortal wound was once there.

The feel of his warm bath water suddenly gone cold shocked him back to the present. Looking around, he decided he had been lost in black memories for about an hour, long enough for the hot water tank to run cold and for his body to register the chill in the once steamy bathroom.

Picking up his shampoo, he began to wash the gore from his body, the tangles of dried blood from his hair, all thoughts of pity for Balthazar and those of his ilk, flowing down the drain.

* * * * *

"He wasn't going to hurt me," Tali whispered into her mirror as she sat and made her plans. "He was going to...I don't know what he was going to do, but it didn't involve hurting me."

She sighed at her reflection then made a face at herself.

"So who are you trying to convince," she snorted as she stared into her glassy eyes.

They looked different to her, somehow, more vibrant, more alive, more...aware.

Yes, her eyes were now aware.

His name was Kye.

What he was, she was not exactly sure, but she hoped he wasn't dead.

She turned her head and glared in the direction of the walk-in closet, the place where Mari slept during the day, and resisted the urge to open the doors and let the sun shine in!

Then she cursed herself for her mean-spirited and evil thoughts.

How was Mari to know he wasn't going to harm her? She did what she had been doing since the day Mari plucked her from the elite training that her mentor and savior, Balthazar, was providing her. Mari had plucked her up and opened her eyes.

No, Balthazar was not her friend.

No, he was not helping her find her destiny.

Yes, he was the cause of her every misery.

Mari had risked her life in liberating Tali, and she deserved more than her dark thoughts because she'd pierced through the heart with a wooden door frame the man Tali was coming to lust after.

In fact, she would probably laugh about it one day!

Maybe.

I mean, having your first meaningful encounter interrupted by a stake through the heart is enough to make a girl gun shy! she reminded herself.

But Kye had not died.

That proved he was not a vampire! Anything that exploded their hearts killed them, the blood loss too much and their bodies unable to heal it fast enough.

But that also proved he wasn't human.

What was he, besides great at foreplay?

Shaking her head and unable to sleep because of all the questions, Tali rose from her bed to stare at the mirror, still getting no answers.

"Mirror, mirror, on the wall, tell me, mirror, what is wrong."

No answers there.

But there was a place where she could get answers.

Back at the club.

It was now broad daylight and there was no danger of her blood and sun-block challenged friends sneaking up on her. She would discover what the two guys were talking about; who they were shipping out for Balthazar, and then maybe she would find some of the answers she sought.

Like who she really was.

Then she could kill Balthazar with a clear conscience, putting all of that life-long training he had given her to some good use. What better goal was there than ridding the earth of scum?

Just maybe, she would find something about her knight in shining red leather.

Throwing on some jeans and a T-shirt, Tali penned a quick note to Mari, telling her where she had gone and why, then raced out of the apartment.

Today, she was going to get some answers; things were going to be different! She could feel it!

Chapter Fourteen

"Good taste in music," Kye mused as he pushed his dark sunglasses higher up on his face.

Today, he was dressed to blend, and in this district, it meant he could wear just about anything. Today, he wore his favorite black leather pants, the not too tight ones with the silver snaps that ran up both sides. His cream-colored shirt, buttoned to the top of his neck, lent him a touch of innocence that the hip-hugging pants almost instantly took away. But that was all right. All of the important parts were covered. On his feet were his favorite motorcycle boots, polished to perfection and ready for action. He didn't call them shit-kickers for nothing.

Depeche Mode's Enjoy the Silence was gently playing over the stereo as his boots made a clicking sound on the rough tiles of the moderately lit club. For a second, he blinked as his eyes adjusted from the bright summer's day to the interior of the place. Looking around, he saw what the darkness had so easily hid, and strangely he felt at home.

The often-patched curtains that surrounded the stage hung drunkenly on a raw steel beam. Gray patches of stucco covered holes in the walls as bare wires trailed to the elaborate steel beams that helped hold up the lighting equipment. The rich leather chairs of the VIP section were no more than cigarette burned vinyl or pleather, and the whole place reeked of disrepair. Kind of like his soul, he thought as he turned to face the bar.

The scarred and pieced together surface that shone like fine mahogany was nothing more than a poorly stained block of wood, its benches mismatched and cheap looking. It was like a garage sale pile that couldn't be sold.

"Looks like the magic went away," he mused aloud as he pushed a tendril of hair behind his ear. His hair hung in a long braid down his back, except for the ever-present fringe that he could hide behind if he so chose.

"But when that light goes out, oh how it sparkles and shines. The magic returns and the fools live in fantasy-land for a while longer."

He whipped around, his body moving into a fighting stance as he faced the person who spoke.

It was a female, but only a fool would doubt the cunning and strength of a woman. Kye had been a fool for one woman too many. The small sting in his back reminded him of his folly.

"How can I help you?"

The woman stood about five-feet-six-inches tall, but it was her air of command that kept him in his stance.

Dressed in flat-heeled, red calf-high boots that matched the thigh-hugging shorts, she looked ready for action. Her red leather halter-top had to squeeze her breasts uncomfortably, but how was he to really know? He was a man and had never experienced such things. But the tight black braces that fastened around her wrists screamed Dominant. That he could understand.

"By showing me what's going on around here," he said quietly as he eased his stance, relaxing a bit but not letting his guard down.

"You don't look the type. So why not take yourself back up-town before somebody here gives you nightmares?"

He was not moving an inch and that meant he had to make her react first.

So he smiled at her, a slow teasing grin, then turned his back to her.

"I am talking to you." She didn't raise her voice, but the authority there was present.

"I bet you are good for a mind fuck," Kye stated simply. "But mental masturbation was never my thing."

"Who are you?"

"Not some bottom to be cowed, that's for sure."

"For damn sure," she agreed.

Her footfalls let him know she approached him.

"Leather pants and boots do not make you what I am, though they fit you nicely. Why the drag? Though you look comfortable walking around in it, if you are playing games, this is the wrong place for you."

So it was to be the sweet approach. She must lure a lot of slaves that way, give them something nice, then convince them they wanted the noose tightened around their neck.

"You mean this old thing?" he asked as he turned to face her, finally.

At his words, she tilted her head to the side, re-sizing him up, reassessing him in her mind.

"How can I be of service?" She was curious now.

"I am looking for something and I thought that I could find it here."

"You are very pretty," she said as she stepped so close to him he could smell the leather mixed with her own feminine musk. He inhaled deeply and smiled.

Slowly, one hand reached up to caress his face. He allowed the touch.

"Very pretty," she repeated as she ran her fingers firmly along his face. "Such a pretty bottom you would make, aggressive yet beautiful."

"Flip the coin, sister," he retorted with a laugh. "No one tops this pretty boy. No one has ever...moved me enough to allow it, to even crave it."

"I could try."

"Yes you could," he said as he lowered his head in an almost submissive gesture. "But then I would probably scar you for life, though I must admit, you would look pretty cute with your ass red from my hand, your cunt dripping with need, your pretty rainbow eyes filled with tears, my dick gagging your lovely little mouth." Her eyes really were tri-colored, brown, gray, and a touch of blue. The wild mane of honey blonde corkscrew curls that exploded around her head gave her the look of an imp, a very dangerous imp.

"You? Break me? Don't make me laugh, though you talk a good game." She hurriedly took a step back from him and the sudden menace. No! Too strong a word. The strained control that surrounded him. She grabbed a curl and twirled it around her finger as she examined him further.

"Do I make you nervous?" he asked as he stared at her from beneath his fringe of hair, his green-gold eyes flashing. "Or do I make you wet?"

"Actually, you make me curious." She tossed the curl over her shoulder and resumed her commanding stance. "What's your name, stranger? It is not too often we get freaks in here like yourself, commanding Tops, be it as it may."

"You may call me Kye."

"Jaid," she answered as she again took in his measure. "And you don't look the type to beg discipline. Though if you are game, I am more than willing to take you on."

"Enchanting offer," he said quietly. "But I really must pass."

"Then what do you want?" Too many cooks spoiled the stew, she thought as she watched the man in black. He could be dangerous.

"I am looking for my girl. I allowed her to come here as a treat, and she hasn't returned home. Understandably, I am worried."

"Couldn't control her?"

"No. Control is never an issue. Something must have happened to her. She is, shall we say, an extreme case."

"Oh shit," Jaid sighed as she relaxed her stance.

"I am not into scat," Kye replied with a straight face.

"But apparently you are into mindless zombies that cum on command and think you possess the cock of a god."

"And if I am?"

"Then we need to do lunch."

"I take it you have seen her?"

"Thousands like her, Kye. And I have a few hundred of the poor lost souls waiting training now. It may be possible that your beauty slipped into my net while I was trolling."

"Then I want her back."

"I'll think about it."

"Think?"

"Finders keepers, ducks. That's the way it works in this game."

"Not the way I play."

"My turf, my rules."

"If I don't like them?"

"Then you can go and fuck yourself…Kye."

He stared at her, noting she acted unafraid and kept total control of herself. Maybe he would fuck her too. After he had Tali, he could come back to see who was the true Dominant here.

"My rules?" she asked again, as she crossed her arms and tightened the halter across her breasts.

Kye blinked as the outline of a small ring pressed through the form-fitting leather at her left nipple. A true Dom, in action and deed, and that ring marked her for the world to see, if they knew what they were looking for.

"Okay. Your world, your rules, Jaid. For now."

"Spoken like a man I could learn to respect," she snorted, as she turned and led him behind the bar.

"But remember, pretty little Kye, these woman and men are mine, to do with as I see fit. You see something you like, we bargain. You see your girl and I can't hold her, you can take her.

I hate damaging goods for no good reason. Once you have them broken to one hand, it takes too damn long to retrain them. Got it?"

"Understood, Mistress Jaid."

"Just Jaid, I hate that Mistress crap. Makes me feel like something out of a novel I once read. All about abused men and aliens. Not that there is anything wrong with it, but I find that it is better to use one's mind than to use one's whip. They break better that way."

"Voice trained them, have you?"

"Wanna find out?"

"Maybe later."

As they bantered, Jaid pressed a series of codes into a security panel beside the back wall and with an audible click, the door slid open to reveal a dark tunnel.

"After you, Pretty Boy."

"Always," he replied as he stepped into the dark corridor. "My pleasure always comes first. Something you would do well to remember."

"Hmm," Jaid murmured. "I don't know if I should kick your ass or make you my partner. Maybe both."

His laughter preceded them down the hall.

Chapter Fifteen

The air was filled with the smell of baby oil and mint. The light was dim. The sound of human misery was loud and apparent.

There was weeping in one corner, a woman from the sound of it, begging for freedom from the lash. In another corner, a male slave obviously waited for punishment, broken and pleading for mercy. The thing that caught his attention was the spectacle taking place in the center of the large square room.

The other bodies were hidden behind screens, but this event, this show, was taking place dead center. No holds bared action, and Kye was in a front row seat.

"Twenty lashes," the woman said, though her voice rolled like thunder. The man kneeling before her dropped down to kiss the toes of her six-inch heeled boots, but no quarter was granted.

Smiling, her body partially blocked by that of her slave as he rose to his feet, she placed a thick wooden paddle in his mouth and told him to get ready for discipline.

As the slave moved, Kye could see the almost black hair of the woman before him. Her eyes were lost in the shadows, but her cloak of hair almost matched the length of his. She was extremely tall, almost six feet, so he assumed without her boots, she was about five nine. Those hidden eyes focused in on him; he couldn't see it, but how he felt it. Again, he was intrigued.

"Another novitiate, Jaid?" she asked as she took one step forward, the concrete floor absorbing the sound of her boots clicking, something he thought only he was capable of. As she approached, the light from a strategically placed torch gave his eyes the opportunity to adjust to the shifting shadows that caressed her harness-clad body as she moved. Her eyes were brown, deep brown. Her attitude was…nasty. Just how he liked them.

"On your knees, dog! Who gave you permission to stand?"

"Hmm," Kye mused as a curl of amusement twisted his lips. "Since no one took it away, I guess no one gave it to me— permission to stand, that is."

"Julie, meet pretty little Kye. He is looking for a misbehaving child. Naughty of him to let her loose like that," Jaid laughed as she took a step back to watch the fireworks. This would prove amusing.

"Well, then pretty little Kye is shit out of luck! What is in my possession, I keep!"

"You may not possess what you never had in the first place," Kye reminded her as he took a step forward, brushing his hair back behind his ears.

"If it is in my dungeon, I keep it. Be careful you don't end up on a St. Andrews Cross, waiting my pleasure."

As she gestured around her, he noticed she held something in her hand. It appeared to be shiny and metal, and quite large.

"Butt plug?" he asked, his expression blank as he took in what had to be five inches of five-inch thick bullet shaped metal.

"You should be familiar with one, as pretty as you are," Julie assessed as she took a step closer to him. "Why, turns you on?"

"Repels, is more like it," he muttered as he brought his eyes back up to hers. "But apparently, you seem to enjoy…afflicting people with it. Please continue! Don't let me get in your way. I'll just look for my girl and be on my way."

"I think you didn't hear me, pretty little Kye! What is mine I keep! Giving away merchandise is no way to run a business!"

As she spoke, she poked him in the chest with her metal rule enforcer. He winced at the thought of where it possibly had been.

"You know," he said in a low, quiet voice. "We often create our own worst enemies."

As he spoke, his mind went back to Balthazar and the smell of vanilla he used to mask the scent of old blood and death. He thought of the man's laughter as he slaughtered Kye's family, as he turned his own brother on him, as he walked away, knowing what the revenant would do. A revenant, not quite human, not fully vampire—a mindless eating machine.

"Threat, pretty boy?" she asked, a deadly tone entering her voice.

"Observation, pretty lady," he replied as he stood up to her measuring gaze.

"You seem familiar to me," she said. As she tilted her head to the side, her long straight hair brushed against the exposed flesh of her body.

The leather harness did not leave much to the imagination, but what flesh was exposed was firm and filled with youthful vigor. She was only about twenty or so. Young to have such a commanding presence.

"What's the business...Julie, was it? I may be in the market."

"All of these slaves are accounted for...Kye." She paused for a moment, to show her lack of regard for him and his questions.

"So, you profit on human misery?" he asked, waiting for her reaction and answer.

It was not what he expected.

She threw back her head in laughter.

"Oh, that is a good one! Have something against slaves, Kye?" Chuckling she nodded to Jaid who turned on an overhead light. "Please have a look at the people I am abusing!" Still chuckling, she led him to one black screen, the whimpering sound behind it sounding more pitiful in the bright light.

"Some of my best friends were slaves," he said quietly, but followed Julie.

"Some of your best fucks too, I imagine," she said her voice sounding serious.

"I have never fucked a slave, Julie." His eyes rapidly swirled from green to gold as he stared her straight in the eyes. "I have made love to a few, but all in my care left in better condition than when they came." Which was true! All of Balthazar's men left Kye's tender care dead or dying. They found release or a valuable lesson, which left them better monsters for it.

"Then look, Kye! See what I am dealing with."

Stepping back, Julie eased the screen aside, showing the hairless form of a young girl. Well, not quite hairless! She had a thin layer of curls on her head and retained both eyebrows. But other than that, she was denuded of hair.

"Show him your wrists."

Without a word, the young woman resting on a padded cot lifted her right and left hands up, presenting to Kye what she had done.

Two raw red looking scars covered each wrist. Clearly, she had tried to commit suicide, and failed.

"How?" he asked Julie, looking up at her, face impassive.

"Car keys. But your question should be why."

Reaching out, he touched the scars lightly with a finger as he felt a hunger roar through his system. These were fresh wounds! The smell of her young sweet blood filled the air around her. He gripped her wrist, squeezing unconsciously for a moment as he gathered his control, eliciting a gasp from her, before he forced her arms to her sides.

"Why?" he asked, stepping back and returning his attention to Julie. His slip in control was not noticed.

"Because she was being treated worse than dirt. She came here to the club because her pimp wanted her to pick up new customers with bizarre habits. She has no self-esteem, no purpose in life, and no reason for living. She was a thing, an empty shell of walking meat with no direction. I saved her. I gave her a purpose. She will now belong to a master who will care for her, who will treasure her. No more starvation, no more beatings at the hands of a pimp, no more risking her life to disease or injury on the streets."

"No more free will?" He turned to her and awaited her answer.

"Funny from a man searching for a runaway slave."

"Mine all have their will and spirits intact, Julie. I have no zombies. I like conversation too much."

"Fair enough," Julie chuckled as she gestured with her butt plug to the slave she was speaking with earlier.

Before she could speak, a buzzer sounded and Jaid turned to the steps.

"On it!" she called as she walked up the steps, leaving Julie and Kye behind.

"Your whipping boy?" Kye asked reminded her of their conversation.

"Oh yes!" she laughed. "Collin! He is here by choice, Kye."

Then to the slave who knelt by a stool, paddle still in mouth, she called, "To me!"

Eagerly, the slave crawled over to her, kneeling up as he reached her side, paddle in place and eyes to the floor.

"Tell the man why you are here, boy," she snapped.

Looking up at her, he pleaded with his eyes for her to remove the paddle. Smiling, she did and he began to speak in a low voice.

"I need discipline, Ma'am."

Kye stared, waiting. Julie shrugged and tapped him on the head.

"Details, Collin."

"I am a bad boy," he repeated.

"And?"

"And I need to be punished."

"On for heavens sake!" Julie groaned and stuffed the paddle back into his mouth.

"And that is healthy," Kye joked, laughter in his eyes.

"That is...that is Collin! Bad choice! He is being trained as he is a sub...sub. His master wants him that way! I supply! I don't question. Oh!" Suddenly, she motioned for Collin to move back to punishment position as she pointed to a screen.

"Stacey! She is a good example." She walked over to the screen and pushed it aside.

Behind it stood a beautiful woman all of twenty years of age. Her blonde hair was cut in a short pageboy, but her naked body glowed with health and vitality.

"Here, Stacey."

Quietly, she walked over to Julie and lowered her head.

"What would you have of me, Julie?" she asked, meek and submissive in actions.

"Explain to the man why you are here."

She peeked once in curiosity at Kye, before lowering her head and beginning her tale.

"I desired to be owned, Sir. I want to be dominated and pleasured. I need my Master to be stern with me, and show me how I may pleasure him. In pleasing my Master, I get great enjoyment and purpose. It is my will to serve."

"Then he should get married," Kye muttered, before asking her why.

"It is my nature, Sir. And to fight against my nature is pointless."

"And you know what is required of you?"

"Yes, Sir. I revel in it. It is my destiny."

"Good enough?" Julie asked as she dismissed Stacey with a glance.

"Yeah," Kye laughed. "She reminds me of Tali."

"Tali?"

"My lost dove. She came here for a party last night and didn't return home. I gave her permission to be here with the clear knowledge she would return to me." Kye lied, thinking fast and chuckling at the thought of the small spitfire being submissive to him. Laid, maybe, but submissive was a bit of a stretch.

"So all of these questions were for…"

"My education and to know how she was being treated if she were here."

"Buyer?" Julie asked, suddenly all business. "Because all of these, save Stacey, Shelby, and Treva, are going to the same Master."

"Who?"

"Why?"

"I may be he."

"Yeah right!"

"Does the name Balthazar mean anything to you?"

"Shit!" Julie began to laugh as she took in Kye again. "He sent you?"

"Maybe, but I was truly looking for my Tali."

"Well, we recruit here," Julie said as she pushed her screen before Stacey again and turned to face Kye. "But he was supposed to pick up his slaves last night, or send them off with his people! Some jackass started a fight and both of them left without the slaves and left me without a back door! I will go and get your bill!"

"Hey!" Kye argued. "I am just here looking for my girl!"

"Well, you need to tell your boss to pick more appropriate help! Do you know how much it is costing to feed and house his slaves? And how many does he need anyway! I mean this is a small operation! He approached me about suitable applicants and I provide them! What's with this cloak and dagger shit anyway?"

"I just want Tali," Kye insisted, wishing he had kept his mouth shut about Balthazar, but realizing these women were not his human helpers. They were... business Dominatrix.

"Well, I want my money! And I want assurances that these girls and boys will be treated right! >From what I've seen of his help, I'm beginning to worry."

"Don't sell to him," Kye said, eyes going dark with intensity.

"I have a deal with him, and the use of this club basement. I have to, but I need assurances."

"Don't sell. Get away from this place. Pack your stuff and go. I have seen what I needed to see."

He turned and made his way to the exit.

"But what about Tali?"

"Here she is!" a voice intruded. Jaid returned, leading a smallish young woman by the hand. "Kye, I found your girl."

"Tali!" Kye laughed in pleasure! His day was getting better and better! He didn't have to kill the Dominatrix bitches. His new fuck toy was here to greet him!

"Kye!" she gasped. "Oh shit!"

Chapter Sixteen

"Where were you, dove? I was worried."

Kye more than warned her with his eyes as he stepped forward, claiming 'his girl' by the back of the neck, digging his hands through her hair to let her know how easy it would be to snap her neck.

"I...I...went home with a friend." That was true enough. She did leave with a friend. Although that friend left him with a three foot piece of wood hanging from his back!

"So, you ran off and left me all alone. I had plans for you, little one. Remember how I whispered them in your ear?"

"I...remember, Kye," she stammered. He wanted to fuck her raw. She shuddered at the mental pictures her thoughts produced; all of that hair, and golden naked flesh. Ah, what a wonderful hour or two that would be. Him, all sweaty and gasping for breath, manly grunts exploding from his mouth. His body poised above hers, arms straining as he held his weight while his hips thrust to the beat of...what was he doing here?

"Good, then let us depart." Then to the waiting women, "Ladies."

"Wait." Julie was not one to be put off easily. "What information do you have about Balthazar?"

"He is a bad, bad man," Kye said quietly, his eyes swirled eerily from green to gold as he stared intently at Julie.

"What the fuck is that supposed to mean?"

Julie was getting pissed! As she stared at her partner in crime, Jaid had the same look of concern on her face.

Their slaves were special to them. They were broken with love, sort of. But each one held a special place in her heart. Each slave was perfection in its own way and to willingly lend that perfection to some twisted bastard! That was unheard of!

"It means that I'm about to catch a case."

"What?" This from both Jaid and Julie.

"It means that the man does not have a very long time to breathe. It means that soon, his perverted view of the world will lose its glow, and I will be the shadow that robs it of its shine. You do not want to be in that shadow as I rain death and destruction ladies. It isn't…healthy."

With that neat admission of intent to commit murder, both Jaid and Julie took another look at the elegant, yet oddly dressed, man in black.

"You are planning on killing him?"

"What's not to kill?" Kye sighed as he tightened his grip on Tali, who was now eyeing him with a touch of fear. "You agree with me, right?" He looked down at her as a slow grin spread across his face.

"You walk in here searching for a slave," Julie rationalized as she stared at the confident man. For no other word, except for maybe determined, would describe his actions and his statements. "Now you openly admit you are about to commit murder after trying to warn us away. Is there some tong-Pacific-white slavery, kill the other gang-gang colors, thing going on?"

She placed both of her hands on her hips as she glared at the silent couple, the man who looked determined and the woman who looked as if she was ready to run or cry, whichever proved to be an option first.

"It's a world domination thing," Kye answered with complete aplomb.

"You're not from around here, are you?" Jaid asked as he turned to make his way towards the exit, Tali in tow.

"What gave me away?" he called over his shoulder.

"Because in a room where we control over twenty slaves, have unlimited access to weaponry, the knowledge to use it, and a hot line to the man you are about to butcher, you walk in and out like you already own the world. You must be from Europe.

Europeans seem to have that 'my shit don't stink,' attitude. So where are you from?"

"Dark places." Kye turned to face the two women and smiled slowly as the pain exploded in his gums. Exposing your fangs was never a good idea, especially when wearing silk that's easily stained by blood, but he was making a point. His fangs exploded into presence, little red rivers of blood outlining his smile, as he watched the two women recoil in shock. "Places you don't want to go."

Then, leaving the dungeon silent, except for the whimpering of the man with the paddle in his mouth, Kye turned and pulled Tali out of the room.

"What the fuck was that?" Julie gasped as she turned to face her partner.

"Don't ask me, but it was walking in the daylight. I saw it! Damn, what the hell are we going to do?"

"How about vacating the premises post haste?" Julie decided as she turned and gave the orders to pack up.

"Vacate to where?" Jaid wanted to know. "I mean, we have the whole damn dungeon to ourselves and we get lots of business from the freaks upstairs."

As she spoke, she casually reached a hand in her halter to adjust the ring through her left nipple. Damn, she was switching to a bar after this! At least then it wouldn't get caught on things when she was disciplining with the sling. And the last time she got her thin leather straps of her flogger tangled around it! Ouch!

"Well, there is that house in the 'burbs. It has a large basement and the six foot privacy fence."

"The 'burbs? Are they ready for this?"

"What do you mean ready? All of those drunk housewives and husbands banging their secretaries on the weekends? Not to mention the closet cases! Some of those people scare me!"

Julie nodded to emphasize her words, then scratched a place on her back with the still unused butt plug. Damn, but those leather straps itched!

"Okay. The 'burbs it is. But we have to get a mini van. What is the name of that realtor you were mummifying last week? Ron, wasn't it? Maybe he can work us a deal."

"Good old Ron," Julie sighed in remembrance. "His ass used to turn the prettiest shade of red after a bare-handed spanking."

"Okay! 'Burbs it is," Jaid agreed. "Besides, I always wanted to take up writing."

"Writing?" Julie laughed.

"Yeah, about what we do."

"Write about pounding asses and tit torture?"

"And butt plugs and ball spreaders, and cock rings."

"Think there's a market for that?"

"Who the hell knows!" Jaid laughed. "But if I am going suburban, I need a hobby."

Then turning to Stacey, she snarled, "Time to pack! Since we are not giving you over to the guy that made freak boy mad, we need to get you all moved. Start packing. Something tells me we need to be out of here before dusk."

There was a moment of silence, then the sound of shuffling and moving feet. Slave labor was good. It was efficient and quick, and best of all, you paid in hand jobs and ass slaps.

Chapter Seventeen

"We're on the move," Chari whispered into the cell phone as she watched Marti leave the room, her one suitcase in tow. "We are coming in tonight."

"What about the man, Kye, I think is his name? Long dark hair, weird eyes—a very strange vamp."

"Mari, I can't tell you what I don't know," Chari hissed as she looked around.

She only had so much time to get to the car. If she was late…

She didn't want to be late.

"Nothing?"

"No, but something's up with Baltha…with him. He is acting strange. I think I'm being spied on."

"Who would help him?"

"A dancer, perhaps. Someone with something to gain."

As she spoke, Marti returned and looked at her questioningly.

"Okay," she giggled as she tried her best to look amused. "Right, Shelby."

"Yakking with friends when we have to leave this place? Not wise, Chari."

"It was just Shelby," Chari defended as she lifted her suitcase from the bed. It was not heavy, since Balthazar would keep her nude most of the time. He had suddenly taken a liking to parts other than her throat. She didn't know whether to be pleased or horrified. His new sexual excess got her closer to his files and operations, but just the thought of his dead seed entering her body…

"Shelby, whoever she is, will not be able to help you when he gets through with you, Chari. Where's your head?"

Saying nothing, Chari pocketed her phone and made her way to the front door of the mansion.

"She is up to something," Marti muttered as she pulled a phone from her belt and placed a call of her own.

"Angel, we have to talk. Tomorrow, noon. We are coming into town and there are things we must discuss."

She said nothing more; just shut down the line and walked to the front door, knowing the message had been received.

There in the large entrance hall, two women, one red-head in a white linen pant suit and one dark-haired woman in black silk suit, stood.

Raqi and Sheri had arrived.

"On with you, ducky," Sheri chuckled as she looked Marti over.

"What do you suppose this one does?" Raqi laughed as Marti stiffened her back and walked past the two women.

"The last one sucks dick, so maybe this one cleans up after. Are you a little vacuum?" she called out.

Ignoring her, Marti waltzed through the door, wincing as the sun stung her eyes. But she rallied quickly. Pulling on a pair of dark shades, she walked to the limo, ignoring the catcalls from the two women.

"Where is Bri?" Sheri asked, tossing her dark hair behind her and adjusting the fit of her specially cut jacket. It easily hid her custom-made Mac 10 without showing a hint of gun line.

"Oh, you know where Bri is. She's sitting by his coffin waiting for the master of the universe to give her the dark gift."

There was a beat of silence, and then both women cracked up laughing.

"Oh no!" Sheri giggled. "Bri is sitting back calculating his net worth and the effect it will have on her wardrobe."

They both broke out into gales of laughter again.

"The wenches are all loaded," Raqi remarked after their last fit of laughter. "Do you know where we're going?"

"Sheraton on the Waterfront. He booked the whole top floor."

"Must be some party," Raqi mused, as she walked over to the car and took the passenger's seat.

"Bri will be in the big guy's arms and will meet us there. Tomorrow, we hunt. Apparently, somebody's screwing with the big guy's plans. People bleed when that happens." Sheri took off her black jacket, noting that the black of her Glock blended neatly with the silk of her shirt, before taking the driver's seat.

"Well, do we have a target?" Raqi adjusted her seat for comfort and slammed the door.

"Not yet, so it looks like we'll have a little look-see before the festivities. Hope this is more fun than the last one."

"Why? You don't like hearing children squeal?"

"No," Sheri said quietly as she licked her lips. "But they can't take much work. The man should have handed over the scrolls."

"True."

They both sat in silence as they remembered the shopkeeper and those three children, all hung by their heels and bleeding slowly in the jars where Balthazar collected the adrenaline-soaked blood.

"Oh well, I am hungry. Do we stop for donuts before we get there? I know it's only a three-hour trip, but I need my sugar."

Sheri agreed and started the car.

The operation was moving to the City and the hounds had been called in.

* * * * *

"Oh. My. God," Tali whispered as she felt a hand wrap around her neck.

"You call me that after we fuck," Kye offered kindly as he led her from the dim light in the club to the streets outside.

"You are alive!"

"Kind of."

"What the hell are you? Vamps are allergic to sun!"

"And garlic."

"Yes, it didn't bother you. What are you?"

"Kye. Remember the name. Later you will be screaming it."

Tali tried to pull away, but the steel grip he had on her body would not ease. He definitely was not human.

"Missed your heart?"

"Yes," he sighed knowing that she was referring to Mari's wooden...splinter. "And fucked up a nice outfit. I plan on making the replacement out of her hide."

"You leave Mari out of this!"

Tali turned angry eyes onto this...man, for lack of a better description, and tried to pull away again.

"Don't threaten when you can't back it up. You know I can take you, Tali."

He leaned in and breathed in her ear.

"Stop that!" she hissed. "People are watching!"

To the few people who were on the streets that time of day, it was a distraction from the normal dullness of everyday life.

"Like they care."

Kye smiled as he began to pull her towards Charles Street. There was a nice hotel that had hourly rates. He could fuck her brains out and be ready to crash the party at the club by six.

"What do you want with me?" Tali was not as scared as she was supposed to be. She was fascinated by the man, now even more so, because she knew he was out to kill her nemesis. It was one of those 'the enemy of my enemy is my friend,' kind of deal.

"Hot, buck naked sex on a platter," he replied honestly. "Then any information you have on the big bad wolf."

"What makes you think I know anything?" she hissed, but kept walking. By the looks of him, he would have dragged her down the street to get what he wanted.

"One, you tried — and it was a good effort — to take me out at the first Goth club. Second, you show up dressed to party with your pet in tow at that club, the club that Balthazar uses as his main collection area. Third, you happen to show up today. And the most damning of all is your name."

"My name? What's the big deal about that?"

"It ends in 'I', Tali. You and I both know what that 'I' stands for."

"I have no idea what you are…"

Kye stopped suddenly and jerked her into an alley.

"What did you do for him, Tali? Were you a fuck toy, a loaner? How about a collection girl? You run out and recruit other little girls, Tali? Was your hot little cunt in his mouth, feeding his perversions, Tali?"

"I…I never met the man. Take your fucking hands off of me! This game has gone too far!"

"Not far enough Tali. So what did he do to you? Have you ever seen the monster that hides in a man's face? What part do you play?"

"Let me go!"

"When I am damn good and ready!"

With a flick of his wrist, he slammed Tali against the wall of the building. Before she could blink, Kye was there, pressing his body against hers, his anger feeding his desire for the woman beneath him.

"What…"

"I may fuck you here, Tali! But sooner or later, and I bet sooner, you will tell me what you know about him."

He leaned down and licked her face, ran his tongue from her chin to the corner of her eye, savoring the salt of her skin. Kye felt his heart race and the urge to bite began to force his fangs from his gums.

Tali groaned as she felt his body harden against her. Something was running down his thigh and he was very glad to see her. The heat wafted from his body, carrying his scent, vanilla and cinnamon, and musk. It was a smell that would be forever etched into her mind as hot lust.

"Please," she gasped.

"You are a hot little piece aren't you? You ever service the man, Tali? Have you spread these dark golden thighs for his pleasure? You let him feed off of you while he fucks you?"

He leaned close and whispered into her ear, making her writhe against him. The leather did little to hide the heated press of her lower body as she began to grind against him.

"Please!"

"I'll please you, Tali," Kye whispered. "I'll give you everything this flexible little body can take. Then I'll give you more."

Tali closed her eyes and whimpered. The feel of his chest through the silk of his shirt was setting her breasts on fire. Her nipples stood out in desire as her hands, once trapped by uncertainty against the wall, buried themselves in his hair.

"You ever fuck in an alley, Tali?"

"No," she whispered.

"In a hotel, Tali?"

"No." There was no denying the fact that she wanted him, almost as much as he wanted her.

"Where, Tali. Tell me and I will do you one better."

"Never."

"No matter Tali. Keep your secrets. I will still have you."

"I have never done it!" she hissed as she arched her body closer to his.

Kye froze for a moment, all movement stopped.

"Virgin?"

"Yes."

"Not for long."

He pulled away so abruptly that he had to catch her to prevent her from falling to the ground. Then before she got her balance, they were walking again.

"Where are you taking me?"

"To my place," he decided as he adjusted his cock with one hand, ignoring the glances he got from passers-by.

"Why?"

"Oh, I am still going to fuck you, Tali. But if what you say is true, then you have never been with him. That means that you have never passed his final test. It also means that you escaped him. And, that he will want you back."

"What?"

"I may have some bait. After I am done, slightly used bait, but still tempting enough for him."

"Kye!"

"Tali! Nothing personal. Just business."

Chapter Eighteen

I know I should be scared, Tali thought as Kye practically dragged her down the street.

They were headed for the warehouse district, she realized, as Kye practically forced her off of her feet.

Kye — what was he?

Just looking at him sent shivers down her spine.

His large quad muscles were clearly defined in the tight leather pants, his strength apparent in the grip he had on her wrist.

His long hair swayed behind him as he turned left and right, glancing at the street around him, constantly aware of what was going on.

Then there was his ass.

Two solid, rock-hard buns that moved just right. Coupled with his gorgeous legs and incredible flexibility — Tali still remembered his splits in the dance club — he was a hot package.

His broad shoulders were loose, ready for action and the tapering to his tiny waist was delicious.

Kye was not as tall as most men she had met — well, the few men she had met — but what there was of him was perfect!

As he stopped at a crosswalk to let a bus go by, she ran into that wall of muscle he called a back.

She could feel his moist heat and had to resist the urge to rub against him and purr like a cat.

He looked over at her, his green/gold eyes flashing as if he could read her mind.

"Fuck it!" Tali sighed as she felt her heart beat triple! She had to have him, monster or not! After she was done, she could eliminate him if the need arose. The key was discovering his vulnerable points and catching him off guard.

As the bus zoomed by, Tali began to lead him, almost running in her eagerness.

She could feel the damp heat of her arousal soaking into her panties and knew she had to scratch the itch he gave her before anything else could be planned! Maybe blood loss to the brain was not a mere male problem! Lord knows she couldn't think straight until she had him, damn the consequences.

"Where are you going?" Kye's deep voice held a hint of amusement as he let himself be tugged along, but still making visual checks of the area. Old habits died hard.

"To your place to fuck." She paused for a moment. "Got a problem with that?"

"Maybe one," he stated then took a step back as a wild tigress turned on him.

"What would that be?"

Tali turned towards him, eyes blazing as she lifted and jammed one finger into his chest. "You get me all hot and bothered, you attack me in an alley, you make all of these promises, Mr. Big Shot Karate Man, and then you try to renege on the deal? I don't think so! After all the sleepless nights you put me through, I am going to ride your cock like it was the last horse out of purgatory! Then I'm going to fuck you again for good measure! So what is your problem?" another poke to the chest. "What?"

"You don't know where I live."

She blinked twice and pulled her finger from his chest, but not before running it across his skin, testing the firmness of his pecs. Just as hard as she remembered.

"Gonna show me?"

"Are all virgins this high strung?"

"Don't know. I am the only one I know." She grinned up at him, her eyes making one last visual sweep of his taut body. "You gonna help me change my status or what?"

She hardly remembered the rest of the trip to his place.

* * * * *

"Nice place." Tali's voce was husky with her rising arousal as she stepped out of the elevator. His place was on the top floor of an old warehouse. There was plenty of room for him to vamp out, but he was in bright daylight. That still made him an unknown entity. "Do you mind me knowing where you live?"

"Not at all," he assured her as he leaned against the far wall of the elevator and watched her invade his space. "I can kill you easily if you present a problem."

She glared at him over her shoulder. The words yeah right, were implied with that one glance.

Turning back to the room, Tali was a bit taken aback by the stark bareness of the place.

Of course, there was the prerequisite kitchen with its dinette set. There was a frosted block glass wall that she assumed hid a bathroom, there was a fireplace with a massive mantel set with a few framed pictures, and then there was the bed. That was all.

A she stepped deeper into the room, her heels clicked across the white ceramic tile, the clicking sound punctuating her each and every move.

She jumped as the loud slam of the wooden elevator doors closing drowned out the sound of her footsteps.

Kye had entered the room, and from the way he was stalking her, he wanted to play.

Walking over to the bed, Tali was struck with a sudden attack of nerves.

Sure she wanted this, but she was still a woman! It took incredible trust to lie down and open for a man. Then she realized she had to trust him a little to be here like this with him.

Kye narrowed his eyes as he watched Tali's sudden nervous moves, a far cry from her earlier aggressive actions.

He inhaled deeply, taking in her scent and then smiled. She wanted him. That much he could smell, but she was a bit nervous.

Smirking, Kye strode over to the bed and flung himself to his back, arms spread out as he continued to watch her walk around his bedroom, stroking his things.

Tali watched as Kye threw himself across the bed, covered with a very white comforter that contrasted sharply with the darkness that seemed to surround him.

She had to admit, the contrast was sexy. She eyed him, waiting for his next move as she absently ran her fingers across an open armoire that held a receiver.

That caught her attention.

Looking around the room, she counted no less than eight speakers mounted on the walls, sitting in windowsills, on the headboard of that pedestal he called a bed.

Kye was really into his music.

Running her fingers across the dial, she tried to imagine what a creature like Kye would see in music.

"Press play."

His voice, low and growling made her turn to him and raise one eyebrow.

"Chicken?" He was still smirking as he silently laughed at her, daring her to make the next move.

Turning back to the receiver, Tali pressed the play button on what had to be a hundred disk CD player, then cranked the volume up as high as it would go.

Instantly a pulsing drumbeat filled the room.

As her eyes widened, a screeching synth organ and a low haunting voice began to sing.

"Last fire will rise

Behind those eyes

Black house will rock

Blind boys don't lie."

The driving beat, the husky voice of the singer, and added guitar made her senses scream.

Something inside her tingled.

It started from her neck, worked its way down her spine and spread to every body part.

Her hands went to her hair as this feeling threatened to overwhelm her. Clenching her eyes closed, she let the words and the music spill over her.

"Immortal fear

That voice so clear

Through broken walls

That scream I hear!"

"Gerard McMann."

Kye's deep voice penetrated the wall of sensation that surrounded her. Her eyes opened, focused in on him, lying so confidently on his bed, and suddenly she had a focus for all of the energy of these new sensations filling her.

"Cry little sister

Come, come to your brother

Unchain me sister

Love is with your brother."

The words, the rhythm, the melody all seemed to force her feet across the room. Suddenly breathless, Tali closed in on her chosen prey, kicking her shoes to some unknown place, all of her misgivings melting away as the music poured over her.

Kye watched, breathless with anticipation, as Tali moved closer to him. There was a sudden sway to her hips and she unconsciously moved to the beat of the music, her steps slow and sultry. She released her hair, tossing it around her head; her unblinking eyes focused on him.

Kye watched how her nipples hardened from the brush of her shirt, how her thighs rubbed together as she moved, increasing the feeling of hard denim against her most sensitive parts.

Watching her, Kye felt his breath catch. She was untamed beauty, graceful as a leopard and sleek as a panther. He felt his cock begin to throb and fill with blood, to pulse and harden with every beat of the music, with every step she took.

"The masquerade strangers look up

When will they learn

This loneliness?"

She stopped at the foot of the bed. Eyes still trained on his face, she grasped the hem of her blouse in both hands and jerked it over her head, tossing the garment aside like her inhibitions.

Feeling the heat coursing through his blood, Kye slid to the edge of the bed, surrounding her with his leather-clad thighs as his cock began to pound in beat with his racing heart.

"Want fucked?" His low voice sent shivers down her spine as his green/gold eyes narrowed into tiny slits.

"Temptation heat

Beats like a drum

Deep in your veins

I will not lie…to little sister"

It was her hands that went to the fasteners of her bra. Her hands impatiently tore the lace free, exposing her turgid nipples to his gaze. It was her hands that tangled in his hair; that pulled his head to the first berry-colored peak.

"Come, come to your brother

Unchain me sister."

Her hands tangled deeper in his hair, tore at the thong that held it in place as his lips closed hotly, wetly, around the tip.

"Love is with your brother"

The light tinkle of the throwing pins hitting the floor was almost drowned out by the sound of her gasp.

"Pain and pleasure."

Pain as her fingers were pierced by the sharp pins, pleasure as his tongue laved her nipple.

"My Shangri-La

I can't forget

When you were mine

I need you now."

Kye's eyes jerked up, his lips left her breast with a popping sound. He inhaled deeply; his eyes growing wide then dilating as a new hunger took over his body.

Scenting the air, his head jerked up to see her face, suffused with passion, her eyes tightly shut, breathing erratically, then he looked away.

It was calling him. The sweet song of her blood.

It called.

"Cry little sister

Come, come to your brother

Unchain me sister

Love is with your brother"

He closed his eyes as he ran his hand from her waist, over her arms, and to the injured hand.

Growling under his breath, he drew her fingers from his hair and across his face, leaving a sticky red trail behind.

"Why did you stop?"

He opened his eyes and saw the passion still burning within her. But along with desire, confusion filled her face.

He turned away, fighting to maintain some control, but the smell of her life's nectar, around him, on his face, was testing him.

He panted as his grip on her hand tightened, as he wrapped his arms securely around her waist, holding her lest she escape.

Lightning flashed through his veins and pounded in his head. His fangs began to pierce his gums, their keen sharp tips pressing down.

Eyes lowered half-mast, he turned and rubbed his face into the warm skin of her wrist, growling as he nuzzled the flesh there.

Then he sucked her finger into his mouth.

"Cry, little sister!"

Chapter Nineteen

"Kye?"

That was all it took.

With a growl worthy of a forest predator, Kye rose to his feet, his mouth clamped onto the injured finger, his eyes blazing gold, drowning out the green..

Tali gasped and stepped back, her desire beginning to fade with his aggressive movements, but she could not move far.

Sucking her digit deeply into the warm cavern of his mouth, Kye's free hand grasped the front of her jeans and yanked, rending the material into shreds with his preternatural strength.

Before Tali could protest, she felt Kye pull her against his body, his hard masculine form, and envelop her within the heat of his arm, her finger still firmly grasped between his lips.

"Kye?" she asked again, shuddering at the feel of her hard nipples pressed against his unyielding chest. "What...?"

But the lead vocals of Puddle of Mud's Control drowned her out. Not that it mattered. Kye was beyond hearing her.

The sweet taste of her blood combined with the lust he felt for this small human. Her scent filled his nostrils; her presence ignited his soul. Damning the beast that dwelled within him, he pulled his teeth away from her skin, fighting the urge to bite and find more of the divine gift of her blood.

But it was not a gift.

He was stealing this life fluid.

And that made him no better than Balthazar.

"Damn it!"

His roar of rage drowned out the heavy drumbeats of the music and with another muttered oath, he tossed Tali onto the bed.

Chest heaving with her conflicting emotions, Tali tried to figure out if she should run or stay.

Her eyes slid over Kye, taking in every inch of his body.

Even as she watched, he growled softly as he narrowed his eyes on her, his hand absently rubbing the huge bulge of his erection through the black leather of his pants.

Her eyes dropped to that caressing hand and watched it as it erotically and lovingly touched the swollen male flesh that demanded release from its confines.

Unconsciously, she licked her lips, causing a deeper rumble to explode from his chest.

She still wanted him.

Lying on her back, her feet flat on the bed, her knees slightly raised, she thrilled at the quiver of fear that shot through her body.

He was dangerous, untamed, wild. He was going to be the one to ride her body to nirvana.

Tali began to quiver as goosebumps formed on her arms and the coolness of the room pressed against the only covering on her body, the damp panties that shielded her from his sight.

"Staying or going?" Kye growled out as he watched her body react to the nearness of his.

The smell of her arousal was thick in the room. It matched the heat that was rising off of him, creating the scent of raw hot sex that filled the room.

"Staying," she whispered, almost too low for him to hear.

"Fuck."

At her passion husky voice, the last of his restraint fled.

Both hands gripped the tight leather at his waist, and again the tendons in his forearms rippled as he pulled, his eyes locked to hers.

The leather rent neatly at the seams, freeing him all at once to her eyes.

"Oh shit!" Tali felt her eyes glaze as the full magnificence of his cock was exposed. Beer-can thick, the long shaft rose towards his navel, quivering and wet with the dew of his desire. Hung like a horse was the only way she could describe it! It had to be a foot long! Suddenly, she began to have second thoughts.

"Too late, little girl," he hissed, reading her thoughts in her eyes. "You wanted me, you got me. No more teasing."

Tossing his majestic length of his hair behind his shoulders, he placed both knees on the bed, the weight of his body sliding her closer to him.

Dropping to all fours, he began to crawl towards her, his glossy black hair falling around him like a curtain, casting his masculine face in shadows as he came closer to her.

Even though her body thrilled at his approach, Tali began to ease backwards, shivering with excitement as every one of her wet dreams moved towards her, slowly.

The slow play of his muscles under his skin fascinated her, as did the sound of his labored breathing.

Suddenly everything fled, the music, the room, the fears that plagued her, as she felt the first brush of his hair against her feet.

Dropping low, Kye, eyes still locked onto her face, lowered his head and ran his rough tongue against the skin of her ankle, his swinging hair brushing against her legs.

"Oh!" Tali could not hold back her gasp of surprise as the nerves of her leg reacted to his touch. Who knew ankles were an erogenous zone?

A slow grin spread across his face as he felt her reaction. But again his attention was turned towards her legs, the soft flesh, the sweet taste of her skin. He could feel the heat of her blood as it raced through her veins.

Wrapping both hands around her calf, he raised her leg and reared up onto his knees, tossing his hair back with a shake of his head.

"Appetizer," he taunted as he separated her legs, watching her eyes grow even wider.

Tali felt the crotch of her panties cool as the air caressed her wet heat. But she felt no embarrassment. He created this desire in her, and it was about time he cooled the flames.

Feeling the quick return of her lust, Tali pulled her leg close to her, pulling Kye closer to her body. The muscles in her stomach clenched as his body invaded her personal space. His heat was almost magnetic as she felt her inner walls quiver in anticipation.

At her actions, Kye grinned wider, exposing the tips of his growing fangs to Tali, letting his emotions seep through his skin to cover her with his desire.

One rough hand reached out to rip the delicate cotton of her panties from her body, exposing her quivering sex to his anxious gaze.

Tali shuddered as she saw his fangs, but then, she knew he wasn't normal. He wasn't human. He was like a vamp in some respects, but a vamp had never played her body to this level of awareness. She had to admit to herself, that some of her attraction was because of the uniqueness of his person, not fully human and not quite vamp.

She felt her legs part, felt her heat and moisture began to leak from her feminine portals and arched her back, enjoying the rush of excitement that now filled her.

"Hot," he rasped as his eyes followed the trail of one lone dewdrop as it slowly made its way through the thin shielding of hair guarding the portal of her womanhood. The rosy color as well as her scent, lush and feminine, drew him.

Releasing her leg, he slid both hands up to her soft thighs, feeling the developed muscle beneath her skin, and spread her further for his possession.

Tali gasped in shock, as Kye seemed to suddenly loom above her, blotting out the light. Her stomach clenched and she fought to hold in a moan as she felt his presence looming closer and closer.

Eyes flaring with heat, Kye lowered his head to her thigh, his tongue lashing out to lap at the skin there. His lips clamped on to a spot, sucking hard and grazing her flesh with the very tips of his fangs.

"Oh," Tali gasped, her body lurching with the flash of heat his actions brought. "Don't stop!" her voice rasped as she watched his every move.

His tongue danced along her skin, climbing higher and higher to her center, nipping and licking, building sensation upon sensation. His hair, dragging along her damp skin was another shock to her system, bringing tremors of pure delight.

Her arms gave out and she collapsed amidst the pillows near the headboard, panting as he moved closer and closer to his goal.

Kye was nearing frenzy. Her taste swept over him, leaving him wanting more and more. The feel of her firm flesh, the gasping sounds she made as she labored to breathe through the intense arousal, all drove him mad with lust. It was almost too much. Almost.

His fingers trailed up her outer thighs, making her moan and writhe against the white bedspread, preparing her for his possession.

Then his fingers were tracing around her hips, and plunging into her feminine heat.

"Kye!" she screamed as she felt his fingers caress her for the first time. Electric shock waves danced along her spine, making her arch her back as she tossed her head from side to side.

Kye moaned. She was soft and wet, just the way he liked his women to be. Lightly, he traced the lips of her womanhood, feeling the slickness of her juices as her body wept for him. He had to taste.

Lowering his head, he purposely dragged his hair over her clitoris as his tongue again lashed out and he had his first intimate taste of Tali.

"Oh shit!" Tali gasped, her mind reeling with confusion. No man, no woman, no one had ever touched her there! Should she fight, should she let him, should she savor this? Where were her hands supposed to go? The questions swirled around in her head until the ensuing pleasure exploded her senses. Fuck what was proper! This felt good!

"More!" she screamed, her hands digging into the long strands of hair that trailed over her lower body and pulling him closer. "Give me more!"

Happy to oblige, Kye groaned his approval and laved her with his tongue. Inhaling her scent deeply, he used his tongue to part the folds of her flesh and hone in on her clit.

Tracing her delicate bud gently, he felt her lurch towards him, her legs lifting and wrapping around his head.

A light touch here, he decided as he began to flick the tip of his tongue against her.

Tali was lost in feelings, awash in emotions, as her body reacted to the erotic stimuli in ways she never thought possible. His touch was perfect, his tongue giving what she craved; yet she hungered for more.

Catching her breath, she raised her head and moaned as she saw Kye, his head buried between her legs, his long black hair covering her like a silken blanket. Groaning her approval, her head dropped back down as what she saw added an extra element to their sex play.

"Yes, God yes!" she growled as she began to rub his scalp in languid circles. "Eat me."

Deciding she needed more, Kye quickly ran two fingers through the moisture pouring from her body and inserted them into her virgin entrance.

Tali sucked in a deep breath, then blew it out as she felt him penetrate her, felt her walls expand to accept his fingers, felt his fingers strike nerves that had never been touched.

She whimpered.

Kye loved that sound, a lot.

Grinning, he took her clit into his mouth, suckling gently as he laved her with his tongue and explored her hot wet tunnel, looking for the spot that would drive her mad.

"Kye!" Her mewling cry filled his ears and made his cock throb even harder. Tremors shot through his body as he gorged himself at the feast of her body. Soon that was not enough for him. He wanted more.

Delivering one last lingering lap to her clitoris, Kye pushed his body up, easing her legs to his sides while keeping two fingers embedded inside her.

His attention was now focused on her breasts, her beautiful quivering breasts.

Before she could complain about his oral defection, Kye latched on to one berry-colored nipple, wrapping his tongue around the tip.

Tali felt her body tightening, tension building inside her at Kye's actions. Every muscle in her body tingled and trembled uncontrollably. Just as she was sure her body was going to implode from so much sensation, Kye moved. But he didn't move far. Within seconds, his soft wet lips were wrapped around her other nipple and another new sensation made her body twitch.

Her hands, first trying to push his head back down suddenly pulled him tighter to her chest. New sensations tightened her abdomen. Then his fingers began to move, to gently thrust within her sheath.

It was too much! This all was too much! She wanted to stop! She wanted it to continue! She was scared and aroused and she didn't know what to do about it! Frustration beat at her and her head continued to pound. Tears filled her eyes as she began to fight against the feelings swamping her body.

Noticing her distress, Kye let go of his oral pacifier and lifted golden/green eyes to hers.

"Are you afraid?" His fingers continued to work her body, never letting her forget the pleasure that was continuing to build.

"Yes, no, I don't know!"

"Do you like this?" His fingers thrust hard and her body arched backward, fire burning her center, her muscles clenching around his fingers.

"Too much!"

"Never too much," he rasped as his mouth latched onto her neck. The adrenaline rushing though her veins was waking the hunger in him for her blood, a hunger that he thought he had drowned in lust.

"What are you doing to me?"

"Taking you," he mumbled as her teeth grazed her skin again.

"Please," Tali moaned as she turned her neck to the side, offering more skin for him to pleasure. Her confusion was leaving her now that things were slowing down a bit.

"You will please me." Kye growled, using his thumb to nudge her clit.

"Yes."

"You are ready."

"Yes."

"Want fucked?"

"Yes!"

He wiggled his hips between her spread legs and let the damp heat from his mushroom-shaped head drag across her flesh.

"Want this?"

"Yes!"

"There will be no blood, thank God," he growled. He decided her training had broken through her barrier years ago when he slid his finger deep inside her wet clasping heat and felt no blockage, and he was glad of it. At this heightened state of arousal, any small amount of blood could trigger a feeding frenzy he would be hard pressed to control.

"Please," she whimpered, the heat from his cock making her body arch towards him.

"Yes, now."

"Kye!"

Kye pushed and felt the head of his cock ease within her hot opening, stretching her muscles and making a home for himself.

"Oh!" Tali's eyes shot open at the discomfort of his entrance. There was pressure and a sharp stabbing pain and he stopped.

Her body tightened up and her hands flew from his hair to his shoulders her nails digging in deep.

"That hurt."

"Of course," he returned his eyes boring into hers. "You are small and I am big."

Tali glared at him. But the deep feelings of pleasure were beginning to return. Even as she stared at him, her eyes began to grow hazy and her lids drooped. Her body softened around his and her grip on his shoulders lessened.

"So, are you a piss poor lover or are you going to give me what you've been promising?"

Kye smiled.

He kept smiling as he eased his full length within her tight body.

He was still smiling as her body accepted his invasion and he began to grind against her giving flesh.

Her torrid, passion-filled screams reverberated around the room, echoing off of the walls.

Kye ground his cock in as far as he could, striking every nerve in her sheath as he swirled his hips.

"So good!" Tali groaned as her hands slipped in sweat dripping from his back. She tightened her arms around him, wrapped her legs around his waist and urged him on faster, harder, deeper.

"Give it to me!" she screamed as he began to rhythmically thrust against her.

"Take it," he growled in return, his head buried in her neck as his hips slammed into hers, as he worked his cock to drive her into a state of sexual frenzy.

Tali threw back her head, tears pouring down her face as unexpected and even more intense pleasure filled her.

All she could see was Kye! All she could smell, touch, and taste, was Kye.

Her hands traveled to his head, pulling his hair, forcing his mouth to hers.

Snarling, Kye took control of the kiss, thrusting his tongue inside her mouth as his body invaded hers.

Tali groaned, their tongues dueling as she gave herself over to total pleasure.

Faster and harder he thrust, the bed slamming against the headboard blending with the heavy drumbeats pouring from the speakers. This was a loving neither would soon forget.

The soft spread against her back, the hard-thrusting man above her, made the feelings swamp her body!

Tali moaned and savored each sensation.

She opened her eyes and the room seemed to spin. No, she was spinning. As she opened her mouth, Kye sank his teeth into her lip, pricking her flesh lightly, lapping at her mouth.

"Kye."

Hard thrust, lap of the lip, another thrust.

"Damn," she groaned closing her eyes and burying her head in his neck. "Baby, we're flying." He felt so good!

The hard press of his body, the feel of the thick shaft as it slid through her wetness, struck nerves and sent sparks shooting though her bloodstream. She could feel every throbbing inch of him, and every motion was made for her ultimate pleasure.

"Levitating," he growled then groaned as her teeth sank into his flesh.

She was so hot, so wet, so damn perfect!

He felt her hot tunnel tighten around him, felt her moans reverberate through her body, vibrating against the sensitive head of his cock.

The slap of their bodies and the sound of her moans filled his head as he felt control of some of his preternatural strength escape.

As his blood rose higher and his cock grew harder, a light euphoria filled his head. He was on a journey to a place that he rarely visited in his long life, a place where pain and pleasure merged and threatened to overwhelm his senses.

So light did he feel, that his body responded accordingly. They began to drift on a white-hot cushion of pleasure.

"Um...huh," she moaned as colors began to swim behind her eyes. Lightning flashed in her mind and her thought processes shut down.

Then hell broke loose.

"Oh, Kye!"

Tali felt her body lurch as her muscles began to convulse around his hardness, each contraction sending fire and burning hot lava through her being. Her arms tightened around him and she could only scream her pleasure as orgasm took over.

"Fuck! God! Yeah, Tali! Fuck! Here it comes!"

Kye grunted and growled as her tight velvet channel clenched at him, milking him, forcing the release he fought to hold back.

"Take it baby, take it!"

He arched his back and slammed into her one final thrust as his toes curled and he felt the essence of his soul explode into her body.

Uncontrollably, he shook atop her, his body out of his control and his mind delving into the waves of pleasure that rippled though his body. He felt his seed explode from his body, his white-hot cream coating her, making each conclusive thrust even more of a pleasure.

The fact she was still climaxing around his erupting cock was another pleasure.

His heart racing, his breath rasping, Kye let go and rode the waves of ecstasy until his body fell like a limp rag onto her.

"Mmm," Tali moaned, too drained to do anything else.

This was all she had dreamed of, all she hoped she could experience with him. But instead of satisfying her curiosity, it made it stronger. She wanted to do it again, in a different position. She wanted to go down on him, to have him explode in her mouth so she could taste his cum. She wanted to roll on top of him and mount him like a jockey. She wanted him. Anyway she could get him.

Kye shook as he struggled to regulate his breathing. This was not what he expected. A quick roll in the hay was one thing, but Tali exploded all of his reserves of control! No one, well maybe one person, had the ability to affect him this way. The fact that even now they were floating some two feet off of the bed gave testimony to the fact he was slipping! She did this to him.

He peeled open one eye and stared at the shaking, sweating woman under him.

What was so special about her? What drew him to her? This was not good. Actually, this was very bad! His lack of control scared him! She could be the one to distract him from his main objective. That would not do.

But the ringing of the phone brought him out of his dark musings.

"Phone," Tali purred as she opened her eyes and watched the man above her...like a cat watches a mouse he has marked for dinner.

"Let it ring."

"Answer it. Or is it a girlfriend calling?" Jealousy began to rear its ugly head.

"Leave off."

"I'll get it then!"

She threw her arm out, trying to reach a bedside table, but hit only air.

"What the..."

Laughing, Kye released his hold on her, disconnecting his still hard cock from her body and letting her drop to the bed.

She screamed until her ass hit the mattress.

"I said leave off!" he laughed as he floated above her, watching her eyes grow wide in shock.

"What the fuck are you?"

She was not scared, but she wondered what she had just paired off with. Should she have used a condom? Oh hell! Birth control! She didn't use any!

Before she could start the questioning, there was a banging at the door.

"I know you are in there, Kye! Open the door! I have news!"

"Angel," Kye sighed as he gently floated to the bed and eased his body down beside Tali.

"And who is Angel?"

Ignoring her, he rose to his feet and made his way to the elevator door. Smiling and nude, he flipped the latch and slid the door open.

"My love," he teased, opening his arms.

"You stink of sex," was the reply as the tall dark-haired woman brushed past him and entered his home. "And I hope you got rid of the bimbo. And for both of our sakes, go and put some clothes on! This is important!"

Then she noticed that the bimbo was still abed.

"Hello, Angel," Tali snarled as she glared at the woman, the rival, she felt, for Kye. He may be a whatever, but he was her whatever!

"Kind of young, ain't she?" Angel laughed as she turned to Kye.

"She wouldn't take no for an answer," he replied as he walked over to his closet and pulled on a robe. Smirking, he tossed one to Tali who still lay nude in his bed.

"Yeah, I see you crying rape," she snorted. "But if Romper Room is finished, I have something you need to know. Balthazar is on his way here and it's time to deal with that bastard. Remember what you promised?"

"Revenge," he replied, then nodded to Tali. "She may have the info we need to bring him down."

"For a price," Tali answered, as she pulled on his robe and stood to face the two people in the room. "Time to cut a deal, Kye. I get what I want, you get what you want, and we all go away smiling."

"And that is?" Angel asked, sarcasm high in her voice as she unconsciously shook her hair over the scar on her face. The woman's beauty was making her uncomfortable.

"Balthazar dead. If he is coming in tonight, this may be our last shot."

For a moment, silence reigned in the room, then Kye began to smile, his fangs still exposed.

"I'm all ears, baby. Give me what you got."

Chapter Twenty

Bri waited.

She sat at the end of the bed and stared at the object of her most recent desire. And she waited.

His hair lay around him, a dark cloud surrounding a pale, still face.

Holding her head still, her eyes rolled towards the window and watched as the sky exploded into brilliant orange and red colors, watched as the day slowly perished and gave birth to a new night.

Looking again at the figure laying so still and quiet on the bed, she knew that soon her waiting would come to an end.

She had better be prepared.

Balthazar opened his eyes, instantly alert and fully awake, aware of his surroundings. He inhaled once, bringing in the scents that surrounded him, identifying them one by one.

There was the smell of old blood left over from last night's feast. He could still taste the fear that coursed through the struggling woman's veins as he feasted slowly, biting her in different places, increasing her terror with a few well placed slaps and cuts. But never hard enough to bruise. Bruised blood didn't have the same flavor and texture as blood drenched in fear.

There was the smell of vanilla — the candles that lay unlit around his chambers. The smell reminded him enough of his youth so that he would never want to find himself in the same predicaments he had pulled himself out of. It was a strong reminder of who he was, where he came from, and all that he had yet to achieve.

Then there was the smell of her, the smell of power-hungry slut, an intoxicating aroma. Of course, with her scent came the scent of gun oil and silver polish. Polish for the buttons that would line her 'security cut' jacket, the jacket designed to hide the many weapons she carried on her person. And polish for the three deadly blades she always carried within easy reach. One of which rested against his neck right now.

"Kill me or fuck me, Bri. But make up your mind quickly. I have business to attend to."

Bri steadied the hand that held the small silver blade against his throat. It would be so easy to press down; to watch the dark, used, stolen blood bubble from the grotesque smile in his neck that one slice of her blade could create. So damn easy.

But nothing in life worth having was easy.

Nothing.

"Why would I kill you, Balthazar?" she asked, her voice low and singsong. "What would I gain?"

"Absolutely nothing, Bri. Which is the only reason you have stilled your hand. If I die now, you get nothing. And you covet things, my dear mercenary bitch. You covet what I have created."

"Yet you call me to your side?"

"Of course. You will want what I have at its peak of success before you try to kill me for it, Bri. Something I admire in a woman."

He raised one finger, pricking its tip on the sharp blade as he pushed it aside, away from his carotid artery.

"Now to business. And I assume it's business because you are wearing clothes and have delivered no further notices of your intent to 'do away' with me."

Snapping to attention, pleased Balthazar understood her intent, Bri slid the blade into its sheath at her waist, and watched as the man-creature rose to his feet.

"The shipment is on its way and should arrive within the hour."

"Good."

Balthazar ran a hand through his hair and walked across the room to his wardrobe, the dying colors of the dusky sky bathing his bare body in shadows.

"The cargo that was misdirected has not been found, but is easily replaced. One of the other clubs has enough people to ensure the order is met."

"Good."

Not bothering with underwear, Balthazar pulled on black, custom-fitted leather dress pants and turned to select his socks. Oddly enough, the ones he picked were covered in little crosses.

"The one you are looking for certainly has become active of late. But I have my people watching his most likely target."

"Which is?"

"Club Destiny."

"And why is that the most likely target?"

He sat on a bench in the walk-in closet to don his socks and shoes, a pair of butter soft Italian loafers. He rose to his feet and delved once more into his closet, this time selecting a long-sleeved black silk shirt.

"Because it's new, it's large, and you will be meeting a few associates this evening. Overseas trusts, you understand."

"So, they are responding to my requests?"

"Demands, Balthazar. You managed to piss off quite a lot of people. Making my job harder."

"Your job, Bri, is to find the one responsible for upsetting the delicate balance of my business here."

"My job is to keep your ass alive until I can collect what is due me."

"Hmm," Balthazar hummed in delight as he buttoned his shirt and tucked it in, making sure to readjust his favorite play toy, making sure to position it to its best advantage. "Sounds like the same thing to me, Bri. You quibble over words."

Walking over to a dresser, he pulled out a large gold cross suspended by a thin gold chain.

"Strange choice of attire, for a vampire," Bri commented as she watched him fuss around the room.

"Funny, how Christians wear this thing," he laughed. "I mean, their great Savior was crucified on one, so some of them say. Yet they wear the object of his destruction as if it were a relic of creation! Would you wear the dagger that slit your mother's throat, Bri? Or the smoking gun that snatched away the life-force of your father?"

"Probably, Balthazar, but I am not Christian, so the point is moot."

"The point, Bri, my dear little cunning bitch, is that I am both! I am their salvation and their destruction. By the end of this evening, the Ancient Council will know, this meddlesome troublemaker will know, the whole damn city will know, Bri. I am their alpha and omega, and I have come."

Draping the necklace around his neck, he positioned the cross dead center on his chest and turned to glance at the woman, who carried his mark on her name, but was not under his power.

"Very...religious, I think, of you, Balthazar. Oh how the masses will drop to their knees in praise."

Bri rolled her eyes as she checked the positioning of her weapons again.

"But if The Delusional Minute is over, we have work to do."

Before she could blink, Balthazar was on her, his hand wrapped around her neck, her air cut off and her feet hanging off the ground.

"You overstep yourself, Bri," he hissed as he brought her face close to his, close enough so that his slightly mint-scented breath bathed her face, bringing along with it the hint of old blood and anger. "I could have you on your knees if I so choose."

A near silent hiss of her blade clearing leather filled the air a moment before the sharp tip pressed against his heart.

"And you will be on yours," she gasped though her constricted throat, eyes dead and clear of fear or anger. No emotions showed in those flat orbs.

"Your soul is a dead as mine," Balthazar laughed as he shook her to try and make any emotion appear. There was none. Perfect.

"Yet I still draw breath, barely," she choked, her lips turning blue as her oxygen was rapidly depleted.

Smiling, Balthazar lowered her to her feet, pressing against the knife, knowing it could not pierce the silk of his shirt easily.

"One day, you will push until I hurt you," Bri hissed, as she breathed deeply. Pulling air into her lungs, she drew her blade back and sheathed it.

"One day, I will let you," he answered as he turned towards the door. "I think I should like to visit death again, my dear Bri. If I carry you along with me, the trip will be all the sweeter."

Silent as a wraith, Bri followed him out the chamber, but as she recalled where his hands pressed against her throat, she licked her lips in anticipation.

Chapter Twenty-One

"So what's the plan?"

Angel looked condescendingly at Tali before opening her purse and pulling out a pack of smokes, a bottom corner torn out. She hated giving smokes to people and having them touch her filters. You never knew where that hand had been.

"The plan is for me to shower. Then I call my friend to let her know I am safe."

"Could be a set-up," Angel sighed tiredly as she tapped her cigarette against the pack. "Lord knows we can trust so very few."

"Why should I set you up? I've got what I want at the moment. How could I hurt the man I just..." A blush highlighted her cheeks. "Well, you know."

"Easily," Kye finally spoke up. "I could kill you now and not lose a moment of sleep." The words sounded confident, but his eyes, those swirling green/gold orbs looked unsure.

Angel missed the look in his eyes, but turned towards Kye, a laugh on her lips.

"She is such a young thing! So innocent and pure, filled with ideals. I never knew you were into chicken, Kye. Even as oven-ripe as this one is, it needs to be sat on a bit more."

"Chicken?"

"Chicken," Angel answered, turning to face the robe-clad young woman once again. "Chicken, as in bait for chicken hawks. As in what that Bastard Balthazar is into. Chicken, my fine-feathered friend, is a slang term used to describe under-aged screw partners. Since you are obviously under age, in knowledge if not in age, you, my dear, are chicken."

"Fuck you, lady. I have seen enough shit in the last two years of my life that I could never claim to be innocent, not that I would want to. To compare Kye to Balthazar... You are one insane bitch!"

As she spoke, her anger started to rise. Unconsciously, she bent her knees and placed her hands in a defensive position in front of her.

"Ohh!" Angel said after looking Tali up and down. "The chicken pecks. Why should I not compare Kye to Balthazar? Two sides of the same coin."

Tali sucked in a deep breath and turned to face Kye. What was he?

Kye absorbed Angel's words without comment, though inside, he felt the blow. He made damn sure it didn't show! Never give weaknesses away, even to friends.

Looking into the faces of both of the women he had let into his life, Angel by choice, Tali by necessity, he figured he had better say something.

"Well, the man made me what I am." His dry tones filled the silence of the room. "I can easily say that I could kill you both without thought." He threw his hair over his shoulder and he observed the nervous shiver that ran down Angel's body and the disbelief that filled Tali's face.

"So now," he continued. "I am stuck with a bitch and a chicken. Must be my day for farm animals."

"Fuck you," Tali growled.

Before she could move, Kye was again in front of her, breathing in her face.

"If you wanted more, all you had to do was ask."

As he spoke, his fingers ran teasingly over her body. He chuckled as her nipples hardened and her body reacted to his nearness.

"Well, I don't have to sit around here and watch."

At her words, they both turned toward Angel, who, with a shaky hand, lifted her cigarette to her lips and lit up with a lighter she pulled from her pocket.

"You had your shot," Kye teased gently now. Even with all her faults, Angel was a woman to be admired.

"Yeah, and the answer is the same after all of these years." She chuckled a bit at the boyish look on Kye's face before she again shook her hair in front of the scar on her face. "I didn't come here to sharpen my wits on you. I came here because of what is going down tonight."

"Tonight?" Suddenly both Kye and Tali were all business. Kye walked over towards Angel, a question in his eyes. "What is happening tonight?"

"Something big is going down. Word from the inside is that Balthazar has called in the big guns. People from the Bridge, man. Rumor has it they are pissed because they lost a few operatives in the Twin Towers and are looking for someone to take their frustrations out on. Guess who has grabbed their attention?"

"This is great, Angel!" Kye said after a moment of concentration. "I've been searching for a way to bring this to a head for a lot of years. I'm as close as I have ever been."

"Where?" Tali gasped out one word as she walked towards Angel.

Why hadn't Marti told them? Or was Marti inside now giving them the same info? She had to call her friend.

"We will know when my contact gets back with me. Until then, little chicken, we wait."

"Not necessarily." Kye stepped back and walked over to his door. "If something huge is going on, they will be advertising."

He opened the doors and disappeared into the elevator.

"Where are you going?" Two feminine voices chimed in, each filled with dismay.

"To get my paper," he answered as he slammed the doors shut and hit the lever to lower the car. "You ladies play nice while I'm gone. Don't get any blood on my furniture! White is a bitch to get cleaned."

As he disappeared, Tali and Angel glared at each other.

"I wonder how long it takes for him to get a paper?"

"They deliver to his front door, chicken! He probably will be back in a second." Angel blew a smoke ring as she smirked at Tali.

"Don't call me chicken! How the hell was I supposed to know?"

"So you just hop between the sheets," Angel gestured with her cigarette towards the mussed bed, "with every guy you meet?"

"None of your damn business, but the answer is no. Where do you get off asking? Even though you are old enough, I don't need a mother at this late date."

Angel sucked in a breath at Tali's words, and then promptly choked on her own cigarette smoke.

"Someone... (cough)...needs...(cough)...to mother...(cough)...your ass!"

Patting herself on the chest, Angel glared at the scrap of girl glaring defiantly at her.

"And I am not that old!"

"Well you look it to me," Tali snorted as she turned and made her way towards the kitchen area.

"Hard living. While you may know hard, sleeping with Vamp Boy over here, you know dick about living."

"Uh hum," Tali grunted as she smirked at Angel, then opened the refrigerator door. There had to be something to eat in this place, unless he was poor from rent and the stereo equipment.

"I am serious!" Angel snarled as she watched Tali's robe-covered butt waggle like a puppy's tail as she scouted out food. "As serious as a heart attack."

"Watch what you say, grandma! Invoking the gods of myocardial infarction could see you as main character in the next episode of ER. Though I know Hopkins is good, I never heard they specialized in geriatrics."

Angel's eyes widened for a moment! How dare that little bitch insult her! And how dare she do it with her face stuck in the refrigerator?

But as she opened her mouth to deliver a stinging retort, the humor of the situation got to her. She exploded into laughter.

"What's so funny?"

Tali pulled her head out of the fridge long enough to stare at the other woman.

Angel was not that old and was quite striking, despite the scar that marred her face, but Tali's womanly instinct told her the bitch wanted Kye. She instantly put her on the defensive and added insult by speaking to her through the fridge, as if she was of no import.

But Tali hated laughter if she wasn't in on the joke.

"If I am old, you little bitch, it is because of what Balthazar did!"

Angel still whooped with laughter, but she made her way into the kitchen and dropped the cigarette into the sink.

"So why do you want him dead?" Tali asked cautiously as she withdrew from the fridge, a pack of ham and a jar of mustard in her hands. She closed the door with her hip and placed her poison of choice on the small kitchen table.

"You want to know?" Angel asked as she took a seat and pointed to the cupboard behind her.

Tali walked over, keeping her eyes on Angel, and opened the door to discover bread. Looks like it was a sandwich after all.

"I want to know."

Silently, Angel watched as Tali put together a thick sandwich, pulled a plate out of the drying rack, and sat down to eat.

"He killed my man, took my baby, cut my face, killed my child, took away my life and dammit, stole my Bible!"

Angel nearly shouted her words, but the reaction on Tali's face was worth the pain of disclosure.

The girl looked absolutely sick.

"He killed your baby, your child?"

"Took her when she was born. Told me that if I obeyed him, I would get her back. He even sent me pictures to ensure I would behave and be a good little slut to his friends. Then one day a friend in his entourage let it slip he had murdered my child, that I was working for nothing, that I had better let him and his friends run a train on me or I was next. What the hell did he know? His words killed me right there. I was going to go out and end it all, when Kye found me. But he promised me something better."

As she spoke, Angel pulled another cigarette from her pack and lit up.

"He promised me revenge." Through the smoke that surrounded her, Tali could see the deadly glint in her eye and knew this woman lived and breathed to see the end of Balthazar. They had something in common.

"Good. You may be a crusty old broad, but you are filled with hate. I can use that. Balthazar stole my family and my childhood."

She paused to take a bite of her sandwich, winced at the smoke surrounding her, but chewed and swallowed anyway.

"He killed my family to get their child, me. Do you know he has orphanages? That he raised all of us poor abandoned children, and we are grateful for what he does, so fuckin' grateful. He educates us, he trains us to give us careers in security. What better job for an orphan? But he failed to tell us he is the one who arranges the accidents that takes our parents away. And he neglected to tell us that when our training is over, if we don't pass muster, he has us harvested for blood. That only the best little automatons get to be made into what he is, so we are stuck guarding his sorry decrepit ass for all eternity. He kind of failed to mention this in his 'welcome to my home' speech."

Angel said nothing, but another cloud of smoke passed through her lips.

"Maybe I knew your daughter, Angel. Maybe I met her a thousand times and never gave a thought to why we were both there. Maybe I kicked her ass when we sparred, cause he starts us in martial arts young, and maybe she kicked mine. But that thing robbed me of my family, lied to me, and now would probably wring my neck if he got the chance. I am the one who got away, Angel. Like you, I swore to get my revenge."

Silence filled the kitchen as both women were lost in thought.

"What did he do to Kye?" Tali finally asked.

"He made him what he is."

"And what is that?"

"Ask Kye."

Before any more words could be exchanged, the elevator creaked and the car stuttered to a stop.

Kye walked in, a grin on his face, his hair streaming around his body.

"We are in luck! Something big is going down."

He walked into the kitchen and slammed the paper on the table.

The two women eased closer to see what he was pointing at.

"Club Destiny. Fetish party tonight."

"Destiny?" Tali asked.

"Rumored to be one of his spots," Angel added.

"I have to call my friend." Sandwich forgotten, Tali leapt to her feet and looked around for a phone.

"I don't think so," Kye said, eyes going flat.

"Let her," Angel said before Tali could reply. "She has good reason."

Kye arched one eyebrow as he looked from one woman to the other.

"Female bonding?"

"No," Angel said as she rose to her feet. "We understand each other. Some things are universal."

Kye said nothing, but nodded. He would find out the common denominator later.

"I'm going home and see if my contact has more news. Later."

They both watched as Angel walked to the elevator and left a lot quieter than she arrived.

Kye turned towards Tali, but she was already on the phone, having discovered one hanging on the kitchen wall.

Shrugging personal shit off for later, he turned towards his shower. He had to get ready for tonight.

What does one wear to a fetish party?

What else?

Leather.

Chapter Twenty-Two

"Chari, Chari, quite contrary, where do your marbles roll?"

Chari stared at the blinking light on the phone and huddled into a tighter ball.

'Lying on the bed was no way for the best golden throat in the country to behave,' he would say. Or 'Come now, my pretty bitch, sing for me.'

But Chari didn't want to hear anything. She just wanted to drift.

Ever since that evening when he forced her to…service him, the thought of his dead seed, penetrating her body, dissolving and becoming one with her flesh, made her skin crawl.

She knew it was time for her to answer the call, knew she had to pull it together or she could never pass the information she had, but her body refused to answer the dictates of her mind.

"Chari, Chari, quite contrary, where do your marbles go? To hell, I understand, they're in great demand, like grains of sand, they flow."

The red light blinked, Chari curled up tighter, and Balthazar waited.

"Chari!" Marti rushed into the room and quickly scanned the place, searching for the missing woman. "Chari, where are you?"

"I fell," Chari muttered. "I fell and landed in hell."

"You don't know hell, girl! Get your ass up and move! Balthazar is calling for you. He and that pet barracuda just arrived and they expect us to be all turned out for the big event!"

"Big event?"

"Something big is going down, Chari! You have to get yourself together!" Marti crossed the room to sit on the bed beside the shaken woman. "You've got to pull it together!"

"Marti, this is hell," Chari trembled harder.

"Get up, bitch!" Marti screamed suddenly, grabbing Chari by the shoulders and pulling her upright. "You are going to fuck around and get us all killed!"

Blinking rapidly, tears began to fall down her face. But her eyes focused in on Marti.

"Sorry," she muttered as she pushed herself away from the other woman. "Sorry, Marti."

"You will be sorry unless you get a move on, girl! That man is not playing! Something had to happen for him to call in the big guns and that means his temper will be fast."

Chari nodded, remembering her encounter on the desk.

"So pull yourself together! Time is wasting!"

Nodding, Chari pulled herself from the bed and made her way to the phone. Pressing her red message button, she picked up the handset and placed it by her ear.

"Wear nothing, my golden throat. I have decided you shall entertain this evening."

That was it. No names, no greeting, just her orders for the night.

"I'm the entertainment," she said quietly, trying to fight back the lethargy that threatened to take her away from the horror here.

"Shower?" Marti asked, trying to get as much info from the woman as she could. Angel would be interested in knowing this.

"Showered."

"The hair?"

"Wild. I am going to die, Marti."

"You don't know that!" Marti moved a step back from the knowing comment from the half-broken woman, moved back as if the aura of death surrounding Chari would taint her as well.

"I know." As she spoke, her voice got stronger, surer, as if she had some plan. She dropped the handset on the phone, and watched calmly as it rattled and bounced, not exactly fitting in its place, kind of like her.

"Chari…"

"Leave me."

"Chari!"

"Leave! I have to prepare."

Nodding, Marti left the room, leaving the naked but suddenly determined woman alone.

As soon as the door closed, Chari searched for her cell phone. Pressing in the number, she waited the few seconds for the call to be re-routed before she began to speak.

"Mari? We are at the Sheraton. Whatever is happening is happening tonight. If you can figure out where, you will know his plans. I will call you later."

She hung up the phone and walked over to the bathroom mirror.

The dead-eyed, dark-haired woman who stared back at her seemed alien. She looked into those eyes, the eyes that now were beyond jaded, and she smiled. She knew she was going to die, and he was going to go with her.

As she giggled in the mirror, she never noticed the door closing shut, or that another pair of ears were listening in from the hanging handset.

* * * * *

As soon as the sun dipped below the skyline and darkness began to creep through the heavens, Mari walked from her closet and looked around at the empty apartment.

"Damn that girl!" she muttered as she looked around to see if Tali had left her a note.

Before she got too far into her search, her cell phone rang.

"Hello?" she anxiously asked hoping that it was Tali on the other end.

"Mari? Listen up! Tonight! It is happening tonight, but I don't know what it is!"

* * * * *

Angel groaned as she clicked open her cell phone and listened to who was on the other end.

"Marti?"

"Listen!" the voice hissed. "We've got problems! One of the girls is feeding info to somebody. I am not sure who her contact is, but either way it is not good for us! We are at the Sheraton Waterfront Downtown and there are big shots coming in. If you want to make a rush for him here, you had better do it tonight. He has his guards around, but knowing B, he'l insult and leave early, leaving his people to clean up after him. He plans on entertaining, and you know he likes his privacy for that, so he probably will be coming back here with a select few. Where it is going down tonight, I don't know, but it is big! He called in the New York Crew, and the Blackwell Bitch is with him."

"Bri?"

"And her two rent-a-goons! I got to go."

"Marti! Who is coming? Marti?"

Her only answer was the low buzz of the disconnected line.

* * * * *

Mari stared at the buzzing phone, then slammed it onto its jack.

Okay! Now was the time to strike, tonight. But first she had to find Tali. There wasn't much time to waste.

Looking around the room frantically now, she finally saw the small note taped to the mirror.

"Gone back to the hot spot. Need clues to Kye. Daylight, so I am safe. Tali."

"Damn that girl!" Mari fumed as she stared at the letter in her hands. "She is going to get us all killed for a roll in the hay!"

Turning, she raced out of the apartment and missed hearing the ringing of the phone.

* * * * *

"Guess I missed her," Tali mused as Kye walked out of his closet holding a few belts. "What's that?"

"Your outfit for the evening."

"I am not wearing that!" Tali snorted as Kye held up something leather that resembled pants, but were practically all cross ties and no legs.

Kye smiled.

"Really, I am not!"

The smile grew wider.

It was going to be a long night.

Chapter Twenty-Three

"I look like a skank!" Tali hissed as she stared down at what she was wearing.

The pants—and she decided to use the term loosely—were nothing more than a thong with leg straps. But she had to admit when she turned to the side, they made her ass look great.

Soon after Angel left and she'd made her phone calls, Kye had shoved Tali into the shower with orders to scrub until she no longer smelled like yesterday's used whore.

"I smell like you!" she growled back, only to have him grin at her, showing off the sharp points of his fangs that still hung below his gums.

"Must be my smell mixed with yours," he taunted, a strange look in his eyes.

"Well, you were sniffing it in earlier, snort boy!" She blinked as she realized she liked the taunting and teasing that went on between the two of them. It was like a game that had no definable ending. "You know you like it," she called as she followed him to his closet door.

He winked at her, then threw off his robe to walk into his closet. Tali gasped.

It wasn't the large amount of clothing that caught her attention, though Kye was a clotheshorse. It wasn't the amount of leather, though she would swear in a court of law that several herds of cattle had given up their lives to outfit him. It wasn't even the mirrored makeup table that sat across from a huge rack of boots and shoes, not a pair of runners in sight! It was his back.

Kye's back was a series of dull lash marks and scar tissue. Some were flat, some shiny with the growth of new skin, but all gave testament to a lashing that would have killed anyone else.

"Kye..."

"What?" he asked as he tossed his hair over his shoulders, effectively blocking her view of his ravaged back like a curtain dropping over a stage.

"Your back…"

The amusement left his eyes and his lips flattened as he watched her. Slowly his eyes became dull and distant as if the life were drained out of him.

"Yes, Tali?"

Tali blinked, not knowing exactly what to say. So she said the first thing that came to mind.

"Your back is seriously fucked up."

His laughter startled her.

It was a cold empty laugh, and as he expelled the ugly sound from his lungs, he bent forward, letting his hair slide to frame his face, exposing the ruin of flesh once more.

"Darling girl," he chuckled. "I have made women scream and faint at the sight of my back. Grown men have whimpered in fear and vomited in corners. Some sick bastards get turned on by the display and want to duplicate it or better yet, have me do it to them. And you stand there and say that my back is fucked up?"

"Well…" Tali hedged, wondering if she was trapped in the room with a mad man. "Well, to be honest, I didn't know what else to say!"

Abruptly, the laughter ended and his eyes seemed to glow from the cave created by the shadows and his hair. It was eerie, those green/gold swirling orbs shining from all that black…nothingness.

"I bet it hurt?" she offered as she continued to stare at him.

"You bet it hurt?"

Quicker than she could blink, Kye was before her, running his hands through her tousled hair.

"You bet it hurt, my ex-virgin? You're damn right it hurt! Wanna hear a little story, Tali? A little scary story before we go and meet the monsters?"

Tali showed no fear as she stared at the creature before her, the creature who took her virginity and now tried to intimidate her. Maybe if he had done this little act before he had made such feverish, savage love to her, she might have been frightened. Now she was merely curious.

"Tell me a story, Kye."

"Once upon a time there was a family. A mommy and daddy and two sons." As he spoke, he turned to the pictures on the mantel and an almost wistful look entered his eyes.

"The daddy was the son of a slave and a crazy Cheyenne man who saw something special in the runaway's eyes. They had one son who was accepted into the tribe because of the power that ran in his veins. Blood will tell, Tali. The blood will always tell."

He fisted his hands in the back of her hair, pulling her neck up, making her gasp in surprise. Her breathing increased as he moved closer to her, but still she only felt a bit of excitement, no real fear. Then she shuddered as the rough texture of his wet tongue lashed across the soft thin skin of her neck.

"That boy," he breathed, as he buried his nose in the hair behind her ear, his breath cooling her wet skin. "That boy was like his father, searching for something in the Indian women he saw, but never finding it, until he came across a Chinese woman on the run from the railroad bosses. They wanted a little fun and games with the Chink and thought she was an easy mark. But she fought them, Tali. She fought them off until that brave on the back of the horse came to her rescue."

He loosened one hand to slide down the front of her body, parting the robe and cupping her breast in his hand, chuckling as her nipple tightened into a hard peak in his palm.

"Now, he killed the men, left their bodies for carrion, and took the woman for himself. He saw in her something other women lacked. He saw power, Tali. The same power that his father saw in his mother, the Voodoo priestess. Power, Tali, blood calling to blood. They had two tri-breed mutts, Tali. The spirits blessed them with two. Until one day, a man came to call on their village."

He pulled back long enough to look into her eyes, for her to accept what he was saying.

Tali blinked at Kye as the sensations and the story stopped. He waited until awareness filled her eyes, then he slid his hand down to cup her crotch.

"Two sons, Tali, the older was next in line to be Medicine man, the younger was more interested in women and fighting. But this man was called by the power in the blood. He wanted that power for his own. When the family refused to divulge its secrets, he got nasty. Have you ever heard the sounds a woman makes when she is being raped, Tali? It is almost like the sounds she makes as she is forced to watch her man's throat being slit."

Tali jerked at his words, pulled back to look at him, but he lifted her in his arms and tossed her to the bed.

"He almost makes the same wet sounds, Tali, the same wet sounds a man will make when his throat is being ripped out."

Tali fought to break away from Kye, but he held her in place.

"They first tied me and my brother up to the lodge pole of the teepee, Tali. Ripped our shirts from our bodies and forced my parents to watch as they tried to skin us with leather quirts. I so enjoy the feeling of leather, my little ex-nun. I still do! Maybe I am a bit of a freak! But leather hurts, Tali. It hurts when it is used to slice the skin. First it feels cold and familiar, almost like a caress or a kiss. Then the burning starts and the screams start. But you keep your mouth closed. You don't want to torment those watching any more than you have to. So you hold the screams in and they fill your mind."

"Kye, stop!" Now he was hovering over her on all fours, staring down into her eyes, forcing the horror he had experienced into his eyes, willing her to understand.

"Stop! That is what she screamed, Tali! She screamed stop! She pleaded with him! She begged him! Then he slit my father's throat."

Tali closed her eyes and turned her head away, trying to block the horror, but Kye would grant her no escape.

"Then he decided that since the elder child was in training, he would make him talk. He raped my mother Tali. He sliced her clothes from her body and raped her in front of her sons. No man can stand the sight of that happening to his own mother, Tali! But I saw things I was never meant to see! I saw things that haunt me to this very day! He raped my mother, Tali! She bled and cried! Blood and tears are his legacy, Tali! And he made damn sure I would remember!"

Tali sobbed once, tears welling up in the corners of her eyes as she shook her head from side to side, denying what he was telling her! It was too horrible, too sick!

"Don't shake your head at me, little girl! You wanted to know what pain is. I am showing you!"

He buried his hand in her hair, forcing her head still as he willed her eyes to open.

"This is reality, little girl! You had better fucking get used to it! You want to know pain? This is pain!"

"Kye…" Tali forced her eyes open, her lashes spiky with tears, silently pleading for him to let her go.

"Pain, Tali. Pain is when he decided nothing is going to loosen your tongue so he had better try something different. Pain is watching as he rips open your brother's neck and drinks the blood, finds the power. It didn't stop him Tali, it didn't satisfy him! He had a taste of pure power, natural power, and he wanted more. He turned my brother into a mindless machine, Tali. He turned him into a walking stomach with nothing but a growing hunger.

"But the magic did something he didn't expect, Tali. Natural magic rejects unclean things. It tried to reject him, but my brother was not strong enough. He came to his senses after he was gnawing at my neck like a baby at a teat. Then he threw himself into the punishing sun to atone for his sins. You see, Tali, the power was not ripe in his body, his blood was not enriched, as it should have been. But mine was."

"Your brother…"

"My brother was picked apart by vultures, Tali, before my dying eyes. I watched him reform and burn, then I watched as vultures plucked his eyeballs out, and nibbled on his brains."

Tali swallowed hard, forcing herself not to gag as the mental picture filled her head.

"Yes, Tali. How would you like to see your idols' eyes plucked out? How would you like to know he was the meal of the day and nothing you could do would save him?"

Tali closed her eyes again, trying to hold back the terror and helplessness filling Kye's eyes.

"Balthazar likes his privacy, Tali. After killing my parents, we were moved to his cabin in the mountains, so he could learn our secrets in private. It was there he left us, me as dinner and my brother as a mindless servant. It was there that a bunch of runaway slaves found and released me. I made it back to my village and found it burned to the ground. Balthazar's doing. If he couldn't have what he wanted, no one would live. Do you know what the fucked up thing is, Tali? The thing that really is ironic is he never learned jack shit! My father had no secret books or spells. It was always in the blood, Tali. His blood. My blood."

"How did you…" she gasped, then paused as she felt his naked body settle over hers.

"Survive? Live while having the better portion of my neck gone and my blood spilling from my brother's belly into the ground? Easy, Tali. He forced his perverted magic into my brother, and my brother mixed it with the power in mine. Evil doesn't die, Tali. And the good refused to drop its hold on me. Those slaves took care of me, Tali. They preached the gospel to me and tried to understand when I sucked the heart out of every animal I killed and wallowed in its blood. But when they started smelling like food to me, it was time to go.

"So, Tali, you want to know what pain is? Try not knowing what you are or what you are capable of doing. Try hearing the screams of your mother in your head, driving you insane each night. Try living with your brother's whispered words of revenge ringing in your ears, following you into your safest hiding space, crying out for vengeance! Try knowing that the power in your blood is all that is keeping you from becoming like the thing you hate most. That is pain, Tali. You have centuries to plot out your vengeance, Tali, my sweet. Years to try and fail. That is pain, my dear ex-virgin. So my 'fucked up' back is just a reminder, my little one. Just the thing that makes you want to rip the monster's head off and piss down his neck. My back is nothing, when you look at it this way."

As he finished, he began to crawl backwards off of her body, once again pulling his hair and the shadows around him like a cloak of darkness.

"What do you have to say about that?"

Tali lay there for a second, absorbing all that Kye had told her, understanding him and empathizing with him.

As he turned to walk into his closet, Tali called out to him.

"I say that's a real mind fuck, Kye. No wonder you are so screwed up."

He froze at her words, before whirling around, a cyclone of hair and golden skin, to face her.

"Well, it is!" she defended herself. "I would be fucked up in the head just like you if it had happened to me."

"That's it?"

Kye stared at her for a moment as she shrugged her shoulders and sat up, adjusting the robe around her calmly.

"I guess," she said as she rose to her feet.

His laughter exploded over her, this time a sound that sounded strangely healing.

"A mind fuck!" he chuckled as he made his way into his closet.

The result of that trip was now rolled, tugged, and tied around her.

Pants with no front or back, just the seat and the tight black thongs that cross-tied down her legs. Her shirt was a tight black band that forced her boobs into unnatural shapes and lifted them inches above the material. On her feet the pair of stiff leather ankle boots had all sorts of neat pockets.

She and Kye wore the same size, so she fit into his clothes almost as if they were painted on.

"Don't get used to being in my wardrobe," he groused, as he pushed her down onto the seat at his makeup table. "In the future, you get your own leather! I hate lending out my clothes."

Tali tried to hold in a laugh as she realized he had not even noticed his comments about the future, and how he was adding her to it.

Still dressed in his robe, Kye began to make up her face, turning her into some Gothic thug that would scare sinners into saints.

"What are you wearing?" she asked as he grumbled to her not to move or she would lose an eye to the liner pencil.

"Leather," he replied. "And very little of it."

Tali chuckled to herself as she pictured Kye in this little number. Then the laugh dried up as she saw him, muscles flexing, hair flowing eyes flashing. Hmm, she could hardly wait!

Chapter Twenty-Four

Chari padded barefoot down the hall slowly, drawing out the appointed time. Her eyes were glazed slightly and her hands trembled as she moved. Her skin seemed to crawl as she heard imagined whispers and hisses. The muscles in her shoulders tightened as she moved closer and closer to what she knew was her destiny.

"Chari," the walls seemed to hiss, sending shivers down her spine. "Chari, Chari."

In giggly little girl voices, in soft maniacal chants, her name seemed to echo down the hall, filling her heart with dread and her mind with more fear than she ever thought she could cope with.

The voices picked up in intensity as she moved, to the point where they were almost shrieking her name in delight as she reached the door.

"Chari," they giggled. "Chari!" they moaned. "Chari!" they screamed.

Louder and louder the voices screamed and swirled through her head, picking up in volume as she moved her trembling, sweaty palm towards the doorknob.

Louder and faster they came, taunting her, making her body quake with nerves, causing the blood to freeze in her veins. Quicker and quicker they came, until they seemed to reach a crescendo as she turned the knob.

Then suddenly, silence.

Then silence, broken.

"Hello, Chari."

His voice was the same, velvety smooth and filled with Old World charm.

"Balt-Balthazar."

She silently cursed herself as her voice broke and for a moment, abject horror showed in her eyes.

He was dressed in black today, all black except for the gold cross that glittered on a chain on his chest. His hair was long and free, and she shuddered as she remembered the baby soft feel of that mass brushing against her bare breasts and how she had begged for more.

"My little golden throat," he purred. "A talent so unique and trained by me. Chari, you are such a…treasure."

He smiled slowly, baring the points of his fangs. His eyes seemed drained of all life, if that was what filled his dead body. Whatever force kept him animated was a mystery to her. Nothing that vile and evil could have a soul.

"What is it you wish of me?" Her voice still shook, but she ignored that and concentrated on his face, trying to decide if this was the day. It appeared so.

"Come closer, Chari."

Again for a moment, the voices giggled and chanted her name, taunted her with the sound of it, the only thing she could claim as hers, even that altered by the man before her.

She stepped forward and then just as quickly, the voices stopped and the door closed with a click. That small click almost sounded like the conclusion of a long epic.

She automatically turned towards the door, her every sense screaming for her to run, but before she could make her feet move to flee, common sense reigned. She turned and took a step deeper into the room, her body trembling with acceptance and eagerness to get it all over with. She no longer feared death.

"Good girl. Don't make me chase you, Chari."

Again the voices taunted her with that name for only a second, laughing maniacally, but as she took another step forward, they ceased.

"Have you been a good girl, Chari?"

"I have been…what you expected me to be," she replied, her eyes filling with defiance. What had she to lose now?

"Have you now?"

"You of all people know what I am, Balthazar."

"Do you remember why I put the 'I' on the end of your name, Chari?"

"Yes."

"Recite it to me."

"'I' is for the entity, the incubus, that unites us as one. We are all born of that being and in giving part of our souls to he who made us, we accept part of his soul in return, to fill in the empty spot we willingly gave."

Then she glared at him, for the first time in untold years. She let her disdain show.

"I did not willingly give up my soul, Balthazar. You bought it for a suck ass team and an even worse bar tab."

"You get what you pay for, yes," he drawled as he continued to stare at her.

"How may I serve, Master?" she asked as she gracefully dropped to her knees.

"You are in the perfect position for service, Chari, my dear. Crawl to your Master."

Head lowered and hair hiding the spite in her face, Chari crawled over to Balthazar who sat in a chair in the center of the room.

The sound of the zipper was loud in the silent room and Chari winced at the sound.

"Do try not to get any on my outfit. Stains show so terribly on black."

The voices giggled and the room seemed to drop in temperature as the object of her hate came into her view.

A golden pillar topped by a plum-shaped head rose like a tower from the sea of black. His eagerness to have her please him was shown in the drops of pre-cum that leaked from the head, making it shiny and moist.

Whimpering slightly, that she would be forced to do this again, Chari settled back on her heels and reached one hand towards his erection.

Wrapping her hand around the base, she moved her head closer and closer to the tip. Closing her eyes at the last minute, she struggled to hold in her revulsion as he passed her lips.

As she was taught, she ran her tongue over and over the head, lapping off his secretions as she prepared to take him in deep.

She felt a tap on the head and looked up to see Balthazar staring down at her.

"Don't take too long. I have business to attend to."

After breathing through her nose a number of times, Chari took a deep breath and slid the massive cock down the back of her throat.

It never failed to surprise her, the feel of his massive organ searing then filling her throat to the maximum width, blocking off her air passages, making her feel as if she were choking.

But she got her mind to the business at, or rather, in hand. As her mouth dropped down, she fisted the remainder of his base in her hand and pulled up, causing him to moan slightly and lean back in his chair.

"Make it a good one, my little golden throat," he purred. "I need something to remember."

Ignoring his words, Chari eased him back out of her throat and took a needed breath, before again taking the plunge. Her free hand cupped his sac and gently rolled his testicles inside, tugging slightly, just the way he liked.

One of his hands went to her hair; silently encouraging her while the other latched onto the back of the Torc around her throat.

"Faster," he ordered and Chari increased her speed, sucking and humming as she went, applying all the tricks long years had taught her.

"Yes," he complimented as he let his head fall back, enjoying the feel of being deep inside her tight warm throat.

Chari felt his testicles start to lift towards the base of his cock and doubled her efforts to make him explode.

She leaned into his lap and took him deep enough to feel his soft pubic hairs brush her nose and lips.

"Yes," he hissed as his hips began to rise and fall to match her movements and increase it. "Face fucked is so nice, Chari. One of your rarer talents, a throat wide enough to take all of me."

Tears began to flow from Chari's eyes as she once again felt shame mixed with degradation. She fought the urge to bite down and snap off the piece of flesh that he so loved plying his 'angels' with. But that would be stupid. That would mean torture before death and he would probably grow it back anyway.

"Yes!" he hissed and Chari felt his nuts tighten in her palm. He was so close.

But before he exploded down her throat and left her in peace, he pulled back from her.

"No!" Chari let the moan slip out and quickly bit her swollen lip. She knew what his stopping meant. He wanted more from her.

"Yes," he answered as he rose to his feet and, using the hands in her hair and on her Torc, lifted her to hers. "Into the chair, Chari."

When she made to struggle, Balthazar lifted her head, forced her to stare deep into his eyes, and suddenly fighting seemed to be the last thing on her mind.

"Good baby," Balthazar purred as he felt her give in to his mind control. "Good Chari."

Standing tall in his black leather, his wet shiny cock extended from his pants and rising towards his stomach, Balthazar pushed the mute Chari into the chair and lifted her legs over the arms.

"Chari, I would like to introduce you to a few new recruits of mine. Rabi, Jai, please step forward."

Inside Chari screamed and tried to fight free of his compulsion, but his will was too strong. Inside a numb body, Chari watched as the two pale silent men walked from the corners and towards their master.

The voices hissed their laughter around her as the two stopped beside Balthazar.

"They are so hungry, Chari. They are my new elite and they are newly inducted into our little family. If you could speak, I know that you would want to say hi."

Chari's horror at being nude and exposed before these two knew no bounds, but even worse was the hunger that began to burn in their dead eyes. And it wasn't hunger for sex. To them, she was food.

"Now Chari, you know what happens to the newly inducted. You have seen it before, my pretty little bitch. They die and all of their bodily fluids are expelled which leaves them empty inside. Hungry, Chari. Hungry and hungering to fill that which is empty. It is all consuming until they learn to leash that hunger."

As she looked on from inside a body that refused to respond, the one called Rabi, the short dark one dressed in black leather, licked his lips...slowly.

"Would you mind, dear, helping your comrades in arms?"

As she struggled to make some form of denial, to make her lips work, Balthazar stepped forward and effortlessly lifted the chair that she sat upon.

"While they're doing that, I am sure that we can finish off what we started. After all, you are so good at doing more that one thing at a time."

Chari struggled to close her eyes, to not see what was happening, but she was helpless to do anything but watch and feel as Balthazar slammed home.

Mentally she bellowed her rage and pain, but at a suggestion from him, her body grew wet and hungry.

"You want this," he purred softly and immediately her body began to respond. "That part of me that is within you wants only to please me. You know it, Chari. I call to myself within you."

Vain bastard, Chari mentally screamed, but soon all thought of anything but the pleasure lashing her body filled her mind.

Her nipples hardened and her moisture began to flow. Suddenly, her body craved more! She had to have him, to have that massive heat plunging into her, rendering her helpless to anything but the pleasure suffusing her body.

Almost as an afterthought, she felt her arms being moved out and away from her body. But she didn't care! All she lived for in that moment was the next hard pounding thrust from Balthazar's shaft.

"Feast, boys, but don't take too much. Miss Chari is going to feed all of my hungers tonight."

Chari felt her arms being twisted and turned, her hands being drawn back and her wrists extended until the small blue veins popped. But it all blended with the pleasure currently shooting from her weeping opening where Balthazar made himself at home.

Grinning, Balthazar watched as his two new recruits raised her wrists to their mouths, and as if choreographed, opened their mouths to expose their new fangs.

"Enjoy, boys," he urged, and as one, they bit down into the tender flesh of Chari's wrists.

"Uh!" she groaned, the pleasure at their bites so intense it momentarily loosened the mind hold Balthazar had on her. Her body arched in welcome, her arms pushing her closer to their now greedily sucking mouths, but then it was all Balthazar and his pleasure in her body.

"Yes, Chari," he purred. "You give so much. Give more."

Chari whimpered, the pleasure spilling past her lips as he thrust faster and harder, pulling her along to climatic bliss that she had only rarely obtained, even before becoming one of his women.

Tighter and tighter the spiral of desire tightened around her, filling her skin to the point where she felt it would explode. Pressure built as fire lashed though her veins, a fire that refused to be extinguished or denied.

Just as she was about to crest the peak and fall into a bliss known only to heaven, his control snapped away from her body.

Suddenly, it was a painful pounding she was receiving. Suddenly the pleasurable warmth of their suckling mouths was a sharp pain as she felt cold begin to seep into her body.

She looked over and saw them, the two ghouls sucking out her life's blood and ravaging her wrists to get more. She looked up and saw Balthazar slamming away at her body, a cynical twist to his lips.

"Welcome to reality, Chari," he breathed as he thrust even faster into her now cringing body.

Even as her eyes widened in horror, laughter began to bubble up from her lips.

This was it! This is what she was waiting for!

She threw her head back as peals of laughter exploded from her lips.

"Balthazar, you bastard!" she screamed and laughed as tears flowed from her eyes. "I hope they fry your ass! I hope you burn! May you never know the peace of death and may whatever holds you to this existence make you suffer long after your body expires!"

"Yes!" Balthazar shouted as his seed exploded from his body, making his arms tremble as he held the combined weight of her body and the chair aloft. "Oh, you are so good, baby," he taunted before he let the chair drop.

"Argh!" Chari wailed as her wrists were torn from the mouths and teeth of the two pillaging her blood.

They started to reach for her, but at a glance from Balthazar, pulled back, hovering like vultures waiting for the prey to quit moving.

"Pretty curses from that pretty throat. That pretty throat that spilled information about me to an outside source. Not very careful of you, Chari, to leave the phone off the hook. Not careful of you to start blabbing at all."

Chari tried to curl up into a ball in the chair, but her body hurt too badly to move. She felt weak and lightheaded, but she managed to close her legs, shuddering as she felt his wet slippery seed leak from her body. She dropped her head as she cradled her injured arms to her chest, whimpering through laughter that still bubbled from her throat. Her mind was in turmoil and she wanted it all to end. What had she left to live for? Her life was past its usefulness. And as she peeked up through her hair at Balthazar's still face, she knew her time had really come to pass.

"Don't worry, Chari. You will serve me in death as you did in life."

"No!" she gasped as she threw her body from the chair and began to crawl to the nearest corner. "Please don't turn me into one of you!"

"As if I would waste more of myself," he sneered as he shook off his cock and calmly tucked it back into his pants.

"What..." Then more laughs, more wicked giggles escaped her throat. "What the hell does it matter, you bastard?"

She crawled to a corner and spun around, using it to support her body as she crouched on the floor. Tears ran down her cheeks and mucus ran from her nose. She cradled the torn wrists to her body still, but continued to tremble with the force of her emotions. An unholy light filled her eyes as what was left of her mind snapped, her lips curved into an evil smile, a smile that showed madness and delight in death.

"Come and get me, you bastard," she sneered. "I always knew you were going to come for me one day. Surprise, surprise, that day has come!"

Balthazar said nothing, but adjusted the fit of his clothes one final time as he walked towards her.

"She's going to burn your ass!" cackled Chari as she began to sob. His semen was cooling between her legs and caused nasty shivers to travel down her spine.

"She is coming for you!" She wound down as Balthazar cast a shadow over her broken form. "Coming for you."

"Who?" Balthazar asked once. He was not really concerned. If this was the one that was threatening his business, then she would easily be taken care of and soon.

"The one who got away," Chari whispered before she broke down into sobs again.

"Damn it, woman, pick an emotion and stick with it!" he snarled as he knelt before her. "Who got away, Chari?"

"Her," she whimpered shying away as he reached out for her.

"You are a frightful mess," Balthazar said quietly as he watched the ravages of her once beautiful face.

"Don't kill me," she whispered. "I am not ready. There is so much to tell her."

"Yes you are, my not so pretty bitch."

That said, he reached up and yanked a fist full of her hair from her head, causing her to shriek in pain as her body jerked back from the unexpected attack.

Smiling at the bleeding bald spot on her head, Balthazar grabbed her right leg and yanked it out straight.

"I'll clean you up a bit," he murmured as he used her hair to wipe away his seed before throwing the bloody stained mess to the floor.

Chari shuddered in pain as blood dripped into her eyes, covering her vision with a red haze.

Still smiling, Balthazar leaned forward and pressed his lips to the top inside of her thigh, the femoral artery.

"Good-bye Chari," he purred as he pulled back his lips to expose his fangs and struck deep and sure.

She shrieked in pain, and strangely enough, remembered pleasure, as she felt her blood well up to the surface of the bite.

Balthazar covered the wound and sucked deeply, pulling some strange emotion from her, making her body shudder strangely as it exploded into climax, leaving her shuddering and strangely at peace.

Balthazar feasted for several minutes, then carefully pulled away from the spurting artery, moving in just the right direction to avoid getting blood splashed on his solid black clothing.

He motioned to the two men behind them and in almost ecstatic hunger, they rushed to replace their master between her legs.

Chari moaned as one took sustenance from Balthazar's bite and the other bit down into her flesh, creating another drinking fount. But she was too weak; her life force was draining away. She could do nothing more than moan and shake her head as she became a feast for the newly undead.

"Good-bye, Chari," he repeated over the snarls and slurping of his new men.

Chari heard his voice as if it were echoing down a tunnel. The edges of her vision grew black as pitch, black as night, and her awareness centered on one glittering pinpoint, his eyes.

Balthazar's eyes sparkled in humor and amusement as Chari took her last few shuddering breaths.

"I forgive you, child."

His voice almost tinkled to her deadening ears, as her vision blacked out and her head listed to the side. They were the last words she ever heard.

Chapter Twenty-Five

"Um, Kye?"

"Yes, Tali?"

"Where is the crotch in those pants?"

Snickering, Kye held up a small leather codpiece while he preened for her. "You like?"

Tali swallowed as she watched his cock swing freely between his leather clad thighs. The tight…jeans things, encased both his legs like a second skin. But jeans could not be made of leather…right? The shiny black material was supple and soft to the touch, though it looked like glossy latex. There only seemed to be legs, and a waistband. They couldn't be chaps because they had a butt and two neat pockets, but where was the crotch? Did they run out of leather? "Um, where exactly does it, that thing in your hand, fit?"

She spoke through a tight, dry throat, her eyes riveted to his free-swinging manhood. Maybe she should have kept her mouth shut. Maybe she didn't care where it went! The view was…interesting.

"It snaps on," he purred as he purposely took a step towards her, making his cock swing like the clapper in a bell. "Wanna help…contain me?" His green/gold eyes twinkled at her, the gold winning for a moment in the swirling vortex of color, as he took another step closer. He was shirtless and oiled, making each scar on his back stand out like dark veins in golden marble. Kye was dressed to impress and to show his body off to perfection.

To most people, a scarred back might not be their ideal of beauty, but to those who inhabited the sadism clubs, Kye's ruined back was a feast of delight for their senses. They would imagine who laid the lash to his back, how long it took to cause those marks, the sound of splitting flesh and the painful whimpers that would have been forced from his throat.

They would wonder how it felt to be under that lash, how it felt to deliver each blow, and more importantly, the strength of the man to take such a beating and survive. They would all want to be the next to top him, to dominate him, to see if they could break a man that an obviously vicious beating couldn't break. Kye wanted them to try. He wanted to cause a stir so great it would reach the ears of the Big B himself. When Balthazar came to look at what the others were whispering about, Kye would have him.

"I don't think it will fit," Tali finally choked out as she turned her eyes up to gaze at his face. "Where do you find this stuff anyway?"

Kye just smirked at her as he carefully cupped his cock and began snapping the small snaps in place. This left a lot of the skin of his upper thighs exposed, but the snaps seemed to be holding. "It'll fit. It's a custom job, Tali, sized to fit me."

Tali said nothing as he gave his package one final adjustment then turned to his makeup table to complete his preparations. They had started by him locking her out of the bathroom while he "cleansed his body" inside and out. She had an idea of what that meant and had left him to it, right after she asked why.

"Having my presence announced because he can smell yesterday's snack is not on my list of things to do, Tali," he snapped, then slammed the door in her face. Okay! So apparently Balthazar could smell digested food in the body. Eww! But then, Kye could smell when she was aroused, so she guessed it made sense.

Now she watched as he carefully outlined each eye in black, making his large almond eyes almost seem vulnerable. The tear he painted in the corner of his left eye, just on the side of his nose, made him seem fragile. The diamond he placed in the center of that tear added a touch of arrogance. His lips were tinted black and a touch of silver gloss made them shine. She should know. He made her face up almost exactly the same way, except her lips were fire engine red and she had at least three shades of pale blue eye shadow.

Next, he began to work on his hair. It wouldn't do to go through all of this trouble to dress up if no one could see the whole show, mainly his back, so concessions had to be made. His hair was left loose in the front, framing his face, and the back was parted neatly down the center. Each part was tightly plaited and laid over his shoulders, the ends fastened with tight leather strips that tinkled merrily with the sound of the small silver bells he had attached.

Several of the silver throwing pins were threaded into each plait, making them a bit stiff but pliant. You would only notice they were there if you knew what to look for, she thought in amazement. But he was not yet done.

Two long thin leather strips were tied around the ends of the plaits, each containing a small silver wire. Nothing like carrying you own garrote in your hair. From a tangle of jewelry, he pulled a thick leather collar that snapped around his throat. Matching armbands circled the top of each bicep, making each muscle stand out in stark relief. Yummy.

He rose to his feet, carrying a second collar, a malicious glint in his eyes.

"What are you doing with that?" Tali backed away as he approached her, his black tinted lips parting in a smile that made his teeth seem all the whiter, the inside of his mouth a bit pinker.

"You are my slave."

"Hello, fang-boy. I don't think so!" Tali threw up her hands and took another step back.

"Tali, we have to go in. Although it is not uncommon for two Dominates to venture out trolling together, it would seem unbelievable for one of them to question every thing that was done and then gawk like an awkward teen once we get inside."

"And that means?"

"For the night, you are my bottom." At her pout, he added, "My baby bottom. That would explain your unfamiliarity with all things carnal and give you the freedom to gawk and stare all you please. No one would pay any attention to you. It is expected you would be curious and a bit afraid. You are the perfect spy."

"But the collar! Kye, it's demeaning!"

"Wanna know demeaning, Tali? Try selling your ass in New Orleans to some sweet sugar daddy at an Octoroon Ball so you can afford to eat because they don't like half-breeds working in their precious towns. Or try being the yes-man to some spoiled southern bitch so she can show off her "Celestial Nigger" to all of her friends while the slaves in the field, your own people, turn their backs on you 'cause they know you think you are better than them. Or try being told there is no place for you on a Reservation because you are too unusual. A collar won't break you, Tali. But maybe I will!" He narrowed his eyes, the face paint suddenly making him look sinister and evil.

"Okay," Tali growled in the face of his reasoning. "But if I chafe or break out or something, I'm coming after your ass, levitation or not!"

Snorting and knowing he'd won, Kye walked over and locked the collar in place.

"Too tight!" Tali complained as she ran one red-painted talon under the tight leather. She had forgotten about the fake nails until she almost punctured her carotid while trying to get some breathing space.

"Tough!" he retaliated before, seemingly out of nowhere, produced a delicate silver link leash.

"What...?" Before she could ask what he thought he was doing, she was snapped in and locked down tight.

The leash was not a necessity, but sheer perversity on Kye's part. A bit of revenge for making him spill out facts about his life, for him wanting her to understand him a little.

"You are my pet, therefore I get to lead you around. And believe me, I'm keeping you on a short leash!"

Tali glowered at him, before snatching the chain out of his hand. "When we get there, you can play make-believe. Until then, come near this dog chain and I bite a finger off. Got it?"

Kye blinked at the ferocity of her words, then turned away before he exploded into laughter. Instead, he pulled on his boots, the high Dehners that cupped his calves but still gave him enough room to maneuver. The buckles were decorated with small hanging razor blades. Only if you looked closely enough would you discover the ornaments were very real and very sharp. He twisted one heel out and checked that the secret compartment, filled with odorless garlic bombs, was intact and ready. He almost smiled when he remembered these were almost the same things Tali tried to use on him. Satisfied, he turned again to his closet, looking for the perfect something to wear outside. It would not do to send the citizens of Baltimore running for cover at his approach. But his outer clothing had to have style.

Spying his black velvet cloak, he knew he had the perfect garment. The cloak had a hood deep enough to create the shadows he loved to hide in so well. It also had a soft silver silk lining, perfect for stopping blades and spines thrown in his direction or at his back. It also had deep pockets; perfect for concealing the four six-inch silver blades that would not make a metal detector react.

Turning to face Tali, he pulled the cloak from its hanger and handed it to her. "Take this," he muttered, wondering why he was giving her so much...protection. "It will keep you safe."

Now why was that important? He barely knew the trick!

"Nice," Tali muttered as she reached a hand out for it, then winced at the unexpected weight as it dropped into her grasp.

Pulling a similar cloak of deep purple out of his bottomless closet, he turned to her. "It may keep you alive. Be careful. It is fully loaded."

Then again, each of his cloaks were.

"Oh! Do I get the prize vampire killer package?"

"Want to test it out on your little friend?"

"Not funny, Kye," Tali snorted, but swung the cloak over her shoulders, loving running her hand over its surface. It almost felt like his skin, the delicate skin that covered his...

"Why are you looking at me like that?" he asked as he watched her dark eyes glitter from the corner of his eye.

"Um," she cleared her throat. "Are we ready?"

Turning to fully look at her, taking in her great beauty and her powerful body contained in such a small package. "Yeah," he said, turning towards the door. He had to distance himself. Drawing on the familiar darkness that filled what he had left of a soul, Kye motioned her towards the exit. He couldn't allow himself to feel, to experience any emotions now. This night was too important. "Let's go."

Feeding off of his sudden stillness, Tali began to mentally prepare herself, to gird her loins against what she was about to face. It was time.

"Right behind you." They closed the elevator door, the sound of the creaking cables and ancient pulleys drowning out the sound of the ringing phone.

Chapter Twenty-Six

Tali shivered as they approached the single black glass door that made up the entrance to the club.

For an opening night, it was pretty quiet.

"Where's the music?" she hissed at Kye as he led her gently towards the darkened entrance with a tug on her leash.

"This is not your average everyday club," he replied as they paused at the door. "Just remember that. If anyone hassles you, turn to me. If anyone touches you, accept it, but don't make plans. After I deal with Balthazar, I am going to want some."

"Humph," she sniffed as she glared at him, her eyes fierce in the dim light, her face almost swallowed by shadows. "And I thought southern gentlemen knew how to treat a lady!"

"I spent time in the south, darlin'," he drawled in his near perfect plantation owner voice. "But I ain't never seen them treat a lady in any other way than I'm about to treat you."

"What does that mean?"

"Show's on!"

Before she could say anything further, he raised a fist and pounded on the door.

Tali blinked and inhaled deeply as the smell of incense and leather greeted her, as the door was swung open.

The woman standing there was dressed in leather, bright pink leather, and had a serious attitude problem.

"What do you want?" she growled, her breasts barely contained within the straps of leather that passed for a top.

And I complained about my outfit, Tali thought as she took in the two leather straps that covered the woman's boobs and ran down into the tight leather pants. Even her six-inch platform heels were pink—kind of like looking at a walking bottle of Pepto.

"We came for the party," Kye said quietly.

"Really?" the woman asked.

"Yes," Kye said as he inhaled deeply. There was something familiar about her. Then he smiled a little, letting his fangs drop just a bit.

"Twenty-five dollar cover charge and no hitting on the ladies, unless they ask you to. But you are most welcome. You look like you know how to party."

She leered at him, her face painted totally white with big pink lips.

"Yes, Renfield. I just love a good party."

The woman blinked then stepped back, allowing them entrance.

"Renfield?" Tali whispered, but Kye shot her a look that closed her mouth.

Renfield? The rat eating subservient slave in Dracula?

Staring again at the woman in her garish outfit, she decided it fit.

"Master," the woman said as the door silently closed behind them.

Yup, definitely Renfield.

Once inside, Tali blinked at what she saw and nervously stepped back into Kye, instinctively seeking his protection.

The place was packed tightly, but that was not what startled her. The ceremonial flogging on the far stage is what caught her attention.

A tall woman with sleek silver hair dressed in biker chic, was swinging a long leather flogger with some skill. He recognized her from the Goth Club basement. Apparently she had been sold to her new Master, Balthezar.

At each stroke, hundreds of lashes wrapped around the reddening flesh of her lust crazed victim, who hung suspended by his wrists from the ceiling, only his toes touching the floor, whimpering and purring each time the lash kissed his flesh.

At each lash, the crowd chanted in delight and sheer abandonment.

"Shelby! Shelby! Shelby!"

"My, she is good," Kye remarked as the music added accompaniment to the harsh whipping sound as the whip struck the man's back. Her actions gave new meaning to the words, 'I'm just a girl, living in captivity and I've had it up to here!'

"Upstairs, Master," the woman said as she led them past the chanting throng and to a small, dark set of stairs.

Tali shivered, her gaze fixed to the stage as the silver-haired woman took all of the frustrations of the day out on the bound flesh. The man seemed to whimper in pain, but he leaned back, accepting each punishing lash as if it were the next best thing to heaven.

As she watched, his cock began to rise until the full throbbing length stood out from his body at attention and clear strings of pre-cum began to glisten and hang from the end of his cock.

His eyes were at half-mast and his lips parted, his breath exploding in time with his lashes, as an almost serene expression-filled his face.

Sweat began to pour from his already sweat-sheened body, his muscles tightening and loosening in time with the movement of the whip on his arching back, reaching for the sizzlingly ecstatic kiss of the lash, as if begging for favors from a well-pleased Mistress.

A tug on her chain brought Tali's attention back to Kye, and she flushed, thinking how distracted she had become.

But this bondage thing, the real bondage thing, was new to her, and it showed.

"You will get your chance, my pretty," Kye drawled, reaching out his hand to caress her face.

Kye saw her reaction and sought to cover it before she did something that would draw too much attention.

"I know it's been a few days, but if you please me in this, you will feel the sweet fire of the whip warming your ass."

His eyes hardened as he looked at her, as his fingers clamped around her chin and forced her head away from the stage and onto him.

The pink lady might think he was giving her a mild chastisement, but he was warning Tali the only way he could.

She lowered her eyes, and then her head, and again cursed herself for drawing attention.

"Please, Master," she whispered, her discomfort making her voice raspy.

"She is so timid, so new to these delights," he laughed as he turned to the pink lady. "You may proceed, Renfield."

Nodding, the woman led them up the stairs and to a door, which she knocked softly upon.

The door opened and a bright shaft of light illuminated the lady for a moment. Tali gasped at what she saw.

The woman was covered in bites, some old and some weeping, but there were neat punctures, in sets of two, covering every inch of her exposed body, some old and scared and others fresh.

Then the Renfield comment made sense. This had to be the club chew toy.

"They are early," a deep voice said from inside. The voice sounded haunted, but there was a thread of steel there.

"They are the Masters, Scotti," the woman whispered. "Behave."

They walked into the room, and there, quite naked and lying on the floor prostrate, was a man. A gold collar surrounded his neck and his head was bowed, showing a tousled mane of dark brown hair.

"I have been remiss in my duties," the woman continued as she went down on both knees in front of Kye, holding up her wrists, the only unmarred piece of flesh on her exposed body. "Drink and be well."

"I see that others have come before me," Kye said as he released Tali's leash and motioned her to the floor.

Tali was stunned, but she dutifully dropped to the floor, nearly imitating Scotti. But she just couldn't bring herself to drop her head like that! She settled for staring at his feet.

"They shall return, Master. We are here to entertain you until they do."

This was it! Kye could feel it! This was all he had waited for, plotted for, planned for. All of his machinations would bear fruit, and revenge would be his.

"Where are the others?"

Tali looked up at the sudden steel in his voice, and noticed his eyes were swirling, but he made no move to hide them.

"They are…out, Master," the woman stuttered.

"By what name are you called, Renfield?"

"Anita," the woman whispered, still looking at the ground and steady in the face of Kye's otherworldliness showing, if she even noticed.

"Anita, the club chew toy, you are an insult to me."

Tali gasped at Kye's putdown, but kept her head bowed. These were the type of people he was used to dealing with; she would let him handle this.

"Master?" Now she was confused. Anita looked up, suddenly looking sickly in her vibrant pink leather.

"You are to entertain me? You are a used bit of goods, Renfield. You let your body and your precious blood be spilled out for the enjoyment of many. You are a blood slut, a feedbag, nothing more than an easy meal for any common creature with fangs and a thirst. You disgust me."

Instantly, Anita dropped her head to the ground, prostrate, begging for forgiveness.

"Why do you do this?"

"Because…" she whispered, her voice shaking with tension and the beginnings of true fear.

"Because why, human? Answer me!"

Kye looked every bit the Dominant vamp as he stared at the woman who knelt, still as death, waiting to pounce on her every word.

"Because they will…he said that… I want to be what you are."

"Then you are a stupid fool."

At his sharp words, her head slowly rose and as she stared into his eyes — his swirling green/gold eyes — she began to doubt the certainty she held within her soul, the certainty that led her to believe she wanted to be like them.

"You offend me, human, thinking of the power and not of the sacrifice."

"Sacra — sacrifice?"

"Would you give up your soul?"

Kye took a step towards her and gently caressed her face.

"My soul?"

"Or do you care, Renfield? Would you give up your soul? Become a salivating beast, a Pavlov's dog every time a human walked past?"

Unconsciously, she nestled into that hand, the gentle hand that taunted with such harsh words.

"Would you like to see every human you meet as food? Can you imagine running into your mother, Renfield, and lusting after that which runs in her veins? Can you imagine seeing her face, and then picturing yourself tearing her throat out and draining her, making her into a dried-out shell, a tattered corpse? You would regret nothing, until the blood lust was sated for a moment. Then it will be lost as you move to your next victim. Hunger is such a strange thing, Renfield. Makes you want to eat children, babies, the elderly. It is non-selective, Renfield. All the world truly becomes your oyster, and all the people a snack."

Anita, the club chew toy, began to shake in her pretty pink leather as his words sunk in.

"This is your first night, Renfield, in your next step. I can smell it. I can smell the new bites in your flesh, the fresh ones that tell me my people are not too far removed."

Anita trembled, but her eyes grew wide as she watched the man before her. His face was painted strangely, his make-up utterly appealing in some androgynous way, but for the first time since venturing down this path, she was truly frightened.

"Go away, Anita. Run away and never look back. Go home to your mommy and live to see another sunrise. Because if you don't, Renfield. I will be coming for you."

Eyes widening in horror, Anita began to choke as Kye moved his hand, lightning fast, from caressing her cheek to gripping her throat.

Anita gasped and kicked as Kye lifted her to her feet by his hold around her neck, and held her there, letting her feel the strength in his hands, before releasing her.

Anita stumbled to her bottom, then scrambled to her feet, her hands cradling her bruised neck. For the first time since meeting the recruiter, she actually feared death. As she ran to the door, she turned back once more and realized she was indeed afraid of death. He was standing here in black.

As the door slammed, the man, Scotti, began to rise to his feet.

"Very good," he whispered as he rose until he towered over Kye from a height of at least six feet five inches.

"But that shit won't work on me."

He grinned as he flashed his neat set of fangs.

"Am I to be impressed?" Kye asked as he tugged on Tali's leash to make her rise to her feet.

She took one look at the tall lanky vamp and cursed under her breath.

"No, you are to be entertained," he grumbled as he took one step towards them, his eyes burning bright as tension knotted his muscles. He was not happy.

"He is going to entertain us," Kye chuckled as he unclipped the leash from Tali's neck. "Precious One, kick his ass. Make me laugh!"

Two thoughts quickly went thought Tali's head! The first was what? The second followed closely, You bastard!

Tali took one more look at the wildly grinning Scotti, and groaned even as she loosened her body in preparation for the attack.

Damn that Kye, but the show was about to begin.

Chapter Twenty-Seven

Silently, they circled each other, arms loose and at the ready, knees slightly bent for balance.

Tali inhaled deeply while carefully keeping out of the reach of the tall dark-haired man. Naked fighting, she thought as she struggled to keep her attention on his upper body…above his waist and an effective distraction from what she could see of his erection.

But the thought of his endowment was quickly forgotten as Scotti, the gold collared slave, made his first move.

Stepping forward into a quick strike, Scotti, right hand held flat in a knife strike, swung out at her neck, his left pulled back ready to deliver a second blow.

Hissing, Tali swung her right arm up, blocking his strike, holding in a gasp as the shock of the blow momentarily numbed her arm.

Ignoring the discomfort, she quickly delivered a closed-fisted punch to his kidneys.

As he bent backwards, hissing in pain, she sent her knee slamming into his back, and still holding onto his right hand, delivered a knife strike of her own to his neck.

The golden collar absorbed some of the blow, but Scotti still tumbled backwards to the floor.

Tali knew that that was not the last of Scotti's attacks — and genetics blessing him with extra height, weight and reach — and quickly retreated to prepare for his next attack.

"A little slow on that last attack," Kye commented from the sidelines.

Incredulous, Tali spared a sarcastic glance in his direction a moment before Scotti recovered enough to roll to his shoulders and launch himself to his feet.

Damn, Tali thought for a moment before Scotti made his next move to kill her. He sure is hung!

Humiliated, the still silent Scotti snorted through his nose and shot daggers at Tali with his eyes.

Circling quickly, he did a quick two-step with his feet to distract her, before he bent low and his right arm shot out to grab her.

Gasping, Tali had a split second to make up her mind about what she was going to do! But her body reacted far faster than her mind.

Sucking in a deep breath, she sprang backwards, her legs scissoring up to strike out at Scotti, making him break off his assault and move backwards to avoid getting a boot to the chin.

Landing on her feet, Tali quickly executed another backwards flip, putting crucial distance between herself and her attacker, and then another for good measure.

Quickly rising up, she slid into a horse stance, arms up in a neutral position, ready to attack or defend.

"Knee time," Kye called out to Scotti. "Too much knee time. I know what Gold Collars are good at, and it appears to hold true. Scotti, you suck."

Eyes narrowed in rage, Scotti felt his temper snap! Arms raised out in front of him, he rushed Tali, hoping to get her in his grasp and end this stupid game of cat and mouse once and for all.

"Shit!" Tali managed to gasp as at least two hundred pounds of naked enraged male powered towards her. There was only one thing left to do!

She waited for the last possible moment, then hit the deck!

Rolling out of the way, she did not see but clearly heard the sound of the plaster wall exploding as Scotti plunged through.

Then it seemed as if a vacuum bubble popped, for in an instant, the hard sounds of the driving beat, the smell of close bodies and mingled cologne, the heat of the packed crowd, invaded the room.

There was a sudden hush as even the music came to a sudden and succinct halt. The murmurs of the crowd reached Tali's ears as she got to her feet and peered through the hole left by the passage of Scotti's body.

As she drew closer and stuck her head cautiously through, Kye opened his mouth to warn her.

But before he could speak, a hand reached through and yanked her through the crater shaped hole that Scotti created in passing.

The crown went wild, and the DJ, some smart ass, pumped up the music!

"Woo! Yaw gonna make me lose my mind,

Up in here! Up in here!

Yaw gonna make me go all out!

Up in here! Up in here!

Yah gonna make me act the fool!

Up in here! Up in here!

Yaw gonna make me lose my cool!

Up in here! Up in here!"

"Fucking DMX!" Tali screamed as she found herself falling, facing the bright lights and disco balls in the black ceiling.

Instead of instinctively curling her body into the fetal position, Tali relaxed every muscle she could think of. When she crashed into the wooden table, she let it break her fall, not her bones.

Shit, she thought as she felt her back strike solid wood, and kept going through.

But she knew that she had to move! Scotti was still there and he was out for her blood!

As fast as she could, she scrambled to her feet, each muscle protesting her movements, and looked around for her attacker.

The crowd soon overcame their shock and began cheering and hooting, parting to make way for the combatants.

Still naked but covered in plaster dust, Scotti stood near the stage, knees slightly bent, arms out and defensive, hands motioning her forward.

"Fuck this shit!" Tail roared as she began to charge in his direction, intent on putting the golden boy down and out.

"Woo-shah!" she bellowed, pulling every ounce of power into her move as she launched her body, feet first, at Scotti.

Scotti ducked and Tali whizzed by his head, landing on the stage. But with the music pumping behind her, she quickly executed a barrel roll and landed on her feet. Whirling around, she sensed more than felt Scotti leap to the stage, prepared to end the bout for good.

Ignoring the man hanging by his wrists, Tali looked towards Shelby, and held her hand out for her whip.

"May I?" she asked politely though the music drowned out most of her words.

"Get him once for me," Shelby laughed as she handed over her flogger.

"With pleasure," she hissed back as Scotti launched his next attack.

Performing a perfect roundhouse kick, Tali had enough time to bend forward to prevent her head from being knocked from her body. On her way back up, she lashed out, striking Scotti dead in the balls.

Instantly, he dropped to the floor of the stage, a scream of pain exploding from his throat.

It seemed every man, and a few of the women in the club flinched and groaned in sympathy with the man who was valiantly struggling not to vomit as he kissed the wood of the stage.

"Good shot." Shelby winced as she stared at Tali.

Leaping out of the way, Tali knew this was her chance. She had to put him down or he would recover and he would kill her.

Even as the black and red agony receded from his mind, Scotti was struggling to his feet.

Tali moved in and delivered a kick to his stomach, grunting with the effort.

Then Tali got mad!

"Throw me through a wall!" she hissed as he rolled onto his back, the pain and lack of breath overcoming him.

"You," kick, "don't," kick, "hit," kick, "women!" she shrieked as she raised her leg and let an ax-kick fall on his rib cage, hoping a rib would break and pierce his lung.

But Scotti was made of sterner stuff.

As she lifted her foot for another attack, his right arm swung out and swept her leg from beneath her.

Arms flailing wildly, Tali wind-milled, tried to regain her balance, but landed on her butt juxtaposition to Scotti.

She managed to hold on to the flogger.

Even as he rolled in her direction, lips drawn back to expose his dainty baby fangs, she lashed out at his face, hard.

Scotti screamed as the many leather-thronged lash split his face, spilling blood across the stage as he raised his hands to cup his injured flesh.

"My eyes!" he screamed as he flipped to his stomach, head resting on the stage as his body trembled in shock.

DMX was rallying all of his 'street street people' to meet him outside when Tali raised the handle of the flogger.

Good solid wood, she thought as she brought it down across the base of his skull, knocking him unconscious to the delight of the crowd.

"Fuckin'-A!" Shelby crowed in delight as Tali handed the flogger back to her.

"Quality instrument," Tali complimented as she looked up and saw Kye standing at the foot of the stage.

He stared straight into her eyes, before he snapped his fingers and pointed to the ground at his feet.

Tali wrinkled her nose to fight against the urge to curse that smug bastard out, but remembered the reason they were there.

"Revenge," she whispered softly to herself as she walked over to the edge and leapt off of the stage. "Remember, revenge," she whispered again as she walked to stand before Kye.

"Took you long enough," he grunted as he pointed to the ground.

The crowd grew silent as they waited to see what the woman would do. She looked like she could kick any guy's ass, and the short man with the interesting leather outfit just commanded her to kneel. Was she a slave? If so, what did that say about the man who commanded her?

Growling softly, still fighting her adrenaline rush, Tali dropped to her knees in front of Kye and waited while the hated leash was attached.

"Good girl," Kye murmured as he ran his hands through her hair and then down to caress her cheek.

"Thank you, Master," she bit out before she captured the skin at the base of his pinky between her teeth and bit down...hard.

Every muscle in Kye's body tightened as he felt the sharp pain flow through his hand and outward throughout his body.

"Tease," he whispered as he tugged on her leash and urged her to her feet.

"This has been entertaining," he said at large, as the bouncers held back the crowd and moved to retrieve Scotti from the stage. Wouldn't do to let the humans see him heal before their amazed eyes. Real vampirism seemed to spoil the fantasy they played in.

"I'll be back," Kye laughed as he turned to lead Tali out of the club.

The crowd exploded into mad clapping and whistling as Kye made his pronouncement and headed for the door. The crowd parted like water before a tsunami.

There was something compelling about the short, exotic-looking painted man and his slave. If he was going to return that night, they would be waiting right there!

But another set of eyes watched as they made their swift exit from the room

"Damn," Sheri whispered as she flipped open her mobile phone. "Bri?" she asked as the line was answered. "Guess which blast from the past just walked in?"

Chapter Twenty-Eight

Once outside the door, Kye dragged Tali into the nearest alley and slammed her against the wall.

"Biting turns me on," he growled as he began a slow grind of his hips into her, forcing her to feel what her actions had done to him.

Tali inhaled deeply and closed her eyes as she felt her body respond to his touches. Her cunt began to weep and her nipples tingled.

"Adrenaline," she whispered as she bit back a groan and fought the urge to press up into him. "It was the fight."

Growling, Kye tightened his hand around the chain of the leash and pulled her face up to his.

"Don't lie to me," he rasped before he slammed his lips on top of hers, forcing his tongue deep into her mouth.

Tali gasped, inadvertently inviting his possession, then decided, why fight it!

Her hands buried themselves in the braided length of his hair, pulling him tighter to her as she gave in to the urge to lift her leg and wrap it around his waist.

"You know you want it," he breathed as he pulled away to pepper her face with butterfly kisses. "You can't resist me."

"Are you going to brag or fuck me?" Tali returned as her hands went to the snap-on the codpiece that barely restrained his throbbing cock.

Her body shuddered as waves of heat flashed through her. Her breath rasped from her throat as she forced her face into his neck, moaning her pleasure.

Kye smelled so wonderful, so alive, so rich! She had to sample the delights he offered her senses.

Her tongue lashed out and gently massaged the skin beneath his ear, making him grind his aroused body harder into hers.

That they were in an alley, that anyone could walk by and see them at any minute didn't faze her. She knew what she wanted, and what she wanted was nibbling on her neck.

"God, you are hot," he breathed as he released the chain and his fingers crawled through the shirt to caress the skin above her nipples.

"If we were in bed, I'd suckle your clit, baby. I'd suckle it and tongue it, and let my teeth drag over it until your thighs trapped me where I could drink you in."

"Kye," Tali gasped as she dug her nails in and popped the first snap that strained to hold him in check.

She groaned at his words, at the feel of his heat rising from his body, and arched her back into his touch, offering her neck for the licks and nibbles she was sure would follow.

"You are so horny," he growled. "I touch you and you get wet for me! God, that turns me on!"

He bent over her neck and took a bite, not hard enough to break the skin, but enough to make her nerves there scream.

"Fuck me," she gasped as she drove her hand beneath the leather holding him, feeling the soft skin and hard steel of his erection spring into her hand.

"What's the magic word?" he asked almost playfully, biting back a groan as her hand encircled his shaft and began a steady, slow pump. She slowly rubbed the pre-cum he leaked like a faucet over the spongy head of his cock, forcing spasms of pleasure to erupt.

"The magic word?" he urged.

Tali looked up at him, eyes dilated in hunger, lips glistening and parted from their kisses.

"Now." Her words were low and urgent. "Fuck me now!"

Kye gasped as her hand gripped him tightly, her thumb rubbing over the hard knob of his cock, sending a rush of delight through his body.

"Now," he agreed as he took her hands and forced them against the rough brick of the wall, scraping her skin lightly and sending fire through her nerve endings.

There is no greater release than submission, he thought as he released her hands and gripped the waist of her pants.

With practiced ease, he unsnapped her, unzipped her, and exposed her weeping flesh to his demanding fingers.

"You are my bitch now," he spat as he buried his face in her neck, sucking on her sweet flesh.

Damn, he could grow addicted to the taste of her flesh.

Tali whimpered at his words, but that was how she felt. She wanted to be used! She wanted to use him and be used in return. His words were touching a place inside her that she was afraid to go to, afraid to even contemplate. But touching him was so exciting!

"I'm your bitch," she whispered back as her hand continued to manipulate him, while her other hand locked around his long braid, pulling his head back. "But remember, you are my bitch too, Kye. And you had damn well better make this worth the effort. Now shut up and fuck me, you bastard!"

Her words rose in volume as his fingers sank into her wet flesh, his fingers going to that spot on her inner wall and his thumb rolling around her clit.

"Fuck, yes," she hissed as she tightened her grip on his braid and dropped her head back against the wall. "More, damn it! I want more."

Trembling, Kye shoved her pants to her thighs and spun her around to face the brick wall.

Before she could protest, one hand went around her waist to again pluck at her clitoris while the other went under her shirt to caress the sensitive skin of her breasts.

"Yes," she whimpered as he arched her body back into his chest, forcing her ass onto the hot wet marble of his cock. "Give it to me!"

His whole body breaking out in sweat, Kye eased back enough to drag his hardness down the trench of her ass, making her quiver in surprised delight, before he bent his knees and pressed against her steaming feminine opening.

"Fuckin' take it," he hissed as he flexed his knees and slammed himself home.

"Ahh!" Tali's wordless cry filled the alley, echoing off the red brick walls and circling them, igniting their senses with the sound of her surrender.

Tali shuddered as she felt lightning strike, as the hard flesh of him penetrated and dominated her body. He slid inside, stretching her, forging a place for himself deep inside her. She closed her eyes and let the sensations in her flow throughout her body. Immodestly she wanted more.

"God, you are so hot and tight," he whispered in her ear, his warm breath making her tingle and throw her head back in hopes that a nibble would follow. "You gonna make me cum."

"Not before me, stud," she gasped as he pulled out and began another, slower penetration.

Kye held his breath as he felt his fingers and toes began to tingle. His nuts tightened in their sacs and began to rise up to the base of his cock.

He took a deep breath to calm himself down. This was the most excitement he'd had in years and he didn't want it to end just yet.

Gathering himself, he began a slow steady plunge into her heat, moaning softly in her ear as he felt the tight pull of her muscles struggle to keep him inside then open to receive the gift of his thrust.

Tali panted, her breath exploding from her as he pressed his hand against her stomach, ensuring that the spot he found would be stimulated by his whole cock as it was repeatedly thrust in and withdrawn.

"You gonna scream for me, baby?" he whispered in her ear as he began to speed up his movements. "You gonna cream all over me?"

He punctuated his words with a sharp thrust and grind as he touched places deep inside of her that sent shivers of wanton pleasure through her.

Tali could only whimper and tremble as sensations built deep inside. Her whole body was alive and charged with sexual energy, an energy that threatened to consume her, burn her in its flames and reduce her to ashes.

She arched and thrust against Kye, demanding more, searching for that release she so craved.

"Yes, baby," he whispered as he felt his control slipping away. "Yes." His voice grew deeper and louder as the wet sound of their thrusts filled the alley. "Give it to me."

Suddenly all that was Tali spun and swirled, then snapped!

Her muscles tensed and she bore down, trapping him deeply inside her, getting that extra stimulation that sent her tumbling over the end into climatic bliss.

"Kye!" she shrieked as her head whipped back, locked into place and her inner muscles spasmed, clenched, milked his cock.

"Take it!" Kye roared as he pounded her harder and harder, feeling his release almost upon him.

Then he was there! His butt clenched, his muscles tensed, and his cock trembled as his balls forced his seed deep into her body in rhythmic spasms.

"Tali," he groaned as the pleasure was wrung from his body and his cock erupted within her.

He thrust again and again, riding out his climax, extending hers, until he collapsed against her, spent, hips still.

Gasping for breath, Kye collapsed against Tali, pressing her firmly into the wall as he tried to find the energy to move. But his shaking legs and his labored breath told him that recovery just might take some time.

Then all senses were on alert as he spun around, his eyes piercing the darkness...searching.

"To think that is what I have been missing all of these years."

Angel's voice was sarcastic and a bit jealous as she observed the two pressed against the wall.

"To think I raced all the way down here to give you a message."

"Message?" Kye managed as he unconsciously blocked Tali from the intruder into their bit of paradise in an alley and adjusted his clothes.

"Yeah, Marti called. You would not believe what is waiting at a certain hotel for you."

"Balthazar?" Tali gasped. Struggling to get her breast band of a shirt straightened over her boobs and the pants fastened at the same time. Damn, those cross-ties over her thighs!

"If you two can stop fucking around long enough get there."

She looked at both of them, unashamedly letting the hair fall back from the scarred side of her face.

"It's time, kiddies. Strap yourself back into your clothes and get ready to ride. Tonight Balthazar dies."

Chapter Twenty-Nine

Mari stood outside of the club's entrance and groaned when she saw the place was empty.

Where is that girl? she thought to herself as she paced in front of the darkened doorway.

Before she could make a decision to move or to stay, she saw two Goth punks walking her way.

"Place is closed," one of them saw fit to inform her. "You know the new spot over on Charles just opened up. And with a bang, you know? There was this Jackie Chan, Jet Li, psycho bitch trashing the place. It was wicked! Kicked some dude's ass until her Master put her back on a leash."

"Oh dear," Mari murmured to herself, before smiling up at the two who seemed to be waiting for her approving comments.

"Um, bitchin'!" Where did kids come up with their language? "They left?"

"Yeah, but the dude said he would be back. I think he was looking for someone."

That's my cue, Mari thought as she waved her thanks and headed off in that direction.

"Thanks, dudes. That is where I'm headed. I wanna good seat to check out the action."

She made it to the club in mere minutes. It was easy to spot because there was a crowd of people still talking about the Battle Royale that took place earlier.

"Some short bitch," one purple-spiked boy laughed to his friends. "She was wearing, like, a strip of leather and that was about it. Her Master was some long-haired cat who called all the shots. I think he could kick both of their asses, you know? He gave off that kind of vibe."

Mari tried to hide the distress on her face, but she knew she had found the place where Tali and Kye would return.

"Damn that girl and her libido!" she hissed as she made her way inside, past the excited bouncer and onto a large dance floor.

There was a stage set up near the far end and a woman was lashing some man with gusto to the approval of the crowd.

She had just settled into a corner table when there was a ruckus of a different kind.

The words 'Limo' and 'Rich fucks' were bandied about the room like tennis balls.

As she watched, she was suddenly glad that she took precautions not to be seen, if not smelled. Because the smell of them would drown out any other scents nearby.

They smelled like bad blood and old death. She had never seen so many of them together in one place.

Just as she got up the nerve to go and investigate, she saw someone who made her blood run cold.

Wearing a black designer jacket that only emphasized her voluptuous curves, the woman walked ahead of the entourage that held several guards in their center. All eyes were clearly on her, as her presence dominated the small group unmistakably made up of bodyguards.

She moved with authority on five-inch heel shoes. Her custom-made black leather shorts were tight and wrapped snugly around the corded muscles of her thighs.

Her wraparound sunglasses hid eyes that Mari knew were cynical and flat, the eyes of a corpse who hadn't the smarts to lie down and play dead.

"Bri," Mari whispered as she eased back deeper into the shadows, grateful the un-alive bitch didn't have the senses to scent her out.

Un-alive was a good way to describe Bri. Not quite dead enough for the rotting process to start, but not alive enough still to be considered human.

What amazed her more were the two women who eased out of the crowd to meet her.

Raqi and Sheri.

The New York clean-up crew was here. Maybe she and Tali did too good a job of stirring up trouble.

Maybe it was that man, Kye.

* * * * *

"That is impossible," Bri hissed at her two lieutenants as her eyes took in the crowd gathered in the club.

Ever since that last shipment disappeared, Balthazar had been hard pressed to meet the demands of his clients.

The idiots celebrating here, like it was the last day of their lives, would go far in replacing what was lost. Even if they were not fully broken and ready to serve.

"I saw her," Sheri insisted. "She was with some guy with a scarred back and an attitude. Are you sure none of your charges slipped his leash?"

Before she could blink, Sheri found a hand at her throat and was amazed a woman could lift her several inches off the ground with one hand. But then again, the woman was Bri.

Then the choking began.

"Are you implying I can't do my job?" she asked, as she calmly shook her compatriot with her left hand, while her right carefully removed the expensive eyewear from her face.

"Ngh...Ngh..." Sheri tried to answer, but remained calm. Most people got their neck broken while struggling in a tight hold.

"Good," Bri purred as she gently and slowly, a testament to her strength, placed Sheri back on her feet and straightened out her jacket, cut similar to Bri's. "But one may have decided not to join with the other cattle."

She tossed her head back a bit, motioning to the group of seven men and women who stood behind her—surrounded by Balthazar's Elite Guard—who had just entered the club.

"If one is that smart, we had better keep our eyes out for him. You say he had that one who decided not to serve, and yet escaped with her life?"

"I swear to it," Sheri added, nonplused about what had taken place before. Bri had learned from Balthazar, and with that teaching came the expectation of being knocked around some.

"Hmm," Bri murmured as she stood still as a corpse, thinking. "This could mean someone is also making a play for Balthazar's growing power. If the figureheads," again she motioned to the group of vamps behind her, "figure out this is a trap, all hell is going to break loose before the designated time. If this one can offer something that shows weakness on our parts, we will never get their cooperation."

"Weakness?" Raqi wondered out loud.

They had no weaknesses! They were revered for their strength! That was why the European Council fucks were too afraid to step foot in America without written consent, and it had to be written on human flesh with blood.

"Weaknesses like an escaped soldier who could not be caught but shows up in the hands of a rival. One small shoe started a strike that crippled China. What would one reluctant trainee cause?"

"We would be laughed out of our position of power. It is a loss of face we cannot accept." Sheri was adamant, her words clear.

"Where are they now?"

"They arrived early and said they would return. He knew this was the meeting place, so he has to come back here to make his claims."

"So keep an eye out for them," Bri said as she turned to face the group she had brought in. "Balthazar comes and it is time to put our plan into action."

Chapter Thirty

Mari huddled in her corner booth, wondering how long she could hide before they noticed her.

She recognized Bri and the women with her. But who were all the vamps?

She knew Balthazar had not turned Bri, not yet. She proved too useful in daylight hours. So that meant Balthazar had gathered the vamps for some reason. Mari intended to find out why.

Moving closer, hiding within the crowd, she began to hear the complaints and murmurs as Bri and her hired goons herded the centuries-old vamps up the stairs towards the room with the hastily covered hole in the wall.

That hole was valuable, she learned, as she stood near it and listened in.

"This has gone on long enough," one short, red-haired vampire with an exotic accent was saying. "Balthazar has gotten us here to this…place," disgust was evident in her voice, "…around these humans with threats and promises, and he has yet to show his face. What game is he playing here?"

"Rene," Bri's voice intoned. "Don't go there."

"Don't go there? What does this mean?" Rene seemed pissed.

"She means this is some elaborate," that word was emphasized, "hoax Balthazar has cooked up to get us here so he may make his inane pleas to be back in the council's good graces."

"Then he wastes his time, Rod," another female voice inserted. "We could never take him back, not after the way he behaved at our last meeting."

"I believe that was centuries ago, Kate," Bri added tiredly. "And since then, a few changes have occurred."

"Katherine. You will address me by my name, Bri. It is a courtesy to you all that I don't insist you call me by my proper title."

"Sit down!" Bri roared suddenly, the cool indifference disappearing from her voice. "You sons and daughters of bitches are here because we have something you want, or are afraid of. So sit your asses down and wait. Balthazar will be here after he deals with some pressing business. Until then, sit down, shut up, and stop your frigging whining. It is giving me a headache."

Silence descended.

Mari had to stifle a chuckle as she tried to envision the faces of the uptight council members at Bri's words.

But her next thoughts wiped amusement from her face. If Balthazar had the council here, he was either going to control them or kill them. She didn't know which was worse!

If he controlled them, he had more power. Would they be plotting to rid the world of his particular brand of insanity behind his back?

But if he killed them...? Balthazar would reign supreme, unchecked and unmindful of things like the depletion of the human species, rights, democracy, peace...just small things like that.

"I have to find Tali," she whispered as she turned from her spot at the wall and ran into a pair of boobs hard enough to make her think she had run into a man.

"Hello, Mari." Sheri grinned down at her, an evil smile on her face.

She quickly turned to dart into the crowd but was blocked by the equally smirking Raqi.

"'S'up, bitch? Long time no see." Her New York accent was rather pronounced.

"Oh, I think Bri is going to love this one," Sheri continued as she pulled a small spray can out of her pocket and squeezed the trigger in Mari's face.

The odorless garlic hit her like a ton of bricks, incapacitating her, making the world spin and the sound of the pounding music muffle as if she had cotton stuffed in her ears.

"Oh shit," she managed as the world flipped upside down and faded to black.

* * * * *

"Why do I still feel the need for a cigarette?" Angel groused as she stared at Tali and Kye in the back seat.

"Because you are a voyeuristic fuck who gets off on what we never meant to be seen," Tali shot back, grinning sweetly.

"Bitch."

"Your mother."

"Ladies," Kye sighed. "I don't have time for this shit. So Angel, stop baiting Tali and tell me what you know."

"Okay, dear, because you asked so sweetly," she added sarcastically. "Balthazar is at the Sheraton Downtown. He is planning something big and has his New York muscle with him. Something's going down tonight. All of that petty shit we've been doing, the parties we've been crashing, it was meaningless, all of it. It was all leading up to this. His plan is big and involved. If we can get him before he gets back from that club and this meeting he's going to, then we have a shot at taking him off guard and squashing his ass like a bug."

"Um, and how do we do that?" Tali asked, fearful and eager her long quest was almost over. Soon there would be no shadow of Balthazar standing over her life. She and Kye could— when did she start thinking on the level of Kye and anything? Besides, he was revenant, unhuman! What future...?

But they would have no future if Balthazar wasn't dealt with.

She would consider their options after his demise. Until then, her concentration was on getting rid of the parasite that had taken over her life.

"Oh, it's easy to kill a vampire," Kye murmured from the shadows in his corner of the car. "Even the old ones die screaming if you bleed them enough and in just the right way."

The singsong quality of his voice as he spoke caused both women to shudder in fear and uncertainty.

Almost as one, they realized they were hanging on to the tail of a tiger, a tiger that had not turned against them because he expected something of them. When he had it, God help them both. If this tiger decided to turn, there was nothing either one of them could do to prevent it.

They had to trust their instincts and step lightly around him.

Kye never even noticed the strained silence in the car as it sped through the still crowded Baltimore streets. His mind was totally occupied.

Never had he been this close to the beast. Never had he been able to taste victory in his mouth, the flavor of it almost addictive as the tangy sweet taste of fresh blood.

He would not fail. This night, Balthazar would meet his doom and revenge would be his.

He knew it. He could taste it.

Chapter Thirty-One

The feel of a hand slapping her in the face and harsh words being barked at her pulled Mari from the comforting darkness that enveloped her.

"Wake up, bitch! I don't have all day."

Bri snorted and landed another stinging blow to Mari's face.

Her eyes fluttered, opened, and finally focused in on the dark-haired woman who stood over her, a snarl on her face, her sunglasses reflecting her own sorry visage back at her.

"Finally. The dead has arisen—again. I made a funny."

At Mari's still face, Bri shrugged. "The undead never have a sense of humor anyway."

"I wouldn't say that, my love," replied a deep smooth voice that would have caused Mari's bladder to release if she still had those needs. "Because I am having a good chuckle right now."

Balthazar!

"That's right, sugar beets. Miss me?"

Mari hadn't realized she'd spoken out loud until he made his biting remark.

"What's this I hear about an escaped soldier running around, causing me no end of trouble?"

"I…" Mari tried to speak but the garlic was still heavily in her system, making thinking difficult.

"Save your excuses, I want some answers."

Mari swallowed then closed her eyes. She wasn't a praying woman, but right now, she felt the need for some of that Old Time Religion.

What happened? How had they known she was there?

"We knew because we were searching for someone," Bri answered. Mari cursed under her breath. "Someone who has the knowledge and the skill to go up against Balthazar."

"I know it's that whore's whelp that has been causing me no end of trouble," Balthazar picked up. "Using the skills I provided to bite the hand that fed her! She is such an...ungrateful brat."

"I don't know what you are talking about," Mari managed as parts of her began to come alive again.

She was tied to a chair, arms behind her back. But her feet were free. Odd behavior for Bri, unless the bitch had something planned for her feet.

She also was aware they had an audience. Several of the vamps she was spying on now looked at her with glee.

"Is this what you brought us all here to show us?" the woman, Katherine, asked, her eyes rolling in disgust.

"Is that any way to speak to your benefactor?" Balthazar asked politely as he turned to face the small group.

"We are your betters," the unidentified male vamp snorted.

"Russell, you may be better than the shits I stepped on to get into this position, but you will never be fit to lick their smears from my boots."

The crowd gasped at this and began to titter, as much as centuries-old vamps could titter.

"Disgusting," Katherine gasped as she brought an ancient silk fan to her face, fanning furiously as if she wished to dissipate some foul odor that had somehow permeated the room.

"No," Balthazar said as he walked slowly over to the group. "Disgusting is a room filled with corpses so old they're farting dust and refusing to see things my way."

He smiled, the darkness of his outfit emphasizing the whiteness of his growing fangs.

"That, and the fact they are dead and refuse to lay down and rot."

"Are you referring to us?" Russ sneered as he delicately laughed in Balthazar's face.

This vampire, as ancient as he was, still had the face and body of a young man ripe with youth and vigor. His brown hair hung over his forehead and his blue eyes laughed at the man he now stared at.

"You, a lowly servant, banished from our motherland because of your…perverse nature, dare to insult us? I remember when you were but a humble watchdog, Balthazar, a pet for our amusement. But you chose to bite the hand that fed you and, lo and behold! The mighty have fallen. You were always a legend in your own mind, Balthazar. But now that you are, as these boorish Americans say, King Turd on Shit Hill, you feel the need to threaten us. Go ahead, Balthazar. Impress me with your threats. Give me something to laugh about before I rip your head from your body and piss down your neck hole."

Balthazar looked at Russ and laughter poured from his mouth.

"So very amusing!" he chuckled. Blood-tinged tears poured from his eyes. "'Before I rip your head from your throat and piss down you neck hole,'" he mimicked, screwing his face up into some comic visage and puffing out his chest, mocking the ancient vampire. "I am so very scared."

Abruptly his laughter died as he threw out his hand in Russ' direction.

Instantly, the ancient felt his body fly across the room, his neck landing neatly into Balthazar's hands.

"But I guess you haven't learned not to fuck with me, old man."

He tightened his fingers as he easily lifted the struggling vampire above his head and brought his body down sharply across his bended knee.

The crunch of his backbone snapping was nothing compared to the strangled shrieks that exploded from his throat as Balthazar's fingers dug deeper, his nails piercing the skin and drawing blood.

The other vamps rushed to assist their compatriot, but stopped short when Bri and her two thugs waved silver knives and loaded weapons in their faces.

His screams got worse and Balthazar continued to apply pressure. The shrieking became full, ear-shattering wails as a thick wet tearing sound began to fill the room.

Blood suddenly exploded from Russ' middle as Balthazar literally tore him in two, both halves of his body writhing and wiggling as they were separated and dropped with a thud to the floor, his intestines trailing wetly between them.

"Piss down whose neck, bitch?" Balthazar sneered, wiping the splattering of blood and gore from his clothes. "That is what you taught me by sending me to America, land of the free and the home of the brave."

He held out his hand and Bri instantly dropped a pristine white hanky into his blood-soaked palm.

The other vamps looked on in horror as their friend writhed and screamed on the floor, his blood forming a dark pool around his twitching halves, whimpering and slowly dying.

Then almost as one, they turned to stare in horror at Balthazar.

"I learned my lessons when you sent me to this place, this land rich in magic and power. I learned my lessons very well. I managed to absorb most of what was here through hard work, trial and error."

He stepped over the dying vamp and casually kicked the upper body out of the way.

The noise he managed from his mangled throat still filled the room with grisly sounds, so at odds with the pounding music they could still faintly hear from the club.

"You are a mad man," Katherine gasped, turning her eyes away and closing them as if giving a moment of silence for their fallen comrade.

"Yes, I am, Kate, old girl!" he chuckled as he circled them. "But I am a mad man with power, and that makes me very dangerous."

Then turning to the slowly fading Russ, he snapped out, "Oh will you just shut up and die?"

Stomping back over, he raised his foot and slammed it down on the helpless vamp's head, over and over again.

"I hate it when people interrupt me while I'm working!" he snarled as he stomped until the head was almost as flat as the floor and silence filled the room.

The others looked on, horrified, but Bri nodded as if his actions made sense.

Mari thought she would vomit.

"Now that that unpleasantness is over," he continued as he walked away from the corpse, "time for the ultimatum. I get to go home, triumphant, smarter, wiser and more powerful. You get to pay me tribute in blood, flesh, money, and anything else I find appealing. How does that sound?"

"Like you have totally lost it," Rod replied. The short, platinum-haired vampire spoke carefully, showing no fear, in spite of what he had witnessed.

"Why should we give you anything?" Rene asked, not amused and not impressed with Balthazar's show of power.

"Simple. Nuclear weapons."

They all blinked at him before the chuckles began.

"This is not some bad action drama," Rene chuckled. "Really, Balthazar. You almost had me scared for a moment."

Still smiling, he walked over to Bri and pressed a small, almost tender kiss on her forehead.

"Have you ever heard of slavery?" he asked, his back to the room, his attention on Mari once more.

Snorts were his answer.

"Well, some very powerful people I have come to know just love their slaves. They like them old and young, male and female, living and…kind of dead."

The laughter stopped at his words.

"Do you know how easy it is to get what you want when you can deliver an undead army, brain-whipped to do all, including their Masters' greatest demands? An army that doesn't need special clothing or equipment, which feasts on the bodies of its enemies, an army that is practically indestructible?"

"Balthazar! What have you done?" Kate had a growing look of horror on her patrician face.

"I have merely given them what they want, for a price. There are so many Middle Eastern factions that need warriors, Katie," he purred. "In return, I get the most amazing gifts."

He turned to face her. They could all read the dead seriousness in his eyes.

"You…you are mad!" Her eyes widened with horror, as she understood what he was saying.

"You could never get so many people to accept The Dark Kiss!" Rod gasped, losing some of his decorum.

"Get? Get!" Again he exploded into laughter. "Who asks them, Roddy, old boy? Look around you! Why would I ask when they are mine for the taking?"

He gestured widely, arms spread, to the club scene below.

"Anything I want! Warrior types, sex slaves, submissives, sadists, all mine for the taking! A never-ending supply of them. Need a young face to cozy their way into a rival's family life? Who would suspect a child's best friend! Need someone to blend in with the growing nightlife, to get in touch with our troubled youth? Take your pick! I have them all, from gang bangers to those Goth punks." He pointed again to the club beyond the walls of the room they occupied.

"I have them all, and it's a never-ending supply."

"But they are children!" Treva gasped, horrified at the scope of Balthazar's plans, at the means he would go through to meet his ends.

"What of it?"

"They…they…"

"Would slit your throat if they believed it would gain them something. But I digress, and that is disrespectful. I do so hate to be disrespectful of my elders."

He glanced at Russ's remains and chuckled.

"The shipments started going out months ago. I have the weapons, I have the armies, I have the leaders by their balls."

At their puzzled looks, he chuckled again.

"Not everyone believes in vamps, esteemed colleagues. Those who thought me foolish were ravenous enough for the young, human flesh I peddle. A few compromising pictures in the right hands can make or break the leaders of some uncivilized countries."

"Blackmail?" Rod was almost horrified.

"Their nuts are in a noose and I am pulling the rope, Rod. Why not blackmail? I already sell the bodies, why not the souls?"

"You have no soul." Rene sniffed, shuddering as she realized they had no way out.

"The countries you represent, your protectors, will have no feet to stand on if I give the order to expose your lily-white hides to the sun, and you know it."

Several of the elder vamps flinched, knowing the truth behind Balthazar's words. Years of bribes and threats were nothing in comparison to having your power base ripped from under you. They were at the mercy of a mad man, and he knew it.

"You planned this well," Katherine whispered, her aristocratic voice a shadow of its former self.

"For years, I planned this. Revenge is the sweetest dish of all."

"It will be your downfall," Mari finally whispered.

"What? What did you say to me?" Balthazar snarled as he turned to the bound vampire.

"Revenge will be the end of you, Balthazar."

As she spoke, she slid her chair back, close to the plastic patched hole in the wall.

She had to find a way to get this news to Tali! Balthazar was winning, and if they didn't do something, power hungry leaders and their armies of undead would overrun the world.

Did Balthazar tell the leaders that, once their pets were undead, they would be virtually powerless to control them? Did he tell them their undead slaves would turn into vicious man-hungry monsters that would exhaust what they considered their food supply in a matter of months?

He had to be stopped!

"What do you know of it? You won't live to see the end of the night."

He motioned to Bri, who nodded to Raqi.

"Hold her still," Bri said as she pulled what was too long and sharp to be called a knife from a sheath down her back. She handed the blade to Raqi and nodded to the chair legs.

"Start with the feet. They take longer to die that way. They bleed slowly."

Mari scooted the chair back in fright, her eyes beginning to fill with tears of futility. If she failed, who would stop Balthazar? Once he controlled the council, his power would reign unchecked!

She inched backwards, Raqi stepped forward, and Balthazar watched amused.

"The chase is on!" he giggled. "See how we deal with traitors. Punishment is harsh and my justice is swift."

Mari whimpered when her back hit the wall, the large opening behind her and the monster with the blade before her.

"Game over," Raqi giggled, enjoying their brief game of cat and mouse. "You lose."

Raqi advanced, but before she could place herself to angle for Mari's feet, Mari reached up and grabbed her around the waist with her unbound legs, throwing Raqi off balance.

"Whoa!" Swinging her arms rapidly, she tried to regain her footing, but Mari jerked backwards, shoving against the chair. They both neatly flipped over, crashing through the patched wall and falling to the crowd below.

They landed with a bone-jarring thud, Raqi's neck snapping as her chest drove hard against Mari's knees.

The music stopped and the dancers backed away from the scene of an unfamiliar death.

Most of them may have worn skulls on their clothing, worshipping The Grim Reaper, but when faced with his work, they turned tail and ran.

"Vampires," Mari whispered, coming out of her daze quickly as she looked up and saw Balthazar staring down at her.

"Vampires!" she screamed a bit louder, her voice growing in strength. "They are fucking vampires! If you don't want to be killed, get the fuck out!"

Chapter Thirty-Two

"It's too easy," Tali muttered as they exited the lift.

They had no trouble getting to the penthouse suite elevators, curious enough on its own, but to make it unchallenged to the suite itself? Something was wrong.

"Stop complaining," Angel retorted sharply as they slipped out of the elevator and into the spacious entryway. "You want them to make it hard? Let's stake the bastard and get the hell out of here."

"Bee-autch," Tali hissed as she stepped up beside Kye, who remained blessedly silent.

"Your mother," Angel hissed back, before turning and almost running straight into a large coffin.

"What the hell...?"

"Will you both shut the hell up?" Kye suddenly commanded, throwing out his arms and urging both women back.

Angel hissed, but Tali, better conditioned to take orders, instantly fell into an alert stance.

"What...?"

"Shh," Kye hissed again, lifting his head and scenting the air around them.

Before he could respond to their unspoken questions, his eyes darted to the coffin like a wild animal spotting its prey — his stillness total.

Tali turned her attention to the coffin. It was plain, shellacked rosewood, but it looked ordinary to her. Would Balthazar...

Blam.

There was a sharp knock and the coffin vibrated under its impact.

Unconsciously Tali and Angel took another step back.

Blam.

Something struck the lid this time, lifting it several inches before it slammed shut.

"Move," Kye hissed as he shoved Tali and Angel to the side.

The women slammed into each other, a tangle of arms and legs, before they tumbled to the marble floor.

"Kye!" Angel hissed. "You had better…"

The explosion of the coffin lid slamming into the shiny silver elevator doors drowned out whatever Angel said.

She let out a shriek and sank back to the floor as the wind from the passing projectile caressed her cheek and tangled her hair.

Tali, still hugging the ground, turned towards the coffin and gasped as she saw the woman who lurched up and to the side of the coffin, struggling to free herself from the silk-lined box.

"Chari!" she screamed, rising to her feet to face the woman who had been a contact for her and Mari for so many years.

But the woman who stared at her, listless and lifeless, was not the same woman she had known for years.

The gold collar that had become so much a part of her was gone, and in its place, a necklace of fang marks.

The eyes that stared at her, a dull flat brown, did not carry the slightest glimmer of intelligence.

Her skin was dull and ashy, lacking something vital to make her look human.

This creature, this poor drained soul, was not the woman she had known and worried over. There was not even a glimmer of recognition on her face.

This creature was more than dead.

Still, her heart wrenched when Tali saw it.

This Chari, this mindless creature sniffed the air audibly, turning her head as if trying to place some unique fragrance. Then her eyes shot straight to Tali.

There was not enough fluid left in her body to allow her to drool, but the hungry expression on her face was enough to give that impression.

"That is not who you think it is," Kye said quietly to Tali as the thing opened its mouth to expose its small fangs. "It's a revenant. It's not human."

Before he finished speaking, the creature managed to gain its feet and rolled out of the coffin to land with a meaty thud to the floor.

It slowly rose to all fours, its head dragging low, as it lumbered to its feet.

Then in a move so fast the human eye had no hope of following, it launched itself at Tali.

She had time to emit one shriek before the thing was on her, hands tangling into her hair as it tried to wrench her head to the side and expose her carotid.

Before it could get a good grasp, its weight was just as quickly jerked from her body.

Kye reacted with lightning speed as he saw the thing throw itself at Tali. Before it managed to get a good enough grip to bite down on her with its underdeveloped teeth, he was on it, tossing it aside like so much garbage.

But it didn't stay down.

Almost immediately it threw itself at Kye; where it got the strength, he had no idea, as malnourished as it was.

Bracing himself, Kye twisted his upper body, centering his balance, before he threw up his right leg, twisted sharply, and launched a perfect roundhouse kick, striking what was left of

Chari in the chest, dead center, knocking her towards the empty coffin.

When it hit the ground, it threw its head back and loud, piercing shrieks filled the air, making both Tali and Angel clap their hands over their ears to block it out.

It was a sound of pain, anger, frustration, and most of all, hunger.

Chari was blood starved, and she was going to get her blood feast, or die trying.

Stumbling to her feet, arms outstretched, she dove, not for Kye, but for Tali.

Maybe it was a bit of familiarity, maybe it was because she was the smallest one there, maybe it was because some part of Chari's degenerated mind recalled the friendship she shared with the woman, maybe it was because Tali felt horror and compassion for what she was. But Chari went after Tali with desperation reserved for beings fighting for not only their lives, but for their very souls.

"Chari! No!"

But the thing that once went by that name kept coming.

Chari felt pain.

It overwhelmed her; it washed over her in waves, drowning out every sensation but pain.

All consuming never-ending pain.

And hunger.

Instinctively, she knew there was only one thing that could make it better.

Blood.

The blood that smelled the most familiar to her, the most enticing, and the headiest, belonged to that thing in the corner.

She no longer recognized people, just things that tried to keep her from what she wanted.

Her sight was dim, things fading in and out. But the one thing she saw was the deep burning glow centered within each of them.

It pulsed and ran in a warm fragrant river, beckoning her, tempting her.

She had to have it, at any cost.

She dove towards the first container, the one that she'd first scented. It would help her — it would ease the ache.

With all that was in her, she threw herself toward it, mouth open and eager to drain what was hers!

Tali froze, for all of a second, as the cold fleshy weight of the thing pressed her to the floor. She inhaled the scent of it — rank cold and sweetly sickening. It smelled of evil...and death.

But before she could react, the weight of it, no longer her friend Chari, was torn from her. It landed with a sickening splat off to her right.

She looked up to see Kye standing there, chest heaving, eyes glowing eerily green.

* * * * *

Everyone in the room paused for one complete second.

Faces stared at faces, the paint not masking the fear and anxiety that spread across some.

Bodies paused in mid-gyration, some arms still held up high, frozen in the midst of their personal celebration of life.

Others shook their heads as if they didn't believe what their eyes were telling them, what their ears were hearing.

But when the small, dark-haired woman slithered out of the shattered chair, her back twisted at some strange angle, they all stared.

In the silence of the room, she grabbed her neck, forced back by the fall from the hole in the wall, and jerked it sharply forward.

It corrected its alignment with a sharp snap of bone.

Some winced, others gagged, and still a few more felt faint.

But when she realigned her body with a twist and a muffled curse, all hell broke loose.

The DJ, in a fit of fancy, began to play a rousing rendition of Drowning Pool's Let the Bodies Hit the Floor.

The whispered intro was enough to start people moving, but as the lead singer wailed out the first chords and the hard hitting driving beat kicked in, just about all were ready for…panic.

Some screamed and a mass exodus towards the front entrance started.

Others turned towards the strange collection of people who were exiting by way of the stairs. Some of the dancers had visions of becoming someone's bloodsucking valentine, while others had death in their eyes. They would not be controlled by these creatures. They would be the masters.

Seeing the panic begin, Mari began to encourage it by rushing some groups, herding them towards the doors as the music screamed and the laser lights pulsed to the beat of the music.

I have to get out of here, she thought. I have to warn Tali.

But as she ducked behind one group of screaming twinks and teenage club hoppers breaking for the door, she looked up into the dark sunglasses of the one woman she truly feared.

Bri stood tall and silent, a buoy in the sea of frantically moving bodies. Even as Mari watched and was tugged closer to the vision of famine and death in black, Bri lifted one finger, pointed it straight at her heart and mouthed the words, "Bang. You're dead."

"Shit!" Mari cursed as the heat and the tension in the room began to get to her.

Back-peddling as fast as she could, she ran straight into the woman who had performed the whipping with great authority.

Before she could speak, the woman gripped her arm and tugged her towards the stage.

The screaming was drowning out the music, and the panicked shouts were making her head ache, but Mari could make out what the woman was saying.

"Vamps? You got to be shitting me!"

"Do I fucking look like I am playing a game?" Mari shouted back as she saw the remaining members of Bri's New York Gang struggling to move in her direction.

"So, are you a good one or a bad one?" Shelby asked as she slowly reached into the side of her leather pants and drew out what had to be a foot of metal, sharp and glistening.

"Fuck!" was all that Mari could gasp, before the woman reached out and wrapped her strong arm around her throat.

"I am figuring you are good, but I'd better take you out, just to be sure."

Mari's brain finally kicked into action, and she jerked away from the woman, just in time for one of the vampire leaders to leap up on the stage with a low growl.

The short, red-haired vampire reached for Mari, tearing her out of Shelby's clutches.

"Where is he?" Rene hissed, her eyes flashing like fire and her fangs hanging low. "Tell us, bitch! What are his plans?"

"No fuckin' way!" Shelby spat back before she reached out and spun the elder vampire around.

Before she could counter, a fist planted itself neatly into Shelby's face, dropping her to the floor as Rene turned and reached for the stunned Mari.

With one fist knotted in her shirt, Rene lifted the younger vamp and with a nasty sneer to her face, lifted her about two feet off of the ground, and held her there.

"What are his plans?"

Rene's nails dug into her throat, piercing the skin, and Mari automatically threw her hands around the woman's wrists, tearing at her fingers to free herself.

"You don't play fair," a voice growled from behind.

Rene turned to face an enraged Shelby, blood dripping from her nose, as she sniffed and wiped the flow away with the back of her hand. "And you are not paying attention."

"What are you going to do to me, human?" Rene laughed as she turned her head to stare at the woman, then turned back to her quarry, intent on finding out what she wanted to know.

"As I was say…uggh!"

As Rene opened her mouth, a grunt and a hiss escaped before her arms started shaking. Slowly, she lowered Mari to the stage and began to turn.

Before she could complete her move, the thin metal rod exploded from her chest roughly where her heart used to be.

"That was easy," Shelby commented as she watched the vampire cough up her own blood.

"Give me that!" Mari screamed as she raced around the gasping vamp and began to turn and twist the blade.

"Take out the heart, you fool! Take out the heart, the blood can't circulate, and it drains out!"

Mari knew if Shelby had removed the blade, an ancient like Rene would have turned and ripped her throat out and used the flying blood to heal herself.

Rene grunted again, then collapsed to the stage, her fingers digging furrows into the dark wood as she felt her death approach, her heart so much pulp.

She lifted her head again, trying to gasp out something, but blood, red and old, poured freely from her mouth instead.

She coughed once, spraying those around her with her fluids, then her head hit the floor with a thump.

"That is how you kill a vampire," Mari hissed as she turned to face Shelby, and a second blade, pointed right at her heart.

"Thanks for telling me," Shelby said with a smile as she pressed the tip into Mari's chest. "That is good to know."

"Oh hell!"

Chapter Thirty-Three

Tali watched, feeling a touch of fear as she stared into Kye's dead eyes.

Then he exploded in a flurry of motion, so fast it was hard for her to follow.

Chari, enraged by the denial of her meal, turned and rushed at the thing that wanted to keep her from what she needed.

Now she was a thing—once human, stripped down to its basest needs and emotions-hunger and anger.

Lumbering gracelessly to her feet, Chari, both arms extended, rushed at Kye, but he was already in motion.

He ran straight at her, easily side-stepping her waving arms, and jammed the heel of one palm straight into her chin.

The angry roars from her throat ceased instantly as her head snapped back with a crunch.

Before she could recover or fall, the choice was taken out of her hands.

Kye automatically widened his stance, centered his balance, threw his weight to the right and delivered a stunning flying roundhouse kick to her chest, using so much force that the snapping of her ribs was audible to all in the foyer.

As he landed, knees bent and flatfooted, the thing named Chari flew backwards, landing across the remains of her coffin.

It labored to breath, its punctured lungs struggling within shattered rib bones, its rasping breaths filling the air with a wet gasping sound.

It turned its head pitifully, in the direction of the meal desired and denied, and a low wail took the place of its pitiful attempts at breathing.

Slowly it pulled itself up on one arm, struggling to stay on its feet, and it whimpered, throwing one arm out as if in supplication.

No mercy was found in any of the watching eyes.

Kye looked over at Tali once, who only murmured, "Do it," then turned away.

As Chari sensed Kye's approach, the one that had caused her so much pain, its whimpers became growls and it bared its immature teeth in his direction.

It lunged once, but Kye's hand caught her outstreached wrist and pulled. Using her own momentum, he kept a hard grip on her arm, stepped behind her and trapped both of their arms under her neck, immobilizing her.

Her free arm lashed up and back, trying to hit his eyes, his throat, any vulnerable part. But his free arm caught her hand, and with a vicious tug, tore the arm free out of its joint. It swung at her side, dangling and useless.

"I release you," he whispered, his eyes glowing gold with power as he nudged her dislocated arm aside and plunged his hand in.

Chari shrieked and her vision faded to red-streaked gray as Kye's hand broke through what was left of her rib cage and gripped her heart in his hand.

There was a frozen moment, where Kye felt the power of life and death within his hands, when he felt like a god.

Then he crushed her heart like tissue paper.

Chari gasped once as her body spasmed violently in his hands. Then she collapsed, as if she was a puppet that had had its strings cut.

Kye looked down at the shell of what once had been an attractive woman, shrugged his shoulders, and, emotionlessly, let it drop to the floor.

"Time to go," was all he said as he looked at the bloodless thing on the floor.

In fact, other than the heart matter, his hand came out clean.

"Pitiful starved bastard," he added as he turned to walk away.

"Chari or you?" Tali softly asked as she watched him walk away from the death he'd so easily caused.

Kye paused for a quick moment, a moment so fast neither woman noticed it, then continued on his way.

He had no time for foolish women or senseless emotions. He had a job to do.

Revenge was at hand.

* * * * *

Mari blinked as she stared at the mad woman with the long hair and the sharp knife.

"Oh, what are you going to do?"

Her words seemed to echo as the music paused then changed to Ramstone's Firefly.

As the lead singer screamed "Bang Bang," Shelby looked silently down at the body at her feet, then up at the vamp who had seemed to help her.

All around them, pandemonium ruled. The crazed Goths, both for and against those with the vampire gift, ran, screamed, and fought with frenzied abandon.

Mari turned to watch for a moment, thinking that, to the humans here, this must be a vision of what their hell looked like—unless they were turned on by the spectacle.

She blinked as she saw Bri headed in her direction, determination stamped across her face.

"Make up your mind quick," Mari hissed as she took an involuntary step back from the edge of the stage. "My time is just about up."

Bri took another step and someone, one of her henchmen, Sheri, gripped her arm.

She whispered something to her and the woman glared at Mari for a long moment, then turned and forced her way through the crowd.

"I guess I can kill more later," Shelby finally answered.

"Yes, you can. In fact, there are a lot of them coming...now!"

Mari practically wailed that last word as wave after wave of Balthazar's troops filled the area.

Knowing that bastard as well as she did, Mari was sure the order to exterminate anything moving had been given. That was why Bri and her bitch had pulled out so easily. They had to be covering the bastard's retreat.

"How can I get out of here?" she asked as she turned towards the woman again.

"They vamps?" she asked and nodded her head towards the group that was now busy cracking heads and breaking bones.

"Yes, but I am after the big one."

"Killing vamps is not so hard."

"Good! Then get me out of here and you can mop up the rest of them." Mari watched the woman crack her knuckles in anticipation and thought that left to her own devices, she probably could.

"Back there," Shelby growled before pointing towards the back of the stage and the black curtain that concealed an emergency exit. "No one ever thinks to look there."

Mari nodded her thanks, and shook her head as the woman, with a rebel yell, leaped off the stage and dove into the fray.

Where do they find these people? she thought before she made her way towards the exit, hopefully to cut Balthazar off.

What she would do when she found him was anyone's guess. But she had to know where he was going.

She managed to make it through the hidden metal door and ran down the damp alley towards the front of the building, just in time to see Balthazar's limo take off.

"Shit! Damn! Fuck!" she bellowed as she stamped her foot in futility.

She turned to go back to the club, maybe bust a few heads to make herself feel better. Maybe even get some info about the slippery bastard's whereabouts, too.

She turned right into a hard muscled wall of chest.

She looked up in time to see the platinium-haired vamp, Rod, staring down at her.

"You want Balthazar?" he asked as he gripped her shoulders in his powerful ancient hands.

"I want him dead," she hissed, struggling to get away.

"He is at the Sheraton," he replied as he let her go. "We will do nothing to aid him, or assist you. The council must be impartial."

"But you just told me where he was!" Mari exclaimed. Then realization dawned on her. "You want him dead. He has all of you between a rock and a hard place. You're hoping we can do what you can't."

Rod smiled.

"As I said, we will do nothing to assist you or aid him."

With that, the ancient melted into the shadows as if he had never been.

"Right," Mari sighed as she turned and attempted to do the impossible.

Hail a cab in downtown Baltimore, in the middle of the night, on a street where a known Goth club was jumping.

"The things I do for that girl!" she sighed and began her quest.

Chapter Thirty-Four

"Stupid bitch," Angel hissed as she watched Kye forge on ahead.

"I am not in the mood for your shit," Tali snarled back, as she stared at the remains of her friend on the floor.

"Well, you are going to get it," Angel replied instead.

She reached out and grabbed Tali's arm, preventing the other woman from following Kye.

"Let go of me," Tali said, enunciating each word beyond the point of proper English.

Angel let her arm go, taking one step back as Tali quickly followed behind Kye.

But she didn't get far.

Kye was systematically opening doors and slamming them, searching for the man, no, demon, that had eluded him for years.

Standing at the beginning of a long hallway, Tali waited, eyes narrowed in anger, for some sign she was needed.

Again, Angel spoke her piece.

"You don't deserve to stand in his shadow, let alone fuck him."

"Jealous?"

"As I said, you are a stupid bitch. I heard your little comment there. He didn't deserve it."

"He killed my friend like she was some trash he found on the street. Chari stayed behind so she could feed us information. She is dead because of me."

"She is dead because of that maniacal bastard that Kye is trying to take out. Don't paint him with your guilty brush."

"Guilty?"

"You don't think I have friends on the inside?" Angel rolled her eyes at Tali then shook her head as if amused by her naiveté.

"Are your friends dead? Did Kye rip their hearts out?"

"If he has to."

That cold statement stopped whatever Tali was going to say next.

"That wasn't your friend in there, Tali. That was some shadow, some physical shade of what had been. Your friend was dead long before Kye pulled her cord. It's just that no one saw fit to tell her that her electricity was turned off."

"But I saw her! She was staring at me!"

"She was staring at dinner. Did you see any blood flying from her body? Did you see any blood on the floor? Balthazar drained her and left her as a fuckin' watch dog. You should thank Kye for getting your friend out of that living hell. If you should be pissed at anyone, you should be mad at the monster that made her."

Tali stared at Angel, almost hating to admit the woman was right.

"If it was your friend?"

"I would kill that monster if Kye didn't do it. Now is not the time for mercy."

Tali stared down the hall as Kye systematically searched another room and slammed out of the door, moving onto the next.

"As if he has any."

"Mercy is for the weak."

Angel walked around Tali, bumbling into her as if she was of no consequence, and walked behind Kye.

Before Tali could retaliate, there was a loud shriek, followed by several other feminine yowls. The two women raced down the hall.

The room they came to had to be one of the largest in the hotel.

But it was the corner filled with hysterical women in all states of undress that held their attention.

In the very center, defending the weakest women, was Marti.

"Who the fuck are you?" she was screaming, her deceptively sleek muscular dancer's body coiled and ready for action.

Kye stood there, shaking his head, as he watched Balthazar's whores trying to protect each other.

"Do I have to murder all of you, or are you going to tell me where he is?"

"Who are you?" Marti repeated as if Kye was stupid.

"I am... Call me The Slayer. That is all you need to know."

"Fuckin' slay this!"

She dove at him the same time Tali and Angel entered the room.

"Marti!" Angel screamed out and the woman pulled herself short, skidding across the floor in the effort to slow down her headlong rush.

"Angel?" the bewildered woman gasped. Then horror filled her eyes. "Its dangerous here, Angel! Get out!"

"I told you I had help." Angel laughed in relief as she ran to Marti and took the dancer in her arms.

After a heart-felt hug, she turned and pointed to Kye.

"Marti, meet Help."

The woman shook her head and giggled again as she took in the man who stood silent and still as she rushed at him, as if she would be light work to him.

"Who is this cute little Blackanese boy you brought me, Angel? I was hoping for nuclear weapons and you bring me your delivery boy."

But Kye was beyond witty comebacks and sarcastic one-liners.

"Where is the bastard?"

Marti blinked as she stared at the man—the half dressed man. Maybe there was more to him than meets the eye.

"Impatient, aren't we?" she sneered as she stalked around Kye like a buyer at a horse auction.

"I have little time left, woman. I have wasted far too much of it on ungrateful women."

"Ungrateful!" both Marti and Tali cried out at the same time.

"I don't even know you, let alone feel the need to be grateful to you," Marti sneered.

"You just killed my friend!" Tali cried out.

"You brought me a killer?" Marti asked, suddenly not so gloomy about her prospects with Kye.

"Chari's dead." Angel spoke in a dead tone, nodding back the way they came.

"Chari has been dead for a long time." Marti sighed. "But why would Balthazar take out one of his informers?"

"Informer?" Tali hissed, turning her angry gaze on the woman stalking her man. "Chari gave us valuable information about Balthazar's whereabouts and movements. Look what it got her! She got turned into some...some mindless thing. She tried to kill me! She wanted to drink my blood!"

"That's what revenants do," Kye said as he turned away from the women and searched the room.

"That? He turned your brother into that?"

Kye said nothing, but took a deep breath as he remembered that dark time in his life.

He shuddered as he recalled how his brother screamed, how his flesh was torn from his body, how he begged for a death that never came. How he could not free his brother from his living hell.

But he had freed the woman, Chari. Now he would ensure that no other woman, no other man, no other human being, would ever be turned into one of those mindless creatures again, by ripping Balthazar's throat out with his bare hands.

Marti paled as she heard this. What color she had slowly drained out of her face, giving her a milky complexion.

"You mean she wasn't an informant?" Marti gasped as she looked back at the women behind her.

"No." Tali tried to take in the other woman's shock and wondered why she seemed so distraught. "She got me and Mari where we are today. She saved my life too many times to count."

Marti slowly ran her hands over her face, pulling the skin down and moaning as the obvious became clear to her.

"If I had only known," she whispered as she turned her eyes back to Tali. "We could have...we could have helped each other. Tali, I was informing on Balthazar too! If I had known, I could have helped her! That poor, poor woman."

"What did he do to her?" Tali wanted to know.

Angel walked over and placed her hands on Tali's shoulders, only to have them shaken off violently.

"What did that bastard do?"

"He," Marti started, took a deep breath and started again. "She was his favorite gold throat. She, uh," she swallowed again. "She didn't have a gag reflex. He...she was his favorite play thing."

"Then why did he do that to her? Why did he turn her into...that?"

"Because he could!" Marti screamed out. "Because he wanted to! Because she got careless. Because she lost it! Don't you get it? Don't you understand? We," she gestured wildly to the women and men behind her, "we are his cattle! He can do to us whatever he wants! There is no escape! We have no escape until he is dead!"

By this time, Marti was screaming as she stared at the defiant young woman who stared back at her with condemnation in her eyes.

"He has destroyed all of our lives," Angel whispered. "He has taken something from all of us. We all thirst for revenge, Tali! We all need to make him pay for what he has done."

Before more could be said, a small chime sounded and the people began to scatter.

"He's here," Marti said as she turned towards Kye. "You want him, you got him. And his minions. If they are returning this early, things went really good or really bad. Either way, he will be in a mood to abuse us."

She turned and walked towards a door hidden in the rear.

"His office is in there. I can guarantee none here will bother you. Most of us want him gone, although a few like what he tosses at their feet. We will keep those faithful away from you. Either way, he will have Bri and her bitches with him. We can do nothing against them. But Balthazar is here. You wanted him, you got him. Now kill him."

She turned, and after whispering to a few of the remaining women, rushed off towards the empty rooms.

"If we had only known," Angel whispered as she turned to Tali. "If we had known, Tali, we could have all been working together. We could have taken him out before now. All of these deaths, all of this pain, could have been avoided."

Tali said nothing.

She turned to Kye and nodded in his direction.

"I was wrong, about what I said," she spoke quietly. "You had to do what you had to do. I thank you for doing it, because I couldn't have."

Kye blinked, as he looked over at her, the young girl dressed in his leather and trying to be so big and tough. She was big and tough, but not tough enough.

Chapter Thirty-Five

"What the hell was that?" Balthazar growled as he climbed out of his limo, Bri as always on his heels. "Just what the fuck was that, Bri? One fucking weak-assed vampire! One that should have been dead a long time ago!"

"Raqi screwed up," was Bri's calm reply.

"Raqi is dead, Bri! Dead! That bitch started a riot in the middle of what should have been my crowning achievement, Bri. My coup de grace! Do you know what that means, Bri?"

"Yes."

"Well, just in case you don't, it means done deal. A done deal, Bri, that is not so done now!"

Eyes narrowed in frustration, and gritting his teeth, Balthazar stalked towards the private elevators that would deliver him straight to his penthouse floor.

Bri followed behind, torn between laughter and fear as Sheri followed, the smile wiped from her face.

She had lost a good friend that night, and she wanted revenge.

"I am not stupid, Balthazar." Bri removed her glasses as the elevator doors shut. "I know what happened. Raqi was careless and she paid for it with her life. Too bad it had to come to that, but these things happen."

"Happen?" Balthazar growled, his eyes shooting fire at her. "These things happen? These things do not happen to me!"

Bri shrugged as she mentally plotted how she would kill him when the time was right. She could use that god complex of his to...

"If you are thinking what I would be thinking in your situation, Bri," Balthazar purred, "you had better be sure to make sure all of my fail-safes are down. If I go, bitch, you go with me."

Bri actually managed to make wide innocent eyes as she stared at Balthazar.

"Me? What would…what could I do?"

"You never took me for a fool before, Bri. Don't fuckin' toy with me now. We have things to take care of before we can recover some of this night's work."

Bri grunted in acknowledgment and turned her thoughts to this evening and how to recoup their losses.

Balthazar ran his hands through his hair as he watched the numbers climb. His mind was beginning to find means to twist this disaster into something that would work for him.

"Okay," he began. "The council, or rather what's left of it, will be trying to regroup. Damn, they die easily."

Bri nodded in agreement.

"So the best thing for me to do is to show them I am serious."

"You did that," Bri interjected. "You ripped out throats and ordered the club vamps to kill everyone that moved."

"Yes," he agreed. "But the ancients will be prepared for that."

"Want me to start a hunt?"

She raised one eyebrow as she asked this question. Hunting was her specialty.

"No, I don't want you dead."

"I didn't know you cared," she muttered as she rolled her eyes.

"I don't," he was quick to reply. "But I own your ass. I will choose when and where you die for me. Is that understood?"

Bri turned and observed the man beside her.

His long flowing hair was free, outlining a face of deadly beauty. His eyes shone with the self-knowledge of his own power — that, or madness.

Still, she felt herself drawn to him.

Him or his power, and she didn't know which was the bigger draw.

She let her eyes travel the length of his body, taking in the firm slabs of muscle that made up his chest and the large knot in the crotch of his pants.

He was fuckable. Insane with power, but extremely fuckable.

"If you say so," was all she said.

"I want you to discover what our little Mari was after in that club. Then I want you to bring me who she was looking for."

"Who?"

"Maybe the sighting you had before is connected."

"Tali and Mari?"

"Stranger things have happened, my little bitch," he purred as the elevator doors began to open.

But Balthazar stopped them from exiting, throwing out one long arm to halt their movements.

"Vanilla and cinnamon," he whispered as the other two looked at him strangely.

"You wear vanilla," Bri reminded him, but drew her gun as she waited for his next action.

"Good of you to notice, pet," he drawled. "But this smell is not my own. Someone's been in my house, ladies. And, it is still here."

"You recognize the smell?"

Balthazar thought back to his first club in Baltimore, to the strangely painted man and woman, to the fight that amused him, until he sent his own people to settle it. Was there a connection?

"Mari does not have the skill," he mused as he allowed them to enter the foyer. "But Tali does."

He removed his arm and the three stopped all forward motion as the crushed coffin lid caught their eye.

"Hmm, my pet is out. I wonder where she got to."

Balthazar's words were almost crooning as his eyes scanned the room.

"There seems to be company with my stalker, ladies. I smell the sweet scent of well-used pussy and desperation. And I believe Angel is here."

"Angel and Tali?" Bri whispered as she spotted a heap of hair and skin on the floor. "Impossible!"

"It's dead."

Balthazar's words reached her as she used her shoe to nudge what appeared to be a human body.

It was Chari.

Chari with a hole in the side of her chest, and most amazingly, a small smile on her face.

"Guess that's one way to be free of you," Bri said, her voice cold as she looked around to find what had caused this carnage. It was so much less...messy, than what Balthazar would have done.

"I don't think that, Bri. Tali and Angel together could not have gotten rid of my little watchdog. Someone is helping them, someone who smells like vanilla and cinnamon. I believe I will go and...sniff out the competition," Balthazar chuckled as he straightened his collar and strode confidently down the hall. "You take care of the reunion-goers, if you will, Bri. I feel a need to go and introduce myself to whoever has no respect for pets. I may even call the ASPCA."

That brought a grin even to Bri's face as she began checking rooms.

Looked like there would be no reason to plan a hunt. The prey had come to her. Not as entertaining, but a kill was a kill.

Chapter Thirty-Six

Balthazar stalked, each step slow and cautious as he turned his head and surveyed the halls of his domain.

Someone was watching him, some force, some malevolent entity that followed his every move.

Lesser men would have shivered at the dark intent directed at him, but Balthazar smiled, enjoying the tingling rush that filled his veins.

How long had it been since he had been challenged? Even Bri at her worse was leashed, to some great extent.

But this…this was different. It felt personal.

Someone had gone to enough trouble to make him a personal quest.

He was flattered.

Out of the corner of his eye, he caught the glimpse of something darting past, just a shadow of a form. By the time his keen, supersensitive eyes adjusted, it was gone. *Some feat, to move faster than my supernatural eyes*, he thought.

As he was contemplating that thought, he felt a rush of air that made his hair stand on end even as it moved with the vanilla and cinnamon scented breeze.

Fascinating, he mused. *The stalker had become the stalked.*

He turned again and just a hint of laughter filled the air, a sound that chilled even his cold heart and caused that long-dead organ to beat, just once.

Then he heard the chanting.

Low and rhythmic, it filled the air around him, taking him back over the many rituals he had learned.

"I know that sound," he whispered as he continued to move forward, ever forward. "But from where?"

He lifted his face again, scenting the air that suddenly was filled with vanilla and that touch of cinnamon, and flinched as the breeze brushed past his face.

Not just a breeze, he thought as a stinging sensation filled his face.

Slowly, he lifted his hand and felt the cold drops of blood that beaded up on his pale flesh.

Amazed, he raised his hands to his eyes, seeing what he had not seen for centuries. His own blood. The stolen blood that rested in his veins. His eyes widened in fascination.

Before he could move again, there was another breath of air, the brush of skin, and the gold cross around his neck snapped with a sharp tug.

He watched, as it seemed to fall to the floor in slow motion, then paused inches from the ground.

There, it did a merry dance, spinning and twirling, its gold a bright star in a room that began to darken with tension. It spun faster and faster, rising and falling like some insane dancer, until it stopped, right before his eyes.

There, it pulsed and shimmered and it seemed to breathe, its inhales and exhales filling the room with an intense silence as Balthazar watched.

Suddenly it exploded, flinging sharp metal barbs into his face, slashing open his skin and bloodying his flesh.

"Son of a bitch!" Balthazar roared as he flinched back, throwing up his hands to protect his eyes. The pain was sharp and immediate! Not at all what he expected, but then he smiled. It looked like he faced a worthy opponent after all.

The chanting began again. With a grin, Balthazar felt his fangs explode in his mouth, a welcome pain that added to the ache in his face.

The hunt was on. He tossed aside the veneer of civility he had polished to perfection over the years.

With a snarl, his eyes blazed bright red and his breath heaved in his chest.

The demon had been released and it relished its freedom.

With a growl of triumph, it launched itself down the hall.

The hunt was well and truly engaged.

But who the prey was, was anybody's guess.

* * * * *

"I don't like this," Angel muttered as she paced the room Kye had sent them to for safe keeping. "What is that man's plan?"

Tali said nothing, just paced the floor and kept a watchful eye on the door.

"I mean, what is he going to do when faced with that…that monster?"

"Shut up."

"He can easily kill him and where does that leave the two of us?"

"Shut up."

"Balthazar never travels alone. I should have brought more ammunition."

"Shut the fuck up!"

Before Angel could turn, Tali was on her, spinning her around and shaking her shoulders with fingers that bruised with their intensity.

"He is out there trying to keep that monster from killing us, you bitch! And we are going to watch his back!"

Tali's eyes blazed with her seriousness as she shook the shorter woman.

"He told us to stay here," Angel said, her voice going cold as she shoved both hands in front of her, between their two bodies and swinging them out to the sides, easily breaking Tali's hold.

"Since when did you ever listen to him?"

"Action. That's what I need," Angel decided as she reached into her jacket pocket and pulled out a very impressive CZ-75, a sleek 9 mm caliber double action handgun.

She grabbed a handful of clips from the other pocket and began methodically checking the bullets.

When she was sure all was in readiness, she nodded to Tali, who stood there, mouth agape.

"What? You think I was the weekend booty call or something? This is a war, doll face. All of us are involved. What kind of soldier would I be if I didn't utilize my talents?"

"Humph," Tali snorted as she walked towards the door. "I never thought you were a booty call. You have to be open and, well, not such a cold fish to get laid. I always assumed you were just a spy. You know, the sneaky little worm that hides in corners and gets off vicariously while mucking around in the filth to learn little bits of what we already knew."

"You bitch!"

"Thank you, doll face. Takes one to know one."

"As long as you recognize it," Angel snorted, humor floating in her eyes as she walked towards the door, planning on following the other woman out into danger. "As long as you do, recognize this — you go first. Your lower form of bitchiness makes a perfect target. I'm Batman, you're Robin."

"I always liked Robin," Tali protested as she gathered herself to face what was on the other side of the door.

"So did I," Angel replied. "He always drew the fire. You never saw Batman dodging bullets when he didn't have to."

Tali immediately exploded into giggles as she turned to face the other woman.

"That was almost witty. I am impressed. Too bad you won't survive the fight to amuse me some more."

"Planning on taking me out?" Angel asked, lifting one eyebrow in curiosity and shaking the hair back from her face, exposing her scar to Tali's eyes.

"No. Sarcasm and wit are used by weak people who have no physical ability to back up their words. Good bye, Angel. It's been...interesting."

Before a reply could be heard, she quietly swung the door open and began to stealthily make her way down the hall.

"Damn, I love a good exit," she chuckled to herself as she turned a corner...and ran straight into a black-coated figure.

"Me too," the woman responded as she leveled the barrel of what had to be a cannon in the center of her forehead. "Good bye."

Chapter Thirty-Seven

"Where are you, you son of a bitch?"

Balthazar's chest heaved and spit ran down his fangs as his red eyes searched the corridors of the floor he inhabited.

He was rather enjoying this!

He was almost at a run as he frantically tore open one door then another.

He felt an odd burning in his loins and smiled as he realized his blood was running out for the kill.

He scented the air again as he tore the buttons from his shirt, scattering them to the ground as he closed in on his prey.

* * * * *

Kye followed Balthazar and felt a killing rage build up in him. Bile rose in his throat and his body shook as he chanted the ancient chants he had refused to let himself practice all these years while waiting for him.

Now that the hour of his destruction was at hand, Kye had to dig his nails into his hands to prevent himself from going out and rushing the man-demon.

Balthazar looked just as he remembered him, calm and cool, suave, if you will. The air of menace that hung over him was still the same.

He appeared more powerful than Kye remembered, but then, he was remembering him from the eyes of an abused boy, a child not confident in his own abilities or power.

He had learned a lot over the years, learned a lot about himself and the world around him. And he knew one thing that gave him an edge.

When you had nothing to lose, you had everything to gain.

Again he rushed the older vampire, chuckling eerily into the room as he again laid his flesh open, this time aiming for his broad chest.

Balthazar turned towards the strike, raced in that direction, never realizing his tormentor was herding him in the direction he wanted him to go.

* * * * *

"Hello, Tali," Sheri chuckled as she leveled her gun on the woman she had caught. "Of all people, fancy meeting you here."

Tali's eyes grew big as she slowly rose to her feet. This was something she had not expected.

"Well, this is singular, meeting you here," she spoke quietly. "I mean, I thought you would still be hanging on to your mommy's tit. I didn't know Bri let you stray so far from her apron strings."

"Oh, she lets us out from time to time," Sheri chuckled.

"To clean up your paper and hose out your cages?"

"And to take care of light work," Sheri giggled, refusing to rise to the bait Tali offered. "I believe light work would be you."

"I kicked your ass a few times, I recall," Tali countered as she spread her legs and centered her balance.

Sheri smiled as she took a step back, distancing herself from Tali and whatever tricks she was trying to pull.

"That was then, baby girl. This is now."

"So how about it? Wanna go a few rounds, stretch the old muscles, get your ass kicked once more for old time's sake?"

Tali tightened her muscles as she prepared to strike.

"Nah," Sheri sighed as she began to tighten her finger on the trigger of her Desert Eagle. "I think I'll just shoot you. If that's okay with you."

"Damn," Tali muttered before a shot exploded and she slammed her arms over her eyes.

Feeling no point of entry or pain—she often knew that pain came after the wound was inflicted—Tali removed her arms and peered over at the hit woman.

Sheri had a stunned look on her face as she slowly reached up and touched a small dark spot on her immaculate sea of black. A spot that got shiny and grew by the second.

"I forgot there were two of you," she gasped as her trigger finger lost the ability to maintain a steady grip. "Ironic."

"Shit!" Tali gasped as she dove out of the way.

Sheri's finger jerked and the sensitive hair-trigger went off, sounding very much like a cannon as a chunk of plaster exploded where Tali's head had been.

Before she could react, another shot rang out and the side of Sheri's head exploded.

Bits of bone and gray gelatinous brain matter rained over Tali, clinging to her hair and covering her face in gore as Sheri's body jerked and slammed lifelessly to the floor, the gun falling out of her limp fingers.

Tali focused on the gun as it spun on the floor, slowing until the barrel pointed directly at her.

"You owe me your ass," Angel said as she walked over to the inert form bleeding on the floor and spit in her face.

"Next time, try not to splatter her over me," Tali joked weakly. "Kye is going to kill me over his leather."

"Whatever."

Angel stood staring at the body as a tear rolled down her face.

"You knew her?" Tali asked as she rose to her feet, wiping gore off of her face and slinging Sheri's remains onto the floor.

"That's the bitch that carried my baby away from me. She laughed while she did it."

"I'm…I don't know what to say."

"Then shut the fuck up," Angel said as she pushed past Tali and all but ran in the opposite direction.

Still wiping bits of Sheri out of her eyes, Tali took one last look at the dead woman and knew Bri would not like this.

Not one bit.

* * * * *

Bri heard the gunshots and immediately moved in the direction they had come from.

Breaking into a run, she exploded from the room she was exploring and raced into the hallway, gun at the ready.

Something dropping over her head was the last thing she expected.

"Quick!" Marti hissed as she tried to hold onto a struggling Bri. "I can't hold her arms!"

Waiting outside the room, Marti and a few like-minded angels jumped the taller woman as she emerged from the room.

Using a bedspread, they managed to get her covered, but it was a struggle to keep her that way.

Two more pairs of arms joined in, holding her gun arm down, while another equipped with silk scarves struggled to bind the woman.

"I can't hold her much longer!" Marti complained as the woman, ever silent, began flexing and bucking, planning her escape.

"She moves too damn much!" CeeJai, a dancer-in-training under Marti, complained. "I can't get a grip."

"She's going to kill us!" a voice wailed and Marti shot the owner a withering glance.

"She's right," Bri hissed from underneath the blackness of the spread.

How dare these bitches try and trap her? She would see to them all when she was done. She may even get Sheri to do that 'whip the skin off an inch at a time' trick she so enjoyed.

She felt the brush of silk against her wrist but maintained her grip on her gun. She expanded her body as much as she could. She had enough sense not to try and fire while blind—she might hit her own people.

As soon as the silk was looped, she felt the bindings tighten around her wrist, and with a shove she toppled over, moving her finger just far enough not to activate the hair trigger.

She hit the ground hard and the breath whooshed out of her chest.

She heard giggles, light feminine giggles, and then footsteps running away.

"Trussed like some damned roast at a butcher shop," she groused as she began to twist her wrist and ease her body out of her confines.

"Stupid bitches," she hissed as the ropes slackened enough for her to begin working them down her body. "Never even checked to see if I was adding girth."

It was the oldest trick in the book; expand your body so that when you relaxed and let your body sink to its normal size, the ropes would be slack.

But then, she thought as the ropes slid to her ankles, they were trying to slow me down, not stop me.

The scarves at her feet, she whipped the spread off and stood, a scowl on her face.

They'd wrinkled her suit.

They'd mussed her hair.

They must die.

Chapter Thirty-Eight

"Scatter!"

At Marti's command, the women who had assisted her in tying up Bri broke in different directions. They all raced to their chosen hiding spots.

If Balthazar did not die this evening, they could disavow any knowledge of the goings on here and wait for another day for their vengeance, and with that, their freedom.

"I'm going with you," CeeJai insisted as she raced beside Marti.

"You may be running to your death," she warned as she raced along the halls, never missing a stride. "That won't hold Bri for long and I know she's going to want revenge. She could be after us even now."

"Yeah, but what other choice do I have? Stick around and be another Chari, waiting to get popped? I'd rather meet my end here instead of waiting for a living death."

"Right on."

The women ran, darting through the halls, marveling at the sheer size of this hotel, as they looked for Angel and Tali.

They slammed into something that knocked them both off of their feet.

"Fuck!" a feminine voice snorted as they fell to the ground in a tangle of arms and legs.

Before the word finished echoing though the hall, a single shot fired and a metallic sounding plink was heard, like something metal had been struck.

It had.

The sprinklers began to shower them with rain, the sound of it almost deafening among the squeals from the startled women.

"Nice shot, Mr. Magoo," Tali hissed at Angel, who managed a blush despite the fact her hair was dripping with water and hair spray.

"I was trying to improve your look, Frank-en-furter!" Angel snorted back, as she checked her grip on her gun and thumbed the safety on.

That taken care of, she swiped the long strands of her hair back behind her head, and swept at the water falling on her face.

Tali was doing no better as mascara and liner ran in black rivers down her face.

Snorting and shaking her head like a cat, she rose to her feet and grimaced as she saw Marti and another woman staring at her as if she had grown another head.

"What?"

There was another moment of silence.

"Are…these the people who are supposed to be saving our asses?" CeeJai asked as she looked up at the unimpressive sight before her.

"Um, yeah," Marti answered, ignoring the scowl both women shot her.

But it was the screech that made them all move.

"My clothes! My hair!"

"Bri!" they all exclaimed at the same time. After a glance at each other, they all took off in the opposite direction.

"Go get her!" CeeJai yelled as she kept stride with the women.

"When she calms down!" Angel replied as they turned another corner. "Why borrow trouble?"

"Our great heroes," CeeJai said rather loudly to Marti as they continued to run.

"Wanna do it by yourself?" Angel returned. "We can go home, you know. Kye has Balthazar and we really are here just keeping Bri and her goons off of your tails."

A sudden explosion made them all hit the deck.

Four women slid in the build-up of water, splashing and leaving quite a wake behind them as they all dove for cover.

Tali felt the heat of the bullet whiz past her face a moment before Angel rolled over and returned fire, twice.

Just as the sound of the second explosion faded away, the water abruptly stopped, leaving the women staring at an enraged Bri.

Her hair dripping in her face and her clothes sticking wetly to her body, Bri looked mad enough to spit the bullets she was planning to shoot at them. Chest heaving and face scrunched into an evil countenance, Bri threw her gun to the side and rushed the women.

"You bitches!" she screamed before she broke into an impressive sprint for a woman wearing five-inch heels.

Before anyone could make a move, Tali rose to her feet and raced headlong to meet her charge. Screaming out her rage, she launched herself into a drop kick, her right leg extended fully, her left tucked neatly underneath her.

Bri abruptly spun, with the grace of a ballerina, and missed the devastating kick by mere inches.

Spinning around to face her enraged opponent, Tali came face to face with a woman she hoped never to see again.

"Bri."

"Tali. Still not dead?" the other woman hissed before she stepped forward and delivered a reverse roundhouse to Tali's chest, easily balancing in her heels.

Tali threw both arms up in an arm bar. Easily countering the move, she lashed out with her right leg, hoping to knock the larger woman to the ground.

But Bri jumped up, threw her body vertical while swinging her free leg around, neatly connecting with Tali's face and knocking her sideways to the ground.

"I taught you that," Bri hissed after she regained her stance, legs apart, knees slightly bent.

"How could I have forgotten," Tali growled as she launched herself to her feet and took a defensive position.

Smiling, Bri gave a slight hop, then kicked her right leg straight up, bringing it down into an ax kick, aiming for the top of Tali's head.

Swinging her right arm forward, she easily blocked the kick, then with the same arm, delivered a harsh chop to Bri's solar plexus.

Predictably, Bri jerked forward, then Tali swung her knee up, connecting with the other woman's chin.

Bri flew back and landed on her butt in a puddle of soggy carpet, dazed for a moment, shaking her head, tying to clear out the fog threatening to take over her mind.

"Run!" Tali screamed to the three wide-eyed women in the temporary lull in the fighting. "Get out of here, or go and help Kye. This bitch is mine!"

Before she could turn around, the bitch in question jumped her, wrapping both arms around her, pinning her arms to her sides and lifting her off of the ground.

Tali grunted as the air hissed out of her body.

Legs pedaling, she tried to kick Bri in the shins or at least knock her off balance.

But Bri expected that maneuver, and had centered herself well.

In desperation, Tali threw her head back with all the strength in her body, blindly aiming for Bri's nose.

The pained gasp and the sound of bone grinding, not to mention the fire that exploded in the back of her head, told her she had made her mark.

Ignoring the eye-watering pain, she drew her head down and delivered another blow, this time gaining her release as Bri's arms loosened.

Not giving her a second to recover, Tali spun around, swinging her right leg around, and kicked Bri in the side of her face, knocking the woman to the side.

As she regained her balance, she looked down at the woman who had terrified others for so long, and wondered what she was ever afraid of.

The woman lay in a puddle of pinkening water, pinkening because of the blood that ran freely from her broken nose. Already her eyes were beginning to darken and bruise and Tali knew the woman would have one hell of a shiner.

Snorting, she turned to walk away.

Then Bri reminded her why people were so terrified of her.

Some unknown instinct made her duck, just as a bullet whizzed over her head.

"You think you could get rid of me that easily?" Bri hissed through her clogged nose as she swiped the blood away from her face.

When faced with an enraged woman with a broken nose and a gun, Tali made the only choice she felt made sense.

She ran, zigzagging down the hall, ducking and dodging as Bri gave chase.

She hoped she could lose Bri in the maze of halls up ahead.

Chapter Thirty-Nine

"Fuckin' come out and play with me! Fucking tease!" Balthazar screamed as he stood in the large corner suite he had set up as his office.

Blood ran freely down his face and soaked what was left of his shirt. He left a trail of shredded black silk wherever he stepped, bits and pieces of his shirt and pants lying on the wet carpeted floor.

His arms were flexed to the max, massive veins showing clearly through the skin as blood flowed through them.

His eyes were an eerie shade of red that had bled into the whites. That combined with his heavy breathing and twisted visage gave him the look of a rampaging demon.

His nostrils flared as he followed the trail of vanilla and cinnamon, followed the chanting, followed his tormentor into what appeared to be a dead end.

The sprinklers sending cold showers down upon them had been a surprise, almost as much as their abrupt stop. Now it was time to bring this game to an end.

Levitating above, Kye slowly twisted his hair into a long braid, the tinkling bells he had placed on the end signaling the end of his game. He would not have gotten as far as he had if the bastard had just looked up.

At the sound, Balthazar's gaze flew up and locked onto the small dark shadow that hovered above him, as a vanilla and cinnamon scented drop of water landed on his nose.

"A fuckin' kid!" he snarled as he clenched his fists and prepared to leap.

Before he could move, a small ball of leather and flesh launched itself at him, hitting him squarely in the chest and knocking him on his ass.

Snarling, he leapt to his feet, his hand reaching out, faster than the eye could follow, and left a string of furrows down Kye's cheek.

Laughing, Balthazar lifted his fingers and slowly lapped the blood from his fingers as the small man stood there, staring at him.

"Your blood flows through my veins, cub. I can track you now, you and your Master who sent you."

"Funny," Kye answered as he slowly licked drops of blood from his own fingers. "I was thinking the same thing."

Balthazar looked stunned for a moment, then reached up to feel identical slashes on his face, from his cheekbone to his lip.

"Touché', cub," Balthazar giggled with madness as his eyes glowed in bloodlust. "No one has ever been able to do that before. I'll be proud to carry your blood, after I take away your life."

Kye snorted as he balanced his body.

"You doubt me?"

"Your taint already runs through my veins," Kye snarled as he bent over and launched himself into the air, his body spinning in a perfect circle as he spun like an arrow towards his target. In mid-air he suddenly spun and aimed his feet towards his target.

Balthazar stepped back to avoid the flying feet, but discounted the danger of the hair, as the long braid with its wickedly tinkling bells slashed across his face, opening the skin above his eyes like a small blood-drooling mouth.

Balthazar's startled hands went to his face while his gaze shot to Kye.

"Who the fuck are you?"

"What? Don't recognize me without my breechclout?"

Before he could recover, Kye jumped and delivered a snap kick to his chin, knocking him into a neat backwards arch before he again landed on his ass.

"What the hell are you talking about?" Balthazar asked, as he again leapt to his feet, seemingly unfazed by the attack.

"Does this ring a bell?" Kye whispered in his native language, startling the man as his eyes opened wide. "Think back, you bastard. About a hundred and fifty years."

"You!"

"Remembering, are we?" he sneered, as he leapt forward, creating rivers of blood on Balthazar's chest before he could swat him away.

"You fucking Indian!"

"You do remember," Kye growled as he ran his fingers slowly down his face, from forehead to lips, making war paint out of his enemy's blood.

"I thought you would have died at your brother's hand. Stupid redskin bastard."

"Oh, he died, the same way my mother died. The same way my father died. Dead is dead, Balthazar. It's time for me to send you on the same journey."

Balthazar threw back his head and his laughter filled the room.

"I remember you as well as your mother. The Chinky-eyed bitch, right? Man, she was a good lay. I had her squealing under me like a good bitch in heat should. And your father, prime piece of ass. Too bad I never got a chance to fuck it before I slit his lying In-jinn," he sneered the insult, "throat. That was almost as much fun."

Balthazar taunted Kye, waiting to see if the younger man would lose control and attack him.

"Lying?"

"What I can't understand, Tonto, is how you managed to survive. I know your brother turned out to be a big waste of time, bad blood or something. Must be all the sage you people smoked. But an eating machine like that won't give a damn if you are brother or not. He should have torn your throat out and gone looking for more. Yet here you stand, all red cheeked and healthy. There is no justice in the world, I'll tell you. No justice at all."

"Oh, there is justice," Kye responded as he watched the man try and taunt him into attacking. Kye had waited too long for this to forget his plan, his reason for living…no, existing…all those years. "That is what I am, Balthazar. I am Justice, living vengeance, come to rain all over your undead ass."

"Yes, I can see that you will try, and fail like the rest," Balthazar muttered as he touched the damage to his chest, glad to note that it, like his face, had started healing. "But the why is what I don't understand."

"It's the power, Balthazar. The power you were too stupid to see."

"What are you referring to, boy? Be quick. I have to kill you and take care of a mess."

"A mess I created, Oh Wise One," Kye sneered. "You are stupid, a stupid forked-tongue white-eyes that couldn't recognize true power when you saw it."

"I recognized it. Apparently your father loved his power over the lives of his sons and wife. Ignorant bastard. If he had shared…"

"You would have killed us anyway," Kye cut in.

"Probably right, but at least the trip into those forsaken mountains would not have been a waste."

"Like I said, you ignorant stupid bastard, you never recognized true power."

"I told you, boy, that… Well, I'll be damned. The old man didn't lie after all. He really was just teaching the way of it. Neither he nor his oldest papoose had any idea what true power was."

"Apparently, the talent skips a few generations from time to time," Kye chuckled as the green and gold in his eyes warred for dominance. "Apparently, you seemed to have overlooked the second son."

"Indeed, I did," Balthazar breathed as he stared at the man. "But your brother…"

"Bit me, passed this taint, your taint, on to me. My talent prevented me from changing all the way, but it looks like you created a new creature, Balthazar. Or should I say, Daddy?"

"My blood runs through your veins?"

"Soon your blood will run on the floor, you bastard!"

"You should be thanking me!" Balthazar whispered as he backed away. He could feel…something, building in the boy. Something foreign, like the thing he chased up into the mountains in the first place. Had it been lying dormant in this second child all these years? All these years when it could have been his!

"For murdering my family and turning me into a freak?" Kye screamed as he threw out his hand, and an invisible fist slammed, then pinned Balthazar to the wall across from him, the dark shadows cast by the two windows across from him bracketing him in a paler shadow.

Balthazar could not move. But he could talk. Maybe he could talk him into making a mistake.

"I made you what you are, boy! Think! I shaped you into my own powerful image."

"An image that is now pinned to a wall like a spider in a web. You speak as if you were a god, Balthazar, a true god. If that is the case, then it's time for a sacrifice."

"I made you!" Balthazar shouted as Kye slowly walked towards him. "I created you!"

"So now the son kills the father."

As he walked, Kye pulled a dagger from his boot, and took aim.

* * * * *

It was the masculine screams that led the three women, plus Tali down the hall towards the far suite of rooms.

Even Bri turned in that direction, suddenly her attack on Tali not that important anymore.

* * * * *

"You sadistic bastard!" Balthazar screamed as Kye drove the dagger through his wrist, the sound of bone grating on steel loud in the room, even above his pained howls.

"See? I do take after you," Kye commented as he gave the knife a twist, making Balthazar suck in a deeper breath, and securing him to the wall as the hilt touched his skin.

"We could rule this place together!" Balthazar panted, his eyes wide with pain and his chest heaving, pleading with a mad man. Pale red drops began to appear on his forehead as he sweated blood in the face of the man who had stalked him for so long. For the first time, Balthazar felt a very real fear.

Kye calmly pulled another dagger from his boot and thoughtfully ran the tip over his face, his eyes contemplating the man pinned to the wall.

"Nah, I think not."

Balthazar had time to suck in a deep breath before Kye grabbed his other wrist.

"I think I'm going to enjoy this."

He plunged the dagger home, through flesh and bone and the wallboard that supported him. Drove the dagger in until the hilt kissed the bloodied skin of his wrist.

Balthazar's shriek sounded piercing and inhuman as the windows began to shake.

"You will not get away with this!" he screamed as a fresh wave of pain pierced his body.

Kye had drawn another dagger and was now cutting away what was left of the shirt, baring the pale flesh in its entirety to his eyes.

"Who will stop me?" Kye asked as he suddenly released his otherworldly hold on Balthazar and his body sagged against the weight of the blades imbedded in his body.

"Ah! Fuck! No!" Balthazar screamed as his eyes slammed shut to try and ride out these fresh waves of pain.

When he again opened them, the red haze of bloodlust had faded, leaving only fear and pain behind.

Then hope filled him as he noticed Bri's still form from across the room.

"Bri!" he screamed. "Help me!"

"Here I thought I would be the one to do it," the woman muttered, her voice sounding odd with her ruined nose.

"Want some?" Kye asked, turning around, dagger drawn, as he waited for the woman's reaction. "Death, I mean."

"Uh," in a reflex she raised her gun, but at a glance from Kye, the weapon went spinning across the room out of her hands. "No, thank you. Carry on. I'll just see myself out."

Tugging on her soaked, ruined jacket, Bri turned on her five-inch heels and stalked out of the room.

"Fuck!" Balthazar screamed with some feeling. "Bri! Get your ass back in here!"

"Looks like it's just you and me." Kye smiled as those words rolled off his tongue in Crow.

Whatever color left in Balthazar's face drained out to the floor, along with his blood as he stared into the eyes of a true killer, a true mad man.

If the old saying was true, 'those the gods would favor, they first drive mad', then Kye had the blessings of every deity known and unknown to man.

Chapter Forty

Tali, Angel, and the two dancers skidded around the corner in time to see Bri leaving the room they had tried so hard to find.

"Shit!" CeeJai gasped, causing the woman to turn and face the quartet that bungled into the death shrine, then walk away.

"Hail, hail!" Balthazar whispered, surprise in his voice. "The gang's all here."

"Oh my god!" CeeJai backed up, holding onto Marti as if the woman was a lifeline. "What the fuck...?"

"Kye!" Tali gasped, her eyes going from her lover to the man pinned to the wall.

"Mother and daughter, united at last."

"What the fuck are you talking about?"

"Did you fuck them both?" he taunted Kye. "I never kept it in the family like that. Too Royal Family, too West Virginia. Too...gauche."

Balthazar knew he was dead. Now he was desperately trying to anger Kye into killing him quicker. Maybe one of the women would...

"What are you saying?" Angel stepped forward, a sneaking suspicion filling her mind.

"You mean, you don't know?"

At her confused look, Balthazar threw back his head in laughter.

"Oh, this is too rich," he gasped, trying to catch his breath. The pain was catching up with him, and his little burst of humor aided it in its return.

"What...?" Tali began, but he continued to speak.

"You found her, I see," Balthazar cackled. "You found your daughter, Angel. You should thank me for raising her the way I did. Tali turned out to be such a spunky fighter."

Angel turned her eyes to the woman she had alternately hated and relied upon these past few days. Horror and awe filled those dark orbs, spilling over into tears as her mind accepted what Balthazar was saying.

"Tali? My daughter?" Suddenly Bri's earlier remarks made sense.

"I gave her such a beautiful name, too. Tali, as in Tali marks, The Tali marks. The thousandth baby I took and created in my image. Of course, I didn't know about our red-skinned friend here. I appear to be one number off."

"You bastard!" Angel screamed as she raised her gun and pointed it at his heart.

Now! Balthazar thought as he closed his eyes and prepared to face the end of his torment.

"No!" Kye screamed as sound exploded in the room and the bullet launched itself from the gun.

When nothing else happened, Balthazar opened his eyes and stared in amazement at the bullet spinning inches from his chest.

He turned his shocked eyes to Kye, who had one hand out, holding the bullet in stasis.

"Damn you!" he growled. He watched the end of his quick death when the bullet clinked to the floor.

"No, damn you." Then he turned towards the women. "Angel, come here."

"You bastard!" she shrieked at Kye, flinging the gun away. "Why didn't you let me kill him? Why?"

"Angel," he repeated, the command in his voice obvious. "Come here."

Maybe it was the tone, or their long friendship, but Angel shut her mouth and stalked over to Kye, tears running down her face. Impatiently, she brushed her wet hair back, exposing her scar for all to see.

"Why didn't you let me kill him?" she muttered as he took her in his arms. "Why?"

"Because a bullet is too easy." His voice was cold, as cold as the steel of the blade he pressed into her hand.

Understanding blossomed in her eyes as she pulled away from Kye and turned towards Balthazar.

"Get him where it hurts," he chuckled with an evil laugh.

"No!" Balthazar screamed as he saw more than an unholy glint in her eyes.

"You maniacal prick," Angel hissed as she stepped closer to the man who had turned her into the ugly monster that she believed herself to be. "You took everything away from me!"

Balthazar remained silent as the woman ranted at him, worried about what she would do. Maybe…?

"You are a poor fuck, Angel. You are a poor fuck, an ugly excuse for a woman, and a stupid bitch to add to the total package. A package you couldn't give away."

"Shut up!" she screamed.

"I did Tali a favor. What would she have turned out to be if you had raised her? Another stupid whore waiting to fuck a stranger for a kind word?"

"Shut up!"

"You are pathetic!"

Balthazar saw her intent before she moved. He read murder in her eyes. Where would she strike? Head, neck, or heart. Whatever way, it would be a deathblow. It would send him away from the one called Kye, the one he created, the one who demanded the most painful death, denying him his final revenge.

He closed his eyes and grinned to himself.

"You bastard!"

A feminine shriek, but the wrong tone.

Balthazar opened his eyes as Tali screamed and rushed him.

Kye grabbed her around her waist, but she struggled in his arms.

Balthazar grinned at his final act of destruction, pleased that the sound of their pain would carry him into the next world.

He giggled as he watched them struggle, momentarily forgetting Angel and her dagger.

The little bitch Tali was more amusing and definitely more entertaining. He almost forgot the pain in his arms and wrists.

But his eyes widened as he saw her pluck something from the back of Kye's hair.

He caught a glint of steel, a thin sliver of it, a moment before the loss of the vision in his right eye.

All was silent for a moment, then pain exploded in his brain, a pain so sharp that he could not even draw breath.

"No eyes! Eyes are the windows to the soul, Balthazar. Yours are black and empty. You don't deserve sight, you bastard. You don't deserve to have anything. You deserve to roast."

By this time, Balthazar found that he could take small breaths and control the intense pain.

"Damn," he whispered. The needle did not penetrate his brain.

He had trained Tali well. Maybe too well.

"You don't deserve eyes," Tali continued, chest heaving as she hung limply in Kye's arms.

"Nice shot," Kye whispered as he hugged Tali to his chest.

"I could claw his eyes out for what he did!"

"Can't even kill right. You are your mother's daughter, Tali. Another stupid whore."

This time, the scream came from Angel. She had heard enough.

Chortling gleefully, Balthazar closed his eyes and waited for his death. Head, neck or heart. Those were all guaranteed deaths.

But it was not his head she struck, nor his neck or his heart. She aimed lower, a lot lower.

"Arghhhhhh!"

Balthazar's inhuman shriek filled the air and rattled the glass in the windows as he rent the air with his agony.

Again and again, Angel stabbed Balthazar, his blood flying in her face and coating her body.

"Please! Stop! Gods, stop it!" Balthazar screamed over and over as Angel turned his crotch into a red ruin.

"You took my baby from me!" she screamed as she stabbed, sending flesh and blood to spew on the floor. "You took my life from me! Die, you bastard! Die!"

She stabbed over and over again, delighting in the screams that filled the air, in the feel of his blood running over her face. Delighting in his slow and painful death.

Balthazar's mouth opened, a low groaning sound emerged, as his body shook under her blows.

All he could feel was white-hot pain. It ran in rivers through his body, stealing his breath and his will to live.

Each slice of the blade seemed to be a thousand and never had he felt such an intense agony.

Then the blows stopped.

Balthazar groaned and writhed against the wall, forgetting the pain in his arms and his eye. Never had he prayed for death since he had become one of the undead. But now he prayed that something would intervene, a humiliating situation for one such as he.

"Balthy," he heard but could only moan. "Balthy, open your eyes, well, your eye."

It was him, his ill-gotten spawn that had ruined him and all that he worked for.

"Open it, or I'll give the ladies all my knives and pins and daggers and walk away."

His eye, he was ashamed to say, shot open at the threat.

"Very good," Kye purred.

The man stood over him, the women huddled together in a group, the whore and her whelp staring at each other searchingly.

"You and I both know that if I stop, you'll heal and will be as good as new come the next moonrise."

A smile lit Balthazar's features, gray from the amount of blood loss. If he could make them go, convince him to leave him there…

"I feel the sun, Balthazar," Kye whispered.

And indeed, when he thought past the all-consuming pain that racked his body in shudders, he could feel the stinging press of a new day dawning.

"I didn't realize we had been in here for so long."

Balthazar said nothing, but shifted his head to get a better view of his tormentor.

"But now that the day is dawning, I am glad that I stuck around."

Balthazar looked askance at the man, but he had turned away and walked over to the ladies.

"Leave me," he said in a sad tone. "Leave this place and forget about me. Forget what you have seen here."

Marti made as if to protest, but CeeJai grabbed her arm and pulled her from the room.

"But if you kill him, what happens to us?" Marti demanded, resisting CeeJai's pull.

"Do you want me to let him live?" Kye asked as he stared at the indignant woman.

"No," she hissed, looking inward. "Death is preferable."

"Then we are agreed."

Marti nodded, then turned to Tali. "I am so sorry," she whispered as tears filled her eyes. "If I had known what Chari was up to...I could have..." She sighed as she shook her head, sadness making her bleak despite their obvious victory. "So much time wasted."

"Not your fault," Tali turned away from her mother long enough to whisper. "She is not suffering anymore."

"No suffering," Marti repeated as CeeJai tugged on her arm.

"Not anymore," Angel added as she reached out her hand to touch her daughter's face, the daughter she had thought dead for so many years.

Nodding, Marti allowed CeeJai to pull her from the room.

"You too," Kye said as he looked at the two remaining women.

"What are you going to do?" Tali demanded, turning away from her mother.

"I am ending this."

"What are you going to do?" Anger and frustration showed in her voice as she walked over to Kye, slamming her fists into his chest.

"What needs to be done."

"What? Tell me! Fucking what?"

"Suicide," Balthazar whispered through bloodless lips as he began to chuckle. "Noble savage to the end."

"Is he right?" Tali demanded as she stared at the man she had come to crave in her life. "Is that what you are planning?"

"Tali," he sighed as he gripped her fists in his hand. "I don't belong here."

"You belong with me!"

"I was an accident, Tali. I was an aberration probably created to get rid of the monster creating the monsters."

"No!" she shouted. "I refuse to believe that! Do you hear me? I refuse!"

"There is no other way."

"Why? Why not, Kye?"

"Because," he shouted as he turned and gave her his back, his scared back. "What good am I to you? What good are you to me? Will you stick around and watch me slowly try and turn you into my next meal? Will you ignore the laughter of others as you age and I stay the same? What will you do when you get tired of me looking the way I do, Tali? When I bury your mother and hold your hand as all of the people you know die and I stay the same? Will you get jealous? Will you grow to hate me more as the years age your body and steal away your youth and beauty?"

"I would never…"

"What will you do when I want to fuck you like some wild thing, Tali? When my desire for blood ruins my common sense and I find myself replacing food for sex?"

"Stop it!"

"I am telling you the truth, Tali. You were something for me to use, something for me to fuck and use as bait."

Tali gasped, then straightened reached out and grabbed him by the shoulder.

Instinctively, he pivoted, striking out at the thing that touched his blind side.

Instinctively, Tali blocked, her arm knocking his fist away as it came inches from her face.

"Say that to my face, Kye," she hissed. "You don't know how to be dishonest. Tell me to my face and I'll leave!"

"Go!" he shouted. "Go away and leave me!"

"Tell me!" Tali shouted, her palm swinging around and connecting with the side of his face, smearing away Balthazar's blood mask and reddening his dark skin.

Kye took the blow, accepted it as the force of it turned his face and knocked him back a step.

He closed his eyes for only a moment, then the glowing green orbs stared back at her.

"I...I can't! All right? I can't! You make me wish for things that cannot happen, Tali. You make me want to hope. Hope is dangerous."

"You love me!"

"I don't know what love is!"

"Do you know what it isn't?"

They both turned to look at the husk of Balthazar that still writhed and snapped at them from the wall.

"Fucking idiots," Balthazar laughed, then moaned as a cough shook his body. "If it was me..."

He never got to finish that statement because with a scream of rage, Kye pulled another dagger from his boot and raced at the barely alive man.

Kye's knife caught him in the mouth, pinning his cheek to the wall.

"Shut the fuck up!" he screamed finally losing control.

Turning back to Tali, he screamed, "What if I become what he is? What if I turn into that, Tali! I have the power; I can hear the whisper of my heart telling me to take things I can't have. If I give in, will I become like him? If I give in to my heart and stay with you, is that not the beginning?"

"No!" she screamed as she resisted the urge to shake him. "This is nothing like that! Kye, you have a soul! You have a heart! You have a mind, and if you start to turn, I'll fucking kill you myself!"

"The aging, Tali! Nothing will change that!"

"Make me what you are!"

Kye staggered back from her, as if she'd struck him a mortal blow.

"You don't know what you're saying," he replied, his voice hoarse.

"I know what I just asked you for! I don't care, Kye! I want to be with you!"

"Will you hate me when your mother starts looking like dinner?"

"I...I will be what you are!"

"You can never be what I am Tali! Look at what I did!" he shouted, pointing to Balthazar's pinned form. "I am just as much a monster as he is!"

"You are not! You are Kye! You are my defender!"

"I am nothing. I am what he made."

Kye's shoulders slumped and he turned to face Tali again.

"Please, don't make this any harder. Please, just go. Take your mother and go."

Before she could answer, Marti burst into the room.

"The cops!"

Turning to Tali, Kye gripped her shoulders and pulled her close to him, as close as they could get without their souls shedding their skin and merging as one.

Then his mouth slammed down on hers.

He kissed her with all the anguish and frustration he could feel. He kissed her with all the hope he'd briefly held, and with the passion he had discovered in her, like no other.

He put his desires, his brief joy, his burgeoning feelings of love, his lust, and he thrust it all inside her with his kiss.

Then he slowly pulled away from her, as if reluctant to let go of her tender lips.

"Kye," she began, but he kissed her quickly again, silencing her effectively.

"You can have my leather," he whispered to her as they broke apart.

A sound, mingled laughter mixed with a sound of soul-deep pain exploded from Tali's lips. Tears rolled down her face, tracking through the smudged lipstick and the muck that stained her.

"It...it must be...love," she sniffled as her chest heaved and she fought to hold in her screams of denial.

She had lost him.

"Angel," he called, still gripping Tali's shoulders.

"Yes, Kye?" she asked as she walked to stand beside the man who had offered her life, destroyed her worst enemy, and had given her back her daughter.

"Get her out of here. Out a back way, if you can. The police will never believe this."

"Kye," she began.

"Did I keep my promise to you?" he asked, suddenly pushing Tali into Angel's arms. "Did I give you all that I promised?"

Angel held her daughter in her arms as she stared at the whimpering remains of a once great tyrant pinned on the wall.

"That and more."

"I promised you death, Angel. That is what he shall have. But I need you to do something for me."

"Anything."

"Take her and go."

"Kye..."

"Take her and go! Get her out of here! You know where my paperwork is, Angel. You both keep it. I won't need it anymore."

Without a word Angel nodded, and turned a sobbing Tali towards the door.

"There are others that need killing," he said as they reached the door. "You know what to do."

Angel stiffened, then nodded again, urging her daughter to follow Marti and exit the room.

Turning back to Balthazar, Kye smiled.

"Now, dawn is upon us, Father," he sneered, watching the wounds heal on Balthazar's body. "And it is time for us to leave this world."

He turned and walked over to the double windows that Balthazar faced, watched, as his one eye grew large in fright as Kye caressed the dark draperies.

"You know, one good thing you gave me was this strength, this agility, this speed. I can do anything, be anything, and I never have to hide from the sun."

He chuckled as Balthazar looked at him in amazement.

"Yup, I never had to run from the sun. It killed my brother, you know. One bite of me, one taste of my blood brought him somewhat back to himself, and he fled into the sunlight. I watched him burn and heal for days, Balthazar. Burned because of what you did and healed because of what my talent gave him. Now it's time for you to feel what he went through.

Balthazar struggled to free himself from the wall, tearing at his jaw, pulling at the knives, trying to voice an objection.

But Kye laughed as he reached up high and tore the curtains from their moorings.

Sunlight, bright and dawning, filled the room.

Instantly, Balthazar began to smolder.

As pained yowls emerged from his throat, more smoke, a thicker burning smoke, filled the room.

Kye smiled as he lowered himself, Indian style, in the center of the two windows, hidden in both light and dark, and watched the show.

A popping sound filled the air, and Balthazar's cries turned to shrieks as his skin began to bubble and ripple.

Then with a whooshing sound, his hair caught on fire. It quickly spread as his screams grew louder, and increased in intensity.

He was a ball of red-gold flame as Kye silently watched the destruction of a man he more than despised, more than hated.

Balthazar's body jerked and twisted against the knives holding him captive as the flesh was slowly burned from his body, until the screams stopped and all that was left was a burning shell that once housed a man.

As the smoke began to die down, Kye removed the last silver needle from his hair.

"Good bye, Father," he whispered as he plunged the sharp needle into his carotid.

Chapter Forty-One

"Get out of the way!"

Angel pushed through the throng of reporters and emergency personnel fighting to get inside the hotel. Finally she just gave up and let the crowd doing the mass exodus bit push her and Tali out the front door.

"Almost there, honey," she muttered to her daughter as they were pushed ahead.

Daughter.

Daughter?

Daughter!

Angel fought back the tears that were threatening to flood her face. She had her daughter! Kye had given her back her daughter!

Kye.

Damn.

"Here, baby," Angel muttered as she wrapped her arms tighter around her daughter. "We are almost there."

The new day's sun was almost blinding as they stepped out of the hotel and into the bright dawn of a new day.

"But..." Tali whispered, tears running through the smeared make-up on her face. "But Kye is in there."

"You are in shock, baby," Angel said, still trying to wrap her mind around the fact she was holding her little girl...and Kye was gone. "It'll be all right. We've got each other."

"Who said I wanted to claim you?" Tali snarled as she jerked away from Angel.

"Ungrateful bitch," Angel snarled back. "I've been mourning all these years for my daughter, then I find out it's you?"

"What's wrong with me?"

"You dress funny!"

"What?"

"And I don't like the company you keep!"

"What?"

"And...and you are such a bitch!"

"Then I guess the apple didn't fall far from the tree!"

Tali was trying to start an argument, to do anything to drive away the darkness threatening to take over her soul.

"To think I prayed for you," Angel growled as she scanned the area emergency personnel were herding them to.

"Ask and ye shall receive!"

"Bitch!"

"Whore!"

Slap!

"Oh baby!" Angel covered her mouth with her stinging hand. She had just struck her long-lost baby girl.

Tali stood there, a stunned look on her face, before tears began to flow in earnest.

"Angel," she cried as she stood there, body quivering in anguish. "He's really gone."

Angel lurched towards her, pulling her into her arms as harsh sobs began to wrack her body.

"He left me!" she cried. "He left me alone!"

Not knowing what to do, Angel rocked her daughter in her arms, trying to take on as much of her pain as she could.

"Why? Why, Angel, why?"

"His work was...done," Angel muttered, as she began to shake with her own sobs.

For a moment, they stood there, surrounded by a hustling mob, while they shared their grief.

But the moment was interrupted by a large man in a dingy T-shirt and work jeans.

"You look like you fit the description," he muttered as he tapped Angel on the shoulder. "Are you Tali?"

"My daughter," Angel answered, and felt a warm rush through her body as she muttered those words. "My daughter is Tali."

"Well, you got some woman named Mari in my cab, covered in blankets. She said to pick you up here. Who's gonna pay me?"

"I will," Angel said as Tali tried to pull herself together. "Looks like we got a ride home."

"What happened?" the cabbie asked as they followed him back to his car. "You all have a costume party that got out of control?"

"Something like that," Angel answered as they stopped beside his car and opened the back seat.

"Careful!" a voice hissed from inside. "You know better than that Tali! I could have had a sunstroke."

"She's just wasted," Angel called out as the cabbie climbed into the driver's seat. "She was supposed to meet us here, but I guess the party's over."

"Dead and over," Tali whispered as she carefully eased Mari over to take a seat.

Angel gave the driver the directions to Kye's apartment and they were on their way.

Tali looked back over her shoulder once at the hotel, teeming with life, and had to fight the urge to get out and start killing people at random. How dare they be alive when Kye was dead? Did they even know he gave his life for them, that he stopped an evil infection from spreading?

The rising sun gave no answers.

* * * * *

Hold me now!
I'm six feet from the edge and I'm thinking
Maybe six feet,
Ain't so far down

Tali lay on the bed, the large plush bed where Kye had made such sweet love to her.

She listened to the words by Creed, and slowly the tears rolled down her cheeks, dampening her pillow, creating a pool of anguish to lay her hot face upon.

She was drowning, sinking deeper and deeper into despair, so far down she never thought she would find her way out.

"It's been three days," Mari whispered to Angel as they stood in the doorway watching her mourn. "She needs something, but I don't know what to give her."

Tali tried to block out the voices of her two moms, one who had practically raised her from infancy, the other newly discovered.

She ignored them because they could never give her what she needed. They could never give her life back to her. He was probably a big pile of ash by now.

The media was all alight with stories of gang wars and whole-scale assassinations, but no one really knew the truth. Kye had given them that, at least.

Everyone was focusing on the international business tycoon who, along with several wives, had traveled to this country for a business deal.

Rumors also stated that the Mafia wanted in on his business. When he resisted, they pinned him to a wall and set him on fire.

His grieving widows were now seeing to their future by dividing up his somewhat substantial fortune among themselves and heading off to the great unknown.

The public was entranced as well as horrified by what had taken place. They pitied the poor families and called out for justice to be served.

Murder was bad for tourism.

The FBI said they would investigate, and that was about it.

But Marti did manage to call with the news that the women who were loyal to Balthazar had disappeared soon after they felt him die.

From the burning pain she described at the moment of his death, they would never forget his passing.

So, the ones who had assisted her and fought back, five in all, were dividing up his fortune and trying to go on with their lives.

"The world has changed so much in such a short time," the dancer sighed as she spoke over the phone. "I hope I am up to the challenge of keeping up."

"You will," was all Tali muttered, tears welling up in her eyes as she remembered what transpired in that hotel.

"They never said a word about his body," she quietly added and Tali knew she was speaking of Kye. "We will never forget what he did, Tali. You have our word on that. If you ever need us…"

"Thank you," Tali interrupted. "I'm sure you have things you must do now."

"You're right," Marti sighed. "But we'll stay in touch. If you need us…"

"I'll call."

That had been two days ago.

Since then, she had rifled through Kye's vast music collection, worn his old clothes, and defied anyone to try and drag her out of her misery.

She ignored the ringing of the phone, just as she ignored the two women who watched her worriedly from across the room.

She heard one of them answer, but again lost herself in the melancholy music.

Well, God, she thought, are you holding me now? Are you listening to me now? Where is my justice? Where is my Kye?

"Tali! Oh my God, Tali!" Mari screamed as she raced across the room and bounced on the bed.

"What now?" Tali sniffed, swiping at her wet cheeks with her palms. "Because if it's Marti, I don't feel like talking now."

"Oh Tali! That was the FBI!"

"What do they want?" she all but snarled.

Didn't people see that she wanted to be left alone?

"We have to go down there! Right now!"

"Don't you have people to bite or gangsters to throw out of windows or riots to incite?"

"They have our boy!"

"Boy?"

"They have him just out of critical care!"

"Boy?"

"Kye! They have Kye! He's alive!"

Chapter Forty-Two

"Tali!" Angel called as the frantic young woman barreled past the security desk and raced for the elevators, tears running in a constant stream down her face. "Calm down!"

Calm? How could she be calm? She had her security badge, she had the floor. Now all she needed was a damn elevator.

"Where is it?"

Tali wailed, tears of frustration running down her face as she ran into yet another obstacle that kept her away from her man. She slammed her fist against the button again, as if punishing it more would make the car move faster.

"Patience," Angel tried to soothe. "It'll only be a few moments more."

But the damn elevator was taking forever. It paused for a few moments between each floor as Tali stared up at the blinking lights, just to piss her off more.

"Fuck it," she hissed as she turned towards the wide doors that led to the stairs. "I'll walk. The eighth floor is not that far."

Even before she finished speaking, she sprinted to the aluminum doors and kicked them open.

"Tali!" Angel tried to call, but she was already gone, taking the steps two at a time.

She reached her floor, exploded from the staircase at a run, slamming the doors against the wall behind them, and skidded to a halt in front of the nurse's station.

"Where is he?" she all but screamed into the face of a nurse standing there. "I have to find him!"

She swiped at the tears running down her face, as she practically danced from foot to foot before the bemused woman.

The nurse smiled, used to this excited and impassioned reaction from family and friends of the patients she saw. Having someone on this floor, a step down from critical, was a major step. From the look of things, whoever this young woman was searching for was indeed well loved.

"Where is who, honey? I need a name before I can point you in the right direction."

"Kye!" she breathed, tears again rolling down her cheeks. "Kye Black or Dark or whatever the hell he is calling himself now!"

"Kye Noir?" she asked and Tali all but jumped in glee.

"That's it! Kye Noir! Please," she urged. "Please, tell me where he is."

"You must be Tali Rodgers."

"Tali...?"

Rodgers? It was Angel's last name. She had seen it on her driver's license once.

So now Angel had given her a name. It was strange to contemplate after all these years. She had just always been Tali.

First her mother had given her life, now she was giving her a name.

"Yes," she sniffled, again running her hands through the tears that just seemed to never want to stop. "I'm Tali Rodgers."

"He's been asking for you," the nurse smiled. "But those guys over there want a word with you first."

Tali turned in the direction the nurse pointed, spying three men milling around a door.

Damn them, she thought. They would not keep her away from her Kye.

Before she finished the thought, Tali rushed at the first of the men, a primal scream erupting from her throat as she launched herself into the air, clipping him neatly in the temple with her right foot and sending him flying unconscious to the floor.

She was after the second man instantly.

The second man, alerted and not as slow as the first, adjusted his stance to catch her around her waist.

She saw his ploy and easily sidestepped him, stopping behind him. As he turned to stop her, she gave a small leap, bringing up her left foot to connect neatly with his chin.

He flew a foot up in the air, before falling bonelessly beside his friend.

Even before he hit the ground, Tali had turned and now faced the last man.

But this man was no fool.

He had drawn his gun and was holding it in a two-hand grip as he tried to draw a bead on her.

"Freeze!" he bellowed as he tried to stare her down.

"Let me by!" she yelled back.

"I said…"

"Tali!" Angel screamed breathlessly as she raced around the small pile of dead-to-the-world men and stopped, panting, beside her daughter.

"Tali?" the man repeated, slowly lowering his weapon. "Tali Rodgers?"

"Yes," she cried, clenching her fists as she tried to devise any way around this man and get through the door he was guarding.

Sighing, the man holstered his weapon as he glared at her.

"I need to see some ID."

Tali almost cried out in frustration. Why would she have ID? She had always just been Tali. No ID required to be raised by a vampire!

"Here," Angel reached into her pocket and handed the man an ID.

She turned to stare at Angel as the guard stared between the picture her new mom had happily taken earlier, and her face.

Finally, he handed the laminated card back to her and nodded towards the door. Her worry and fear showed plainly on her tear-streaked face. His heart began to thaw a little.

"You can go in and see him, but as soon as you are done, young lady, we are going to have a chat about you assaulting my men."

"But…"

"The doctor is in there with him now," the man continued. "When you go in, please tell him to come out and check the men that you, um, removed from your path. I may even be able to persuade them not to press charges against you."

"After all," Angel chimed in. "They did get their asses kicked by a girl half their size."

"Your daughter?" he asked as he glanced at the idiots who had underestimated a girl and paid for it. They were beginning to stir and groan. There was still life there after all.

"Chip off of the old block."

"Damn odd chip," the man countered as the door opened and Tali slipped inside.

* * * * *

"Kye," Tali whispered, her arms automatically rising as she reached for the figure that seemed dwarfed by the large bed. Tears ran unchecked down her face as she walked, as if in a trance, deeper into the room, her whole attention on the man who lay there, a silent, still lump in a large sea of white.

"He really is lucky to be alive," the doctor commented as he watched the sobbing young woman approach in something akin to shock. "He is severely anemic and then there is the blood loss…"

His voice trailed off as she ignored him, her total attention on the man in the bed.

"Well then," the doctor smiled as he made his way to the door and quietly slipped out. "What the fuc…" he was heard to mutter as he stepped outside, but the closing of the door cut off his words.

"Kye?" Tali whispered again as she stepped up to the bed, her eyes seeing past the wires and tubes that surrounded her man, her eyes only seeing him.

"I should have died," he whispered, his voice weak, as his eyes slowly opened to look up at her.

"Oh, Kye," she gasped as she stared into his eyes, watched the green and gold war and swirl in them as he looked back at her.

"I should be dead, Tali," he whispered again. His hand shifted under the covers as he slowly snaked it out of the blanket and reached for her.

"No, Kye," she countered. "You should be here, with me." Her whole body trembled as she took his hand into hers, her tears and her grief easing as she felt the warmth of his body touch the cold places that had begun to freeze the moment she thought he was gone from her for good. "How…?"

"They say I am anemic. That I have a low blood sugar count and that I appear to have some strange form of leukemia." He tilted his head in the direction of the bags that hung suspended from his IV pole like so many pouchy tree ornaments. "They tell me that I am not as lucky as my father."

"Your father?" she gasped. "I thought your father was…?"

"Dead. According to them, he died stuck on a wall, the work of organized crime, no less," he sighed as he closed his eyes. "The Mafia must be big this year. But they twisted it around and found some story to suit their needs."

"But how did they come to that conclusion?"

"DNA. Apparently when the old boy changed my brother, his taint affected his DNA. When my brother bit me, I was altered as well. The old bastard and I seem to have the same genetic make-up. So they put two and two together and came up with a failed assassination attempt. They are seeing gangsters everywhere these days."

"Oh, Kye." She giggled as she sat on the bed and inhaled his scent. Of course there was that hospital antiseptic scent, but underneath it, was the faint scent of vanilla and cinnamon.

"I told them the truth. I told them I was there to meet the man who made me. Now they believe I was caught up in his assassination attempt, that I was intended to die watching him burn, as an example to people who don't do what they want."

Even Tali had to shake her head at that one.

"So I was hauled here and plugged with plasma and glucose until I couldn't see straight. Of course they noticed that odd thing with my blood and want to spend all of their time studying me. That's when they called my house and got in contact with you."

"You had me so scared," she whispered as she reached out to caress his face. "I thought I had lost you, Kye."

"I should be dead, Tali," he sighed as he shifted in the bed to stare at her. "I have no reason to be here. What am I supposed to do, Tali?" The anguish in his voice was almost too much for her to bear.

"I have lived my life trying to kill the big evil thing. That is all, Tali. That was what I was designed for. That is what I was created for. Now that the big evil thing is gone, I find I have no purpose. I have no reason for being here, yet God will not let me die."

"You are mine," Tali said quietly, surely. There were no tears in her eyes now and her voice carried a seriousness that it previously lacked. "You were made for me."

Kye looked into her eyes and read determination there.

"Tali," he began. "I am not exactly the most stable guy around," he warned.

"Tell me something I don't know."

"I am being serious, Tali."

"Shut up."

"What?"

"Shut up, you selfish bastard!" Tali hissed as she threw his hand back to the bed. "What the fuck is wrong with you? You just got a second chance, Kye. You got a second chance. How many people Balthazar brushed up against can say the same? Your mother, your father...your brother? No. But you get to start over, Kye. You get a chance at life! Not only that, you get another chance at me, you son of a bitch!"

He blinked as he looked up at her, for once at a loss for words.

"That's right, you get a chance. Who said I was a done deal? You hurt me, Kye. I have been sitting there for the past few days crying my eyes out, pining away for your stupid ass. I have feelings, Kye! I have feelings and emotions and you trampled them, stomped all over them. So I get this call and I come busting my rump to get to you, and all you can do is whine about not knowing what to do with your life. Boo-hoo! Poor Kye. You can fucking float, you bastard! What the hell is wrong with you? Then you talk about wanting to die, no, deserving to die. Well la-de-da! You can't seem to die. Poor little baby! Now stop whining, get over yourself, and think about what you are doing to other people. People who care about you! Like Angel and me!"

"Tali, I..."

"No! You listen, you...you...underdone vamp! You put me through hell! I beat up two FBI agents to get in here to you!"

"FBI?"

"I said shut up! I beat up people to get to you. I wear my heart on my sleeve! I gave up my pride, which is all I apparently own besides my name, and you lay here whining about your fate! Well fuck your fate, Kye! Fuck your fate, and fuck you!"

Tali jumped to her feet and stalked towards the door.

"Tali, I love you!"

She froze, her hand on the doorknob as she paused, shocked.

"I love you, Tali!"

"What?" Her back was still to him, but she was listening.

"I said I love you! When I was lying there, dying—and I was dying Tali—all I could see was you."

"You love me?" she whispered.

"I'm fucked up, Tali. I don't know what I'm going to do. I don't know what is going to happen to me. But I know I love you, Tali. I love you with all of what passes for a soul. I love you."

"Prove it."

"What?"

She turned slowly, her eyes glistening with tears, and a small Mona Lisa smile playing around her lips.

Kye struggled to sit up, his wires and tubes tangling as he reached out one arm towards her, his face desperate and lost.

"Prove it."

"How?"

"You have a lifetime to figure it out, Kye. You have a long shelf life!"

"Will...will you show me how?" he asked quietly, his face showing his exhaustion. "I don't know how, Tali. I don't know how to love."

"Then how can you say you love me?"

"Because I would kill for you."

"You'd kill for Angel."

"I would die for you."

"Will you live for me?"

Silence.

Tali started towards the bed, each step purposeful and sure.

"Will you live for me, Kye? Will you get out of this hospital, go back to your loft, and build a life for me? I understand you will never fit in, Kye. I know you won't age and that I will age and one day die. I know this. I also know you have a lot of ghosts to lay to rest. But will you try to be strong enough to deal with them for me? Will you fight to be with me, Kye? Am I worth it?"

By this time, she was beside his bed, staring at him, chin lifted up in defiance. If she didn't hear what she wanted, she was gone, and he knew it.

"I...I refuse to share my leather. You will have to get your own."

"But we are about the same size," she murmured, a smile pulling at her lips.

"You'll put hip and tit prints in my stuff. You get your own. And we have to find a job."

Her smile widened. "We already have one."

"So what do we do, since you have it all figured out?" he asked.

"We do what we were trained for, my man. We hunt vampires."

Kye stared at her for a moment, then shook his head.

"We hunt vampires. Just like that."

"Well, you are too fucked up to do anything else," she stated as she rolled her eyes at him. "I don't exactly have a past. Maybe we'll be bodyguards, security experts. Something like that."

She shrugged as if it was of no consequence to her either way how their lives turned out. She was just ready to begin living, really and truly living.

"Tali," he said in the face of her surety. "I am scared. I am frustrated and confused. But I am willing to try. I will live for you, Tali. You are mine. Maybe I'll earn the right...to earn your love."

"Kye," Tali whispered as her tears spilled over again. "Damn you, Kye!"

Then she was in his arms, pushing tubes and wires out of her way.

Immediately, his arms came up to enfold her, to pull her closer to him.

"I'll never let you go," he breathed as he tangled his hands in her hair and pulled her face up to his.

Their kiss was one of passion and fire!

He thrust his tongue deep, flicking it against the slick heat of her tongue, teasing her, enticing her to return the caress, which she did with abandon.

Tali groaned as her tongue tangled with his. Then feeling bold, she thrust her tongue inside his mouth and trembled at the heat she felt.

Slowly, she tickled the sharp points of his fangs, moaning as his body shuddered beneath hers. She jerked as one finely-honed canine pricked her tongue, sending a trickle of bittersweet blood in his mouth.

"Tali," he gasped as he pulled away from her, "You are playing a dangerous game."

Tali pulled away enough to touch the tip of one finger to the bleeding tip and touched the little nick. Staring into Kye's wildly swirling green-gold eyes, a small grin spread across her lips.

"Pain is starting to turn me on."

Before she could blink, Kye ripped the tubes from his arm, tangled his hands in her shirt, and with one tear, Tali was bare from the waist up.

"No bra," he hissed as his eyes zeroed in on her berry-colored nipples.

"No time," she gasped as he reached out and palmed both of her breasts, heating them with his touch even as he plucked at her sensitive nipples. "I wanted to get to you."

Growling, Kye pulled her onto the bed, pulling her up and over him until her breasts hung suspended above his watering mouth.

"What else did you leave off?" he purred as she swung her legs around to straddle his body.

Before she could answer, his hand was forcing its way past her waistband and cupping the firm cheeks of her ass, kneading them as he rose up and captured one peaked nipple in to his suckling mouth.

"Oh," Tali gasped as he drew on her flesh, sending sparks flying to her stomach and a humid heat pooling in her groin. "Oh, Kye! I thought I would never see you again!"

His free hand cupped her breast, pulling her closer to his nursing mouth while he began to thrust up into the wide-spread vee of her thighs, forcing his steel hard rod against the swollen flesh of her clit hidden beneath the stiff denim.

Her hands tangled in his hair, pulling his head harder against her, urging him to use her roughly, wanting, needing to feel that he still lived, that he was hers, that she still made him hard and wanting with need.

"Bite me!" she gasped as her body bent protectively over his. "Make me your own, Kye. Use me."

It was a demand he was all too happy to fulfill.

"You are mine," he growled again as he tightened his grip on her and with a twist of his upper body, reversed their positions, slamming her to the bed and hovering above her.

Whimpering and writhing against the sheets, warmed by the heat of his body, Tali forced her eyes to open and felt the crotch of her panties grow ever wetter. The fierce gold in his eyes overtook the green as he stared hungrily at her.

"How could I ever give this up?" he asked more to himself than anyone, as he rose to his knees and gripped the material of her jeans in both hands.

The thick tearing sound of the denim as he rent it from her body momentarily drowned out the heavy breathing that filled the room.

Kye could smell her, smell his mate, and the flimsy barrier of her pants was keeping him away from what was his.

He tossed the pieces of material aside as his gaze dropped to the thin cotton panties that barely covered her woman's mound, his favorite playground.

They had to go too.

But her hands beat him to the task.

"Stop teasing me!" Tali growled as she reached down and ripped at the sides of her underwear, wanting the irritating material gone from her body. Under the slight air-conditioning, the material was becoming uncomfortably cold and she wanted heat.

"Who am I to stand in the way of true lust," Kye purred as he pulled the thin hospital gown away from his body and tossed it aside.

"Love, you bastard," Tali growled as she tossed the ruined cloth away and reached for his hardness.

Heat, she thought, as her hands trailed up the ridges and bumps that made up Kye's throbbing cock.

She watched his eyes flair as she ran one thumb over the wet tip of his cock, and licked her lips as if tasting his salty emissions.

Kye squeezed his eyes shut and threw back his head, his eyes closing at the intense sensations that swamped his body as Tali carefully jacked him.

She knew just where to touch, that spot just beneath his head, and how tightly to grip him as she pumped up and down and up and down.

"You are killing me," he growled as pleasure threatened to make his muscles into jelly and his body a boneless sack.

"Fuck me," she replied. Kye tossed his hair over his shoulders and grinned.

Before she could react, his hands spread her legs wide, exposing her heated center for his enjoyment.

"Hot, baby?" he asked as gentle fingers made exploring forays across her swollen flesh.

"Please," she whispered, drawing her knees up, trapping his callused hand against her as she bit her lip and reached out to him.

"You asked me to bite you," he whispered, as he lowered himself over her, letting the trailing ends of his hair tickle lightly along her body, making her skin so sensitive she had to resist the urge to scream. "But I would rather lick you, Tali. You are so damn sweet."

His eyes bored into hers as he slid lower and lower, until he could feel the damp heat of her caressing his face and he smiled at the pleasure of drowning in her scent.

Then his fingers were parting the wet folds of her flesh, his thumbs peeling back the hood of her clit, exposing the milky white pearl as his hungry mouth descended.

"Kye!"

He lashed out at her with his tongue, stimulating the little bud until she screamed her pleasure and he felt her essence coating his face.

But that was not enough.

He dipped lower, his thumb taking place of his tongue as he began to lap at her feminine opening.

Tali screeched, her hands tangling in his hair, pulling him up against her as his tongue danced around her folds, then darted in between, tasting her from the source.

His hands slid around to her ass, cupping her, lifting her, holding her more fully against his mouth as he feasted in earnest.

Tali arched her back, her hands going to her breasts, pulling at her own nipples as waves of dark fire washed over her.

"Enough, Kye," she gasped as her back arched off the bed. "Enough. Fuck me! Now, damn it!"

With one last lingering lick, Kye again rose above Tali, a dazed look in his eyes.

"Never enough," he purred as he lowered himself over her, his hair encompassing them both, creating a dark shadowy place that felt the finest of silks but smelled of man and woman, of need and sex, of Kye.

Almost roughly, he gripped her thighs, pulling them up and around his waist as he ground his swollen cock against her, teasing her opening and her clitoris with his tip.

Tali's hands went to his head and his back, her nails digging in as a low keening sound filled the room, bringing with it the rushing of feet and a blast of cold air as the door swung open.

"Get out!" Kye growled, never taking his eyes from the form of his lady that lay beneath him, panting in need.

There was a hushed 'excuse me' and the door was swiftly closed, but Kye and Tali paid them no heed, lost in the sensuous battle taking place on the bed, a battle where both would be victorious.

"Fuck me!" Tali gasped again, one hand traveling down to gently tug at his balls, pressing into his perineum, making him jerk against her.

"I thought you wanted me to bite you?"

"I want it all," she breathed back.

Kye closed his eyes and inhaled deeply, the smell of Tali, of sex, and underneath it all, the smell of her sweet hot blood rushing though her veins close to the surface of her skin.

I can do this, he thought. I can take her with me, make her what I am, and then I will never have to lose her again.

Even as these thoughts crossed his mind, his mate's body spasming underneath his touch, his heart rebelled at what he was thinking.

"Tali," he moaned.

But then her hand gripped his steel, guided his dripping head to her gasping opening, and her body seemed to suck him in.

"Oh, fuck," he panted, his eyes closing and his fangs exploding from his gums as her exquisite quivering heat surrounded him.

It was like being stuck in a silken vise, he thought as almost electric-feeling shocks centered low in his stomach, and he felt his balls began to rise against the base of his cock.

It would be so easy, her skin so delicate, the blood hot and powerful, waiting for him, a liquid feast to quench all the fires that raged through his body.

"Oh, Kye!" Tali gasped as she felt him part her with one elongated thrust. "Yes!"

Unaware of the war going on within him, Tali reveled in the feel of his hard steel stretching her, filling her almost to the point of pain, yet fulfilling a yearning that had taken over her from the first time she had seen him.

She closed her eyes and let her body go, following animalistic instinct as she wrapped her body around him and forced the wild coupling she craved.

"Tali," Kye gasped again, burying his face in her neck, nipping at her shoulder, so close yet resisting the pull of her blood.

Could he make his love go through what he was dealing with, looking at every person on the street as an appetizer, never having the hunger fully satisfied, just sated?

"More!" Tali demanded and his hips began a slow rhythm, two long thrusts and a slow grind that made her squeal with delight as his soft pubic hair abraded her clit.

Bringing both hands underneath her back, his hands cupping her shoulders, Kye rested his weight on his elbows and began to slowly increase his speed.

Faster and faster he slammed into her, hoping to drive away the conflict within, to pull himself away from the edge of taking her soul, trying to drown out his need by making her scream in ecstasy.

"Kye, Kye, Kye," she chanted, his name almost a mantra as her legs wrapped higher around his waist, opening herself further to his thrust. "More."

Growling in his neck, almost screaming at the feelings shooting though his cock, Kye began to rise up on his arms, throwing his head back like some wild stallion as he centered the energy of his thrusts directly on her, rubbing her internal hot spot as well as stimulating her throbbing clit.

Tali opened her eyes, stared up at her man, and saw life and death warring in his eyes.

Strangely enough, she was not afraid. She knew Kye would never hurt her. She knew she was a part of him, more than his very thick, very long cock slamming into her cunt.

"Tali," he growled once more, as he reached down and pulled her up.

Spreading his legs wide, he pulled Tali up until her legs gripped his waist and his hands cupped her ass, holding him to her tightly as gravity forced her down deeper onto him.

Tali reached low, gripping his ass, feeling his muscular buns flex and quiver with his every thrust, digging her nails into the pliant flesh and forcing him tighter, harder, faster, inside of her.

It was his chin that nuzzled her, that made her lift her head.

Kye leaned back, one hand traveling up to tangle into her hair as he forced her mouth to his.

Again his tongue invaded her, thrust deep, tasting all that was Tali, eating at her with a hunger that couldn't be denied.

Pulling away, he licked her face, tasting her sweat and her unique flavor as his lips traveled lower to the pulse exploding in her neck.

His body began to tremble, his hands to shake as a powerful blood lust consumed him. He squeezed his eyes shut, his fangs all but burning as the need to put out the fire with the blood in her veins almost consumed him.

His heart pounded faster and faster, a low groaning sound of hunger exploding form his throat as his sharp teeth grazed the skin of her neck.

He drew back, his whole body poised to strike as the first waves of her orgasm rushed over them.

His decision was made.

"You will never be my Renfield," he breathed as he threw back his head, long black hair flying around them, and he gave a mighty thrust with his hips, slamming his hardness inside her, feeling himself swell larger than he had ever been.

"Kye!" Tali screeched his name as things in her lower body tightened and tightened and then snapped for a second time.

Her muscles clenched around him, milking him of his essence even as lightning flashed through her body, up her spine and exploded in her mind.

"Tali!" Kye all but roared as his balls slammed tightly to the base of his cock and his release tore through him.

"Yes, Tali, yes!" he bellowed, punctuating each cry with a pounding thrust, driving himself as deep as he could and letting his hot seed explode from his body, filling her with his life and his passion.

Slowly, he rose up and lowered Tali to the bed, dropping weakly over her, his hair tying them both together as it wound about their passion-soaked limbs.

Breath heaving together, they both gasped for air as a feeling of deep contentment filled them.

Kye felt his fangs slowly recede as his muscles relaxed and he slid to the side, not wanting to crush his woman beneath his dead weight.

"We have to have a name," she whispered as she brushed a lock of his hair from her face. A self-satisfied grin spread her lips and a peace like no other filled her.

"I am a Slayer, Tali. It's all I know," he managed as the blood lust in him cooled, banked by the soft ashes of the aftermath of their coupling.

"All we know. The Slayers," she giggled as his hands buried themselves in her hair and pulled her mouth to his.

"Oh, hell," he sighed. "What are you getting me into? The Slayers," he repeated as he forced his tongue into her mouth, eating at her, as if he were drawing strength for her very presence.

"Bloodsuckers beware," she muttered, before she began to return the kiss, infusing it with all the passion and lust she felt for this man, along with a healthy dose of love.

"And I am not sharing my leather."

"You gave it to me!"

"When I was dead," he whispered back. "Now I'm all alive."

He leered as the feel of her tight body next to his caused a tingle in the cock region. As he began to swell against her hip, he leered at her for all he was worth.

"Want me to prove it?"

"Kye!"

* * * * *

"You have to excuse them, doctor," Angel said as she waved her hand in front of the red-faced physician who had wandered into the middle of their hospital athletics. "They are always doing stuff like that! To think I raised her better than that!"

The doctor tried to gather his dignity as he adjusted the fit of his lab coat and mopped the beads of sweat from his forehead.

"That was a, ah, speedy recovery."

Angel tried not to laugh as the doctor had a word with the agents outside the door and then hurried away.

Looks like life is going to get more interesting from here on out, she mused. She leaned up against the wall to wait as groans and grunts trickled from behind closed doors. Looked like round two had started. This is going to be...fun. Ah, grandchildren!

About the author:

Stephanie Burke welcomes mail from readers. You can write to her c/o Ellora's Cave Publishing at P.O. Box 787, Hudson, Ohio 44236-0787.

Also by STEPHANIE BURKE:

- Keeper of the Flame
- Dangerous Heat
- Lucavarious
- Seascape
- Merlin's Kiss
- Hidden Passions Volume 1
- Hidden Passions Volume 2
- Wicked Wishes anthology with Marly Chance and Joanna Wylde
- Threshold anthology with Shelby Morgen

Why an electronic book?

We live in the Information Age—an exciting time in the history of human civilization in which technology rules supreme and continues to progress in leaps and bounds every minute of every hour of every day. For a multitude of reasons, more and more avid literary fans are opting to purchase e-books instead of paperbacks. The question to those not yet initiated to the world of electronic reading is simply: *why?*

1. *Price.* An electronic title at Ellora's Cave Publishing runs anywhere from 40-75% less than the cover price of the <u>exact same title</u> in paperback format. Why? Cold mathematics. It is less expensive to publish an e-book than it is to publish a paperback, so the savings are passed along to the consumer.

2. *Space.* Running out of room to house your paperback books? That is one worry you will never have with electronic novels. For a low one-time cost, you can purchase a handheld computer designed specifically for e-reading purposes. Many e-readers are larger than the average handheld, giving you plenty of screen room. Better yet, hundreds of titles can be stored within your new library—a single microchip. (Please note that Ellora's Cave does not endorse any specific brands. You can check our website at www.ellorascave.com for customer recommendations we make available to new consumers.)

3. *Mobility.* Because your new library now consists of only a microchip, your entire cache of books can be taken with you wherever you go.

4. *Personal preferences are accounted for.* Are the words you are currently reading too small? Too large? Too...**ANNOYING**? Paperback books cannot be modified according to personal preferences, but e-books can.

5. *Innovation.* The way you read a book is not the only advancement the Information Age has gifted the literary community with. There is also the factor of what you can read. Ellora's Cave Publishing will be introducing a new line of interactive titles that are available in e-book format only.

6. *Instant gratification.* Is it the middle of the night and all the bookstores are closed? Are you tired of waiting days — sometimes weeks — for online and offline bookstores to ship the novels you bought? Ellora's Cave Publishing sells instantaneous downloads 24 hours a day, 7 days a week, 365 days a year. Our e-book delivery system is 100% automated, meaning your order is filled as soon as you pay for it.

Those are a few of the top reasons why electronic novels are displacing paperbacks for many an avid reader. As always, Ellora's Cave Publishing welcomes your questions and comments. We invite you to email us at service@ellorascave.com or write to us directly at: P.O. Box 787, Hudson, Ohio 44236-0787.

Printed in the United States
26388LVS00001BA/55-63

9 781843 606222